MW00617602

EVE AND THE FADERS

A NOVEL

BERNETA L. HAYNES
LORNETT B. VESTAL

Snake Doctor Press

ALSO BY
BERNETA L. HAYNES

Landrien Moriset

Eve and the Faders

This book is a work of fiction. Names, characters, places, and incidents are a product of the author's imagination or are used fictitiously. Any resemblance to actual events, places, or persons, living or dead is coincidental.

Copyright © 2021 by Berneta L. Haynes & Lornett B. Vestal

All rights reserved.

The scanning, uploading, and distribution of this book without permission is theft of the author's intellectual property. If you would like permission to use material from this book (other than for review purposes), please contact snakedoctorpress@gmail.com. Thank you for your support of the author's rights.

Originally published in the United States in 2021 by Snake Doctor Press.

First Edition: January 2021

ISBN 978-1-7359850-0-8 (paperback)
ISBN 978-1-7359850-1-5 (ebook)

Printed in the United States of America

snakedoctorpress.com

To all the invisible heroes who are strong because they have no other choice.

PROLOGUE

Sitting at the kitchen bar, Eve Cooper watched her mother place the cookie sheet on the stove. "I want to try one," said Eve, bouncing with excitement. "Please?"

"That depends," Marie Cooper replied, smiling at her daughter. She brushed aside a few strands of her daughter's wild hair. "If you promise you won't play with your food at dinner?"

"I wasn't playing. I was making art," said Eve. "There's a difference."

Marie put her hands on her hips and shook her head. "Mushed green beans and carrots isn't art, Eve. It's wasted food while some poor kid—"

"Some poor kid wherever is hungry. I know. I know." Eve rolled her eyes but smiled. "Okay, I promise I won't make art with my green beans tonight. Now, can I have a cookie? Please, Mommy."

Marie laughed. "You're too damn precocious for your age."

"What's precocious?"

She placed one chocolate chip cookie on a saucer and handed it to her daughter. "Don't you worry about it. That's the only cookie you're getting for now. Be careful. It's still hot."

Eve bobbed her head as a smile spread across her face. The smell of fresh-baked cookies was tantalizing, and she made sure to sniff the cookie and dip a finger into a melted chocolate chip before licking it. When she bit into the cookie, however, her teeth bumped against something hard as a rock.

She spat the cookie onto her palms and examined the gooey mess. "Mommy..."

Marie beamed. "It's good, isn't it? I added a little cinnamon."

As Eve stared at her hands, they seemed to grow in size. "Why do my hands look weird?" She fell silent when she raised her gaze and saw a bare, windowless room. No longer was she sitting on the bar stool in the bright kitchen of her childhood home. The kitchen and everything in it had vanished, along with her mother. She blinked. "Mommy?"

Something that felt like bolts of electricity shot through her limbs and spread through her body. Against a wet, concrete floor, she lay curled up and shivering.

Alone.

It was the shivering that woke her; the shivering and the pain. Pain like no other she'd known in her life.

Agent Grobeck fixed his vacant green eyes on her and lowered the Taser. "Miss Cooper, it doesn't need to go this far. Don't make it harder on yourself."

"I don't have to answer your goddamn questions. I want a lawyer," she shouted.

"You're not charged with a crime. For all intents and purposes, this place doesn't exist. Your right to an attorney doesn't apply. Now, kindly answer the question, Miss Cooper, and I'll have the guards give you clean clothes. I know you must be eager to change out of those filthy clothes."

Eve looked at her sweat-soaked blouse and dingy jeans. After struggling, she pulled herself up and faced Agent

Grobeck, who was standing just inside the steel door. "I wan my lawyer."

"Please answer the question, Miss Cooper."

"Lawyer. Now."

In too short of a moment for her to register his movement, he raised the gun. A buzzing noise followed, and Eve collapsed onto the floor. Gasping for breath, she rubbed her arms and clutched her chest as an intense heat spread through her.

He squatted to meet her gaze. "Are you ready to answer my questions?"

Coughing, she managed to look at him and, in a display of foolish contempt, spat at his feet. "Lawyer."

He sighed. "Very well."

The second shot from the Taser hit her chest again. This time the agony was so overwhelming she assumed death was a moment away. Over and over, he asked the same question, and each time she spat or glared at him. Each time, pain followed her defiance.

She wondered if any of it was real. Was she dreaming? *That's it. This is a nightmare. I'm going to wake up.*

Tears formed puddles on the floor beneath her while she lay curled in a fetal position. No longer trying to suppress her sobs, she wailed. Sinking into an empty hole of nothingness, she watched as if from outside her body as he towered over her.

So lost was she that she didn't hear him leave. The sound of her own sobbing enveloped her.

A day or several passed between the agent's first visit to her cell and his second. She had no way of knowing how many minutes, hours, and days had slipped away since she'd found him waiting in her living room. She now realized she should've pepper-sprayed him on sight and fled. But curiosity

had gotten the best of her that night. She wondered why the price of curiosity had to be so high.

As she sat alone in the dank room, her stomach and head ached from hunger and thirst. She remembered eating a Subway tuna salad sandwich before returning to her apartment on a rainy evening. Then there was the bottle of water she'd found next to her feet when she woke after the first round of abuse. That was it, not a morsel of food. Just one small bottle of water. She'd drained it in a few gulps, her tongue desperately digging around the bottle for any remaining drops.

"Let me out of here," she'd screamed, throwing the empty bottle at the door. With every word, her parched throat had cracked in pain. "Please, anybody. Please, help me."

Taking deep breaths now, she sat cross-legged on the hard floor. Agent Grobeck wanted her alive. Yet this realization failed to bring her any comfort. She looked up when she heard shuffling of feet outside. If she hid next to the door and waited, perhaps she could tackle the person and make a run for it. *What other chance will I get?*

But as she stood, the door squeaked open. She'd missed her opportunity. *Damn it.*

Agent Grobeck observed her. "Good afternoon, Miss Cooper. I see you're up and about. I hope that means you're ready to talk." He'd brought in a chair and placed it two feet from her. Once he sat, he rested his hands on his knees. In one hand was a recorder and in the other was a Taser. "Agent Yu will no longer serve as your direct supervisor. I've been tasked with the rest of your training. As such, I have questions for you. Are you willing to cooperate now?"

"Training?" she asked, wincing. The very act of speaking hurt her dry throat. Meanwhile, her head was throbbing, and her stomach seemed to be doing somersaults. Nonetheless, she held his unsettling gaze, noting how dilated his pupils

were and how there seemed to be no emotion in his eyes. There was a saying her mother had..."The motor's running, but nobody's behind the wheel." As she studied him, she understood that saying for the first time. She wondered how she'd failed to see it before, and Agent Yu's warning returned to the forefront of her mind. *She tried to warn me.*

"Yes, Miss Cooper. You didn't take to our kinder, gentler training methods. You left us no other choice."

"Wait. Are you serious?"

He smiled. "Yes. And for your sake, Miss Cooper, I suggest you cooperate. From the looks of it, I'm not sure how much longer you can hold up. Are you willing to cooperate?"

She gave a slight nod.

He crossed his legs and leaned forward. "Smart girl. Now, have a seat and let's get started then."

Eve remained standing and didn't move.

"Very well. When did you discover your ability?"

"I don't know."

"When was the first time you were aware that you could become invisible?"

"I don't know."

"Miss Cooper, do I need to remind you—"

She groaned, cold and trembling. "When I was a kid."

Watching him process her response, she realized she wouldn't win against this man, not by being defiant and angry. There was nothing she could do but comply, and even that might not be enough to avoid more torture. She'd have to play along for now. She'd have to come up with a plan.

"Agent Yu," he said, looking straight at Eve, "turn down the AC a bit, will you?"

She looked around to confirm that the two of them were alone in the room. There must be speakers and a microphone in the room somewhere, she surmised. As the interrogation continued, Eve speculated about whether she should try to signal to Agent Yu to help her. *Can I trust her anymore?*

After a while, she grew tired of the interrogation and began tapping her feet against the floor in an effort to distract herself. Out of sheer boredom, she began memorizing every detail of Agent Grobeck's face. The small scar over his left eye, the green eyes that looked blue in some lighting, the pink lips, and the ever-present sneer lurking behind his smile. One day, she'd wipe the satisfied smirk off his pale face, or she at least would die trying.

"That's all for now. Thank you, Miss Cooper," he said, standing up.

"Agent?"

"Yes, Miss Cooper?"

"What happened to my cat?" Try as she might she hadn't been able to erase an image of him strangling Mr. Pebbles and leaving the poor thing for dead in the apartment. But she couldn't be sure if the memory was real. She couldn't be sure if anything was real anymore.

He'd reached the door and didn't bother turning to look at her. "It ran off."

She exhaled, not sure if she believed him. But perhaps Mr. Pebbles was alive and free somewhere, roaming the streets of Chicago. Or maybe he'd found another home already. Maybe Zoey had found him...

Not a minute after the agent left, another man—more squat and rugged-looking—came in carrying a pair of white linen pants and a white T-shirt. He threw them at her and exited without a word. She hastily removed her dirty clothes and put on the clean clothes before the man returned with water and a bowl of soupy oatmeal. He sat the food tray near the exit and locked the door behind him.

Eve rushed to the tray, sniffed the food, and her nose curled up in disgust. The oatmeal smelled like sour milk. But she dug the spoon into the oatmeal anyway and consumed it to the last drop, trying not to gag. She took the glass of water and drank it in a couple of swallows.

Still hungry, she wiped her mouth with her hands and licked her lips. Surely, they would bring her more. They couldn't expect one bowl of oatmeal would be enough after days of no food. She thought about the speakers and microphone hidden somewhere in the cell and considered requesting more food. But the words choked in her throat before they could escape her lips. *I won't beg.*

Instead, she sat in silence, cross-legged with her palms against her knees. Throughout her childhood, her mother had made her sit like this when she was in trouble. Right now, Eve was in serious trouble.

Listening to her stomach grumble, she sat there, immersed in her thoughts and plotting her escape.

TOO GOOD TO BE TRUE

1

TWO MONTHS EARLIER...

The brief Friday afternoon downpour had flooded parts of the street, and Eve avoided the puddles on her way to the bus stop heading home. Her ninth-grade students had been demanding as usual, and she was desperate to plop down on her sofa. The rainy weather only added more stress to an already gloomy day that involved breaking up a fight and giving one of her most passionate students a low grade on his Faulkner paper. Watching his heart shatter as he stared at the C minus was tough. The first assignment always revealed the different learning levels of her students—which students needed to be in an advanced class and which ones required more one-on-one help. He fell into the latter category, and she hoped the private tutor she suggested would help him.

As she reached the people queued up for the bus, the heel of her left shoe broke, and she tumbled to the ground. She shielded her face right before she hit the concrete. Audible gasps sounded from the crowd. Trying not to look at them as she pulled herself up, she cursed under her breath and ignored the pain shooting through her legs.

"Miss, are you all right?" A young man reached out to lift her.

She mumbled, "I'm fine, thanks," slinging her bag over her shoulder and picking up the broken shoe. Her gaze averted, she hobbled to the bus and sat in the first vacant row near the front. As she massaged her foot through the stockings, she turned and stared out the window at the gray sky. High-rise condos sailed by, only to be replaced with modest two-story houses, as the bus turned onto a neighborhood street. What she wouldn't give to get away from the city for a while, to somewhere smaller, warmer, and less rainy. A brief change to her routine. *Aruba.* Zoey had said Aruba was nice. But that took money—lots of it—and one thing Eve didn't have was money.

"What the—" she exclaimed when a heavy weight landed on her lap. She looked at the backpack on her lap and then searched to see the owner. A pink-haired woman who smelled of coffee and cigarettes plopped beside her.

Eve frowned. "Did you seriously just throw your backpack on my lap?" she asked the woman.

The woman turned to Eve and stared blankly but made no effort to grab the backpack. Instead, she scratched her head, knocking a few pink strands out of place, and inserted earplugs.

Stunned, Eve looked around to see if anyone else had noticed the woman's odd behavior. "Excuse me? I know damn well you heard me," she said and thrust the heavy pack at the woman.

At once, the woman leaped up, clutching the backpack against her chest and moving away from the seat. Staring in wide-eyed horror, she pointed at Eve.

About four people watched with alarm.

Eve rolled her eyes. "Oh please. Just drop the theatrics."

At that moment, several individuals in the surrounding

rows scurried from their seats and collided into one another, all of them gawking and pointing at Eve. The bus came to an abrupt stop, and the woman, along with a half-dozen others, went crashing to the floor.

Eve surveyed the scene with increasing concern. *No. It can't be happening again.* The woman was rubbing her backside and looking in Eve's general direction. Yet she wasn't looking *at* Eve. She was looking somewhere in the general vicinity of Eve. In fact, all the people on the bus seemed to be doing the same—looking in Eve's general direction but not at Eve. "Ugh. Come on. Not this crap again," she groaned. As she spoke, two women shrieked and covered their mouths.

"Where is it coming from?" asked one young man, staring in Eve's direction. He approached, his hand outstretched and patting at the air near her face. His cold hand brushed Eve's face, and she staggered. She slapped his hand away, and he jumped back, evoking more frightened screams from the crowd. He gestured at Eve while pressing himself against another passenger who was sitting in an aisle seat. "There's something there."

"Um, yeah, I'm here, and you can keep your hands off me." Eve slid her left foot into the broken shoe and stood.

All at once, everybody started hollering and running to the two exits, toppling over each other, and dropping grocery bags. In a matter of seconds, there were only a dozen passengers on the bus, and the driver was scanning the bus for signs of what had caused the disturbance.

She looked from him to the passengers gathered outside on the sidewalk. They stared at the bus, some of them confused and others looking frightened. *Shit.* She closed her eyes and counted to ten like she always used to do whenever this happened. *Get a grip, Eve.*

As she shuffled toward the front of the bus, no one seemed to notice her. Some passengers fixed their attention on the driver, while others were still staring at the bus as though it was about to attack them. "Excuse me?" asked Eve, tapping the driver's shoulder.

He let out a high-pitched scream and jerked in his seat. When he spun around, he pointed at Eve, his eyes darting left and right. "Something," he said to the passenger behind him, "I felt..." He paused and seemed to reconsider his words.

She could see the panic dancing about his face and imagined what he was thinking. She assumed he was thinking he couldn't afford to have a nervous breakdown, not in front of all these people. They would think he was mentally unstable; word would get back to his employer, and he might lose his job. He couldn't afford to lose his shit in public.

"Are you okay?" asked the passenger.

The driver cleared his throat. "Ah, uh, yes." Scratching his head, he turned to face the rest of the passengers and waved them to come into the bus.

Most of the passengers hesitated and shot wary glances around. No one moved into the seat Eve had used. No one uttered a word. They all stared at him and remained frozen in place. For a moment, it looked like he wasn't going to be able to get his passengers to return to the bus. However, a few passengers whispered to each other and, slowly, walked to the entrance of the bus. Soon, other passengers fell in line and boarded.

"What the hell was all this about? I'm confused," one woman said.

A man replied, "Seems like that one guy was hearing voices or something. Spooked everybody out, I guess."

The woman who had sat next to Eve and sparked the whole event threw them an uncertain glance.

"It's a shame we don't address the mental health crisis in this country. A real shame," the man finished.

The woman chimed in. "True. We need to do better as a

society, don't we?"

Numerous conversations of this nature followed, while others had a good laugh about the incident as they filed onto the bus. On with their normal lives they went, not realizing they had witnessed something extraordinary, something altogether remarkable.

The bus departed, and Eve sat on the bench. She pulled the mirror from her purse and held it up to her face. There was no reflection. She closed her eyes and counted to ten. When she opened them, she held the mirror to her face. No reflection. "Goddamn it," she muttered. Was she losing control again? Her mother's sudden passing had triggered it the last time, four years ago. She thought about how long it had taken her to feel normal again after that year. She never wanted a repeat of those dark days.

Eve slipped the mirror inside her purse and inhaled. She glanced at her broken wet shoe and looked over her shoulder at the shoe store. She limped into the store, gazing at the rows of shoes, and stopping at a pair of black two-inch heels. Two inches were manageable.

Conscious about her clothes, which were soaked and dingy from the fall, she hoped not to draw too much attention to herself. She squatted, pulled out a box, and slipped her feet inside a size nine. They weren't comfortable, but they'd suffice. She searched for the price on the box. *Please don't let it be more than forty dollars.* She had fifty dollars left in her checking account until the next pay over a week away. "Miss?" said Eve, spotting a salesclerk strolling down the next aisle toward her. "How much are these shoes?"

The clerk, a young girl of no more than twenty-five, looked at her and frowned. The girl resumed walking down the aisle.

Realizing she was still invisible, Eve groaned and looked at her soggy clothes and broken shoe. *Oh, fuck it.* With a quick look left and right, she slipped the new black heels on her feet, placed the empty box on the shelf and stuffed her own broken shoes inside the purse. What could it hurt? She couldn't limp all the way home in broken shoes, and she needed that fifty dollars to get groceries this week. A major department store wouldn't miss one pair of shoes, she concluded.

Keeping her head low, she headed straight for the exit.

She broke into a sprint once outside the store and stopped in front of a bank a block away. Looking through the window, she could see a teller counting money and stuffing it inside something beneath the counter, the cash register. Eve's heart quickened as she watched the teller count some bills. She thought about the unpaid property tax bill lying on her kitchen countertop, about her own paltry checking account. If only she could get a loan to pay the bill...but then, that would be more debt on top of her mountain of student loan debt.

When her cell phone vibrated, she was thankful for the distraction from these unpleasant thoughts. "Hey, Zoey," Eve answered.

"Hey, you," Zoey Res Ellis replied. "I'm standing outside your apartment right now and wondering where the hell you are, since you were supposed to meet me here like twenty minutes ago."

"Oh, shit. I'm sorry. I had a—uh—you know how late CTA be sometimes," she said, crossing the street and hurrying toward the Red Line station at Lake Street. "I'm on my way."

The train car was almost empty when she got off at her stop. As an invisible Eve plodded down a quiet neighborhood street to her apartment off Devon and Clark, the cool September breeze brushing against her face, she counted to ten over and over. *Come on. One...two...three.* Just as she reached her corner, she stopped and pulled out the mirror. "Please, please be normal again."

To her immense relief, she saw her reflection at last. She ran her fingers through her tight curls and slipped the mirror inside her purse.

With extra bounce in her step, she walked two more blocks and stopped at an uninviting three-story apartment building with an expansive, gated courtyard. Smiling, she approached a tall dark-haired woman in tight blue jeans and a faux leather jacket.

Zoey held up a paper bag. "I had Chinese delivered while I was waiting on your late ass."

"I'm sorry. It was—"

"A crazy day at work and CTA is crap. Sure," said Zoey. "I know how you can make it up to me." She planted a lingering kiss at the side of Eve's neck.

Eve flushed bright red.

"Wait," said Zoey, surveying her. "Are those new shoes? And why are you all wet and dirty?"

"It was a crazy day. Come on." She entered the gate code, held it open for Zoey, and grasped her free hand. "I'm glad you were thinking about food. I'm starving."

When they entered the muggy apartment, Mr. Pebbles meowed and rubbed against Zoey's ankle. Smiling, Zoey knelt and gave the shaggy sand-colored cat a gentle pat on the head, and he purred. He strolled to the bowl of food under the kitchen table and nibbled at the food leftover from the morning. "It's a little hot in here. I thought your landlord fixed the AC."

"It went out again last week. He's supposed to come by this week to replace it," said Eve, going straight to the refrigerator. She turned up a carton of orange juice and took a swallow.

Zoey shook her head. "You need to find another apartment. That asshole is ripping you off." She stood at the kitchen table and frowned when she looked at the stack of papers and noticed the envelope addressed from the Porter County Treasurer in Valparaiso, Indiana. "Eve, I thought you'd already paid the property tax bill. Didn't you tell me not to worry about it, that you'd found the money?"

Ignoring her, Eve placed the half-empty orange juice carton inside the refrigerator and filled two glasses with water. She made her way to the sofa and sat the glasses on the coffee table.

"Eve?"

"I lied. I don't make enough, so I haven't been able to save the money to pay it. I calculated how long it would take me on my salary to come up with that much money. At least two years. So, no, I haven't paid it."

"What about a payment arrangement—"

"The county already made it clear that no payment arrangement is available." Eve kicked her feet up on the sofa and tried not to look gloomy.

"It's your childhood home, Eve. Your family's property that they frickin' built from the—"

Eve sighed. "Zoey, I feel like shit as it is about it. It's the only thing I own in this world, and I'm about to lose it. Don't rub it in."

She shook her head again and cast Eve a heartbroken look. "You remember I offered to—"

"Stop, Zoey," Eve said, her tone sharper than usual. But a moment later, she smiled. "Bring the food and come join me."

Relenting, Zoey grabbed the bag of food and joined Eve on the sofa. "Well, I still say you need to look for another apartment. It's probably moldy as hell in here with all this mugginess."

"Do you know how much rents are in Chicago nowadays? I'm lucky he isn't charging me more."

"You could take me up on that other offer, you know. You never gave me an answer."

"Look, I'm totally into the idea of us living together. And Gabe's cool and all, but—"

"But what?"

"Call me crazy, but I don't think he'd appreciate the idea of his wife's lover moving in."

"Gabe digs you, Eve. You know that."

"Yeah, and I'm sure he's totally not obsessed with the possibility of watching his super-hot wife have kinky sex with her super-hot girlfriend all over the house. But live there with you guys full-time? Doubt he'd dig that."

Zoey shoved her and laughed. "I'm not suggesting you move in with us permanently. Okay, I am, but I know you won't do that. I have another idea. How about you at least let me find you a nice apartment and set you up for a while until you can get caught up on your bills?"

"So I would be like your 'kept woman'. And you can afford to do that? It's not like you're rich. You're a therapist."

"Gabe will help."

Eve scoffed. "Sure, he will."

"He's already agreed to it."

"What? You asked him?" she groaned. "I'm not a charity case, Zoey."

"No shit, Sherlock. You're the smartest, strongest woman I've ever known. And I enjoy your company. Gabe enjoys your company. You're not a charity case—far from it. But everyone needs help once in a while, Eve. So let me help."

She stared at Zoey, not sure what to say.

"Well, I'm putting it out there on the table. It's up to you."

Eve remained quiet, not sure what to say.

In silence, they dug into the Chinese food. As they

downed noodles and dumplings, Mr. Pebbles sat on the windowsill and watched them with longing.

"You hear your phone ringing, right?" asked Zoey, stuffing her face with dumplings.

"It's probably the same scam call. Been getting a weird repeat call for a couple of weeks. They left a voice message the last time."

"Hmm...about what?"

Eve swallowed her noodles and took a sip of water. "Some fake offer of a job I never applied for. I've tried to block the number."

"Let me guess. It's one of those 'make a bazillion dollars working from home!' scams, isn't it? I've gotten those."

"Actually, no. It's a government job supposedly at some fake agency called S-P-I or some shit no one's ever heard of. Anyway, I'll figure out how to block it soon."

"Interesting." Zoey put down the bowl of dumplings, grabbed her own cell phone from the coffee table, and spoke into it: "S-P-I."

"What are you—"

"Whoa," exclaimed Zoey, eyes wide, as she dragged her finger along the screen. She turned the screen to Eve.

"Special Procurements Initiative?"

They looked at one another.

"Eve, you mean to tell me you never got curious enough to look it up?"

She shrugged. "Nobody gets offered shit they never applied for. I figured the whole thing was fake."

Zoey's eyes were glued to the screen. "It looks like it's a department or division within our intelligence branch."

"Like the CIA?"

"This is kind of creepy now, Eve. Who the fuck gets calls from the CIA?"

"Terrorists."

She put the phone down and smirked at Eve. "Are you trying to tell me something? Because if you're about to tell me you're some sort of James Bond deep undercover operative for, like, the Russian government, then that's just...sexy."

Eve laughed.

"I'm seriously turned on right now."

"You are a mess," Eve said, grinning.

"I understand you can't tell me. Of course, you're sworn to secrecy." Zoey moved closer to her and slipped her hand under Eve's shirt.

"I never knew you were into role play," said Eve, sliding back on the sofa.

Zoey lifted Eve's shirt and unsnapped her bra. "Your secret is totally safe with me...Miss Bond."

Laughing, Eve fell against the sofa as Zoey kissed her mouth, neck, and shoulders. Worries about bills and the incident on the bus faded into the background, mere white noise. All that mattered now was the lavender scent of Zoey's hair, the soft brown hue of her flawless skin, the fluttering sensation of her gentle kisses.

Eve woke before dawn and looked at the clock on the nightstand. Turning over, she rubbed her eyes and groaned. Why was it always so difficult to get a good night's sleep? She sat up, pushed the sheet away, and yawned. She trudged out of the dark room and to the kitchen, where she poured herself a glass of water. As she gulped the ice-cold water, she glimpsed her cell phone next to the envelope on the countertop.

She paused and stared at the sleep screen that showed two missed calls and a voice message. *I'd be foolish to do it...to return the call. Right?* She put the glass in the sink and grabbed the phone. After a deep breath, she listened to the recording.

"I hope this message finds you well. I'm calling to touch

base about an opportunity at SPI. I would love to discuss your suitability for the position."

It was the voice of the same woman who had left a message last week.

When the message finished, Eve hit "replay." She stared at the phone after the message finished a third time. *This is stupid. Don't be desperate, Eve. You know this is a scam. You know it.* Yet she hit "call back" and waited for the number to go to the recipient's mailbox.

To her general surprise, however, a woman answered—the same woman who had left the two messages.

"Hi, Miss Cooper. I can't say I expected you to call at six in the morning."

Eve's mouth hung open, but she didn't say anything.

"I know you're ready to hang up because you're sure this is a trick to get your social security number and whatever else. Let me cut to the chase. This isn't a scam or a trick. We already know your social security number and other sensitive personal identification information. That's of no interest to us. This is an invitation; one we're sincerely hoping you'll accept."

"An invitation to what?"

"That's a...complex question. But I'd be delighted to answer it and more in-person. Meet me at two o'clock today at 1833 South Pulaski."

"Hold on, I didn't say—hello? Hello?"

There was a click and the call disconnected.

When Eve boarded the pink line train that Saturday afternoon, she took a seat next to the door. In the nearly empty train car, one person was standing in the aisle, while several others were seated and staring at their phones. A dark-haired woman, laughing and walking alongside a tall woman with a short-cropped haircut, entered the train and sat in front of Eve. The women whispered to each other and laughed, an infectious sort of laughter. She thought about Zoey, wondering if she should take her offer to move in. *Gabe is nice, but what if he becomes jealous?* Sure, he didn't seem like the jealous sort, but you could never be too sure about people, right?

Eve watched the women lean in close to one another, kiss lightly on the lips, and continue talking in hushed voices. Her gaze drifted to another pair, a woman and a man who were talking animatedly and showing one another something on their phones.

By the time the train reached her stop, the train car was at capacity. She squeezed through the crowd and exited onto the platform. Repeating the address in her mind, she headed toward the escalator. *I could turn back, go home, and forget about this. That's the sensible thing to do. But what if there's money in this? An opportunity to save the house?* She glanced over her shoulder at the platform below. *Oh my God, what am I doing? Oh, fuck it. It's just a meeting. What's the worst that can happen?*

When she emerged from the station, she stopped at the first storefront window she saw and peered at it, searching for her reflection. She closed her eyes. *I need to be unseen, hidden.* Yesterday, she'd lost control and somehow activated her ability. Today, she needed to activate it. *I need to be hidden.*

After a moment, she opened her eyes and saw only the building behind her reflected in the window.

Eve looked at the street sign. Following her phone's GPS, she took a right on Pulaski and walked five blocks. "You have arrived," the GPS announced. She gazed at the boarded-up gray building, searching for the number.

"Where is it?" she mumbled, searching. "This has to be the right address." She looked around for any sign that she was at the right location.

But besides the small shops, one of which appeared

abandoned, the area was desolate. Just greystone apartments and cars parked along the street.

Sighing, she folded her arms across her chest. "Just like I figured. Waste of fucking time."

"I hope to change your mind about that," said a familiar voice.

Startled, Eve spun around and almost lost her balance. She found herself staring into the dark eyes of a woman who was leaning against a black SUV.

"I'm glad you made it, Miss Cooper."

"You...you can see me?" Eve looked at the window of the car and didn't see her reflection.

The woman smirked. "No, of course not. But I can hear you."

"How do—"

"I know about your particular talent? Well, that's exactly what I'd like to speak with you about. But, if you don't mind, I'd prefer to chat inside, since I'm pretty sure it's about to rain." She turned to the car and glanced over her shoulder at Eve. "There's a diner a couple of minutes away. Is that okay with you?"

"No, I'm sorry. I'm not going anywhere until you tell me how you know. I'm careful to never use my ability—well, besides when I had an accident yester—"

"Four years ago, we detected some unusual activity in Indiana. So we sent some of our people there and asked questions. Your father, Jackson Cooper, had some interesting things to say."

"You're lying. My father doesn't know about my ability."

"Right. He doesn't know. But he did describe a weird incident that happened during your mother's funeral. He believes he must've had one too many drinks because it's the only thing that could explain what he saw."

Eve's heart sank. She knew what was next.

"He claims your mother's 'invisible spirit' not only screamed at him for hurting her but also drove off in his pickup truck afterward. He said he couldn't see her, but he recognized her voice. Several funeral guests also reported seeing a pickup truck speed off with apparently nobody behind the wheel. It seems they convinced themselves they had succumbed to some sort of mass hysteria due to grief. Any of this ringing a bell to you?"

Some shadow agency's been watching me for years? Spying on me? Making herself visible again, she glared at the woman. "Who are you?"

"Agent Olivia Yu, Special Procurements Initiative, Chicago Division."

"Okay. And why are we meeting at this abandoned building?"

"Oh, this place? It's convenient. I live about six blocks south near 24th." She paused and looked at the dark clouds that had moved in while they spoke. "So, is a diner okay with you?"

Eve inhaled, looking from the building to the car to Agent Yu. *I may as well find out more about why these people have been watching me.* "Fine."

She read through the first pages of the packet, while Agent Yu sipped coffee and watched her. She slid her index finger along line after line on the page and stopped at a sentence near the bottom of the third page. "This salary...this is monthly?" she asked, hoping no drool was dangling from her mouth. *With this kind of money, I could pay the property tax bill in one month.*

"Yes, the salary is monthly during the initial six-month FIO training period."

Eve cast her a quizzical look.

"Field Intelligence Operative training. After your training, you'll be assigned as an FIO, which results in an immediate salary increase. If the amount noted isn't acceptable, I'm willing to negotiate," said Agent Yu, pouring sugar into her coffee. "New FIO training begins the first week of October."

"Next Monday?"

"Yes, nine days from now. So you'll need to wrap up your affairs at the school in that time."

Eve closed the document and fixed her gaze on the woman. "I haven't accepted." She paused as the waiter arrived with a pitcher.

"More coffee, miss?" he asked Agent Yu.

She shook her head, and he gave her a curt nod before leaving them alone again.

"The problem," said Eve, glancing around before turning to Agent Yu, "is I don't trust this. I don't trust you."

Agent Yu smiled and sipped lukewarm coffee. "I would be worried if you did, Miss Cooper."

"You see, saying things like that isn't the way to inspire confidence in a person."

"All right. Look, the truth is people like you are few and far, and it's exactly why I'm certain you'll excel at SPI."

"People like me? What does that mean?"

She regarded Eve with an inscrutable expression. "You didn't honestly believe you were the only one with gifts, did you?"

Eve sunk a little in her chair. She often had wondered whether there were others like her and whether they, too, had passed through the world as 'normal'. How many others had spent their entire lives hiding this big secret, dreading ever being discovered? As her mind swam with these thoughts, the waiter returned with their orders and refilled her glass of water. "I always knew I couldn't be the only one, that there had to be others. But..." she muttered, peering at her plate.

"But you've never met another?"

"No. At least, I don't think so."

"That must be lonely."

"You've no idea." She spooned potatoes into her mouth.

"Go on," said Agent Yu. "Tell me more about your life up till now."

"I'm pretty sure you already know everything there is to know about me."

She sipped the water and wiped her mouth. "Technically, yes. But I'm particularly curious about why a woman with your gifts settled for being a teacher, why you never used your gift."

"I didn't 'settle'. Being a teacher was my calling."

"Was?"

"*Is* my calling. Teaching is my calling." Eve stared at her plate, at the potatoes and peppered bacon. "And I figured if I ever used my 'gift' it would blow up in my face. I'd be a freak, an outcast."

"Because you thought you were the only one?"

Eve nodded.

"So this..." said Agent Yu, in between chewing, "mediocrity...is the life you envisioned for yourself instead?"

"You know what? I'm not interested in the offer. I'm good," she replied, rising and gathering her purse.

"I'm sorry. That was rude. I shouldn't have said that. Please have a seat, Miss Cooper."

"I don't want the job," said Eve, turning toward the exit.

"So you're going to walk away from this? From a chance to do something extraordinary? From a salary that would allow you to save your family's home?"

"How do you know about—"

"Like you said—we already know everything there is to know about you." Agent Yu wiped her mouth with the napkin. "Now, please sit and let me start over."

Eve glanced around the empty diner, exhaled, and

resumed her seat.

2

Eve retrieved three plates from the cabinet, humming and swaying her hips to the electronic dance music blaring from the television's speakers. She finished setting the table, placing the plates alongside empty glasses and silverware. After filling each glass with lemon water, Eve looked at the table.

Once she returned the water pitcher to the refrigerator, she grabbed the half-empty wine glass from the kitchen counter and turned it up. The song changed, and she closed her eyes as it washed over her. Her arms followed the thrusts of her hips, responding to the bass of the melody. Losing herself in the solace of dance, her mind drifted back to the conversation with Agent Yu and a smile curled her lips.

Just as the vocalist cut in and matched the pleading tone of the melody, a light knock at the door distracted her from the song, and she opened her eyes. She took a quick sip of wine, sat the glass on the kitchen counter, patted her hair, and checked her reflection in the glass of the microwave door. Sparing another glance at the table, she inhaled and hurried to the front door.

When Eve opened the door, Zoey and Gabriel greeted her with bright smiles. Gabriel, a lean man with large brown eyes, was holding a small red vase of dahlias. "What are the flowers for?" asked Eve, looking from him to Zoey.

"Zoey saw them at the store during our grocery run earlier and said they reminded her of you," he replied, grinning at his wife.

"Aren't they beautiful?" said Zoey.

Eve's face flushed as she stepped aside for them to enter. "I remind you of dahlias?"

"I read somewhere that they symbolize strength," said Zoey.

"Actually, in the Victorian era they symbolized an important bond. Probably why they often use them for weddings nowadays," said Gabriel.

Shutting the door, Eve chuckled. "You two are like walking encyclopedias."

They laughed.

"Anyway, I could use a little color in this room," said Eve, looking around. "I think they'll go nicely over there on the window."

"Over there?" Gabriel pointed, and she nodded. He placed the vase on the window ledge and remarked, "They should keep for over a week. Flowers from Whole Foods last a while."

"They're pretty. Thanks, you guys," said Eve. She was about to switch the topic to dinner, but Zoey interjected.

"Eve, I don't know if I'm imagining it, but you're glowing. You look positively...happy."

"Are you saying I usually look miserable, Zoey?"

Zoey laughed. "No. But I've never seen you looking like this. Not to mention you invited us both to dinner out of the blue, and from the looks of it—the music, the wine glass over there—you're in here basically partying by yourself. Something's up."

"Well," said Eve, walking to the kitchen to retrieve her

wine glass. "I have good news, actually. But first..." She filled two wine glasses and handed them to Zoey and Gabriel.

Silently, they sipped their wine while watching her finish off the wine in her glass and pour herself more. "So..." said Zoey, approaching Eve, "are you going to tell us?" She closed the space between them and sat her glass on the counter behind Eve. "Or are you going to keep us in suspense all evening?"

Eve's heart quickened as Zoey's lips brushed against the crevice of her neck. Soon, Zoey's mouth met hers.

"I don't mind a little suspense," Zoey whispered.

Eve looked over Zoey's shoulder and extended her hand to Gabriel, who was standing nearby. He came forward and took her hand as she met his gaze. Looking into his eyes, Eve asked, "Is this okay with you?"

"As long as it's okay with you. Is it?"

As Zoey kissed her shoulders, Eve breathed in and kept her eyes fixed on Gabriel. She brought his hand to her lips. "Yes."

"All right," Zoey whispered, kissing Eve's chest, "now that you two have settled that..." She lifted Eve's shirt and brought it over her head, gently undressing her until she was left in nothing but lace panties.

For what seemed like the fiftieth time already, Eve blushed. Zoey and Gabriel were kissing her shoulders, and their hands were wandering everywhere, and she knew if heaven existed, she was there now.

"Hey," said Eve, sitting up, and pulling the sheet over her naked body. She smiled at her lovers—Zoey was resting against Gabriel, who was running his fingers through her hair. "This isn't...you know I've never done anything like this before."

"A threesome?" Zoey caressed Eve's cheek. "It was the

first time for us, too. Not that we hadn't thought about it. But Gabe insisted we leave that ball in your court."

Gabriel planted a kiss on the side of Zoey's forehead and clasped Eve's hand. "Look, you two have a closeness that's special. I accepted that before Zoey and I married. I wasn't going to get in the middle of it, unless invited."

"How very feminist of you," Eve teased and glanced between them. "So, what do we do now?"

"We can start with the dinner you prepared," said Zoey.

"You know what I mean."

"Yes." Zoey kissed her lips. "I know what you mean. We can do whatever we want. But, first, we should eat." She got up, fully nude, and looked around for her clothes.

Gabriel scooted toward Eve and reached for her hand. He squeezed it gently and met her gaze. "We'll figure it out together. I'm guessing Zoey already mentioned that you can live with us, right?"

"Yeah," said Eve and glanced at Zoey, who was half-dressed now. "I just don't want to be a third wheel, you know."

Zoey laughed, pulling the shirt over her head. "You underestimate yourself, Eve, and how much we love you. It's endearing but sometimes kind of annoying." She sat in front of Eve and gazed at her two lovers before shaking her head and smiling. "I really am the luckiest woman in the world."

For a while, there was silence as they sat on Eve's bed and enjoyed what could only be described as a moment of pure happiness. Moments that were rare for Eve. The last time she'd felt anything akin to this was when she first met Zoey during her senior year of college—that night they'd shared a kiss at a New Year's celebration. They'd been friends and frequent lovers ever since, no matter Zoey's marriage to Gabriel after college or Eve's flings with other women. She wasn't sure if she believed in soul mates, but she assumed

Zoey was as close as she'd get to finding one.

"Well, before we eat, are you going to tell us why you invited us here tonight?" asked Zoey.

"Oh, right," Eve replied. "You know that weird job offer?"

"The CIA job?"

"Actually, it's the Special Procurements Initiative. But, yeah, that one. I met with the woman who'd contacted me, and she gave me more details." Eve paused. "I start next Monday."

Zoey's eyes widened. "Wait...what? You accepted?"

"Yeah," said Eve, grinning. "It's a chance for me to make a difference in the world. Instead of wasting away at CPS where they're laying off teachers left and right and barely paying the ones they keep. I mean, I love teaching—and I'm going to miss my kids—but I'm tired of struggling to pay bills. This opportunity...it's once in a lifetime, you know. And the salary is amazing compared to my CPS salary."

"Wow," said Zoey. "That's awesome. I'm proud of you for taking the leap."

She frowned as she watched Zoey's expression go from shocked to concerned. "But? There's a 'but' written all over your face right now."

Zoey stood again and paced a few times before facing Eve. "Are you sure you're not having a quarter-life crisis? As long as I've known you, all you ever wanted to do was teach. It seems so sudden, this change. Also, I'm a little confused about what made them interested in recruiting a schoolteacher."

She silently chastised herself for not realizing that Zoey might ask this question.

"Eve?"

"What does it matter? It's a legitimate opportunity to do something meaningful with my life, to make a decent income for a change."

"But I don't under—"

"Zoey," Gabriel began. "I'm sure Eve made the decision she felt was right for her."

Eve appreciated his support but also wanted to assuage Zoey's concerns. "And you checked out the place yourself, Zoey. It's legit."

"I'm not saying it's not legit. I'm saying I don't understand what makes them so interested in you, considering that nothing on your resume equips you to work at an intelligence agency."

Eve averted her eyes. *I can't tell them.* "Zoey, you're my best friend. But there are things you don't know about me."

"What the hell does that mean?"

"Zoey, please drop it," said Gabriel. "Everyone has secrets."

Eve sighed and stared at Zoey. "It just means you should trust me not to make this decision without thinking it through. I know what I'm doing." Clutching the sheet against her, she stood and approached Zoey, who turned away, folding her arms across her chest. "Look at me, please."

"Why do I feel like you're hiding a big secret from me? Like you're afraid I can't handle it or something," said Zoey.

"It's not whether you can handle it. It's whether I can handle you knowing." With her free hand, Eve lifted Zoey's chin and kissed her lips. "I promise I'll tell you when I'm ready. I promise."

"Is it that bad, Eve?"

She shook her head and smiled. "It's not bad at all."

"Then why—"

"You have to trust me. Okay?"

At last, Zoey nodded. "You promise you'll tell me."

"I swear. In time."

"All right, fine." Zoey smiled brightly. "I mean, the thought of you having some big secret is kind of sexy, actually. If I'm honest it's turning me on again. So I suggest we go eat now before I get something started again."

Eve laughed. "Everything is always about sex with you, isn't it?"

"And what? That's a problem?" Zoey scoffed and winked.

"I'm not complaining," said Eve.

"Me neither," Gabriel added.

As she walked into Martin Delaney High School on Monday, she headed straight for the principal's office. It was best to start the day off with her resignation instead of delaying it, she'd decided. She'd rehearsed her speech the night before.

"Hey, Miss Cooper!" yelled a lanky student from her third period English class.

She waved at him and, at once, experienced a surge of guilt. The first surge of guilt she'd felt since deciding to take the SPI job. Her students were the only thing that made the job worth it, even if they drove her near the edge of sanity some days. How would she explain her decision to them?

"Hey, Pierce. Hope you memorized that poem. You know I'll be calling on you this afternoon."

"I got you, Miss Cooper. I got you."

"All right then," she said, chuckling as she opened the door to the administrative office.

"Is Don in yet?" she asked the secretary, who pointed her toward his office.

"He has ten minutes or so before his meeting."

"Thanks," she replied, wondering why she'd never committed the woman's name to memory. She turned the corner toward Principal Gray's office and knocked twice.

"Come in," said a deep, commanding voice. His face lit up when she opened the door. "Eve, how are you?"

"Oh, I'm great. I just need a quick word..."

"No problem. What can I do for you?"

She sat across from him and smiled some more. Recalling her rehearsed speech, she launched into a long monologue about how much she'd enjoyed working at Martin Delaney but that she'd found a "calling" elsewhere. As she said it, she hoped she didn't sound as disingenuous as she felt saying it. After all, she couldn't quite consider the job at SPI a "calling"—in light of Zoey's reaction, she still wondered if she'd made a mistake in accepting the offer—but she knew that word would resonate with him. What she'd wanted to say was simpler: that he and the district didn't pay enough for anyone to live on, and she couldn't tolerate living like a pauper much longer. But she figured it was wiser to resign on a positive note instead of pissing in the water. *Never know when I might need to come back to this place.*

When she was done, he leaned back in his chair and shook his head. "I don't know what to say. We won't be able to replace you, that's for sure."

If I'm so irreplaceable, why didn't you pay me more? She fought the urge to roll her eyes.

"But a calling can't be ignored," he went on.

She smiled.

He glimpsed his watch and stood. "Well, I would like to discuss the process of your transition, but unfortunately, I have a meeting in a minute. Can you plan to stop by again at lunch?"

Eve rose and gathered her purse. "No problem. I'll see you at lunch."

He walked her to the door and, before she left, said, "Eve, congrats. I look forward to hearing more about the new job."

She nodded and exited his office. Breathing a sigh of relief, she hurried to her first period class.

After school, she lounged under a gazebo at the lakefront and peered at the teal blue expanse and closed her eyes. Silent and still, Eve shut her eyes. Images from her childhood flickered in her mind. Like an old film roll, the images flashed across her mind. There she was, sitting on the porch while her mother braided her hair, helping her mother pick cherry tomatoes from the tiny backyard garden, stepping in between her parents during one of their many fights, hanging upside on the monkey bars at the playground during recess until the boys approached...

The boys shoved her around the circle while shouting and laughing. Two girls with pigtails watched, one of them frowning and the other wearing an excited expression that matched the ones on the boys' faces. Eve covered her face with her arms as they pushed her to the rocky ground and kicked her stomach and legs. Something that tasted metallic filled her mouth, and when she coughed, she saw red flecks on the ground beneath her. Anger flooded through her like a tsunami as she recoiled from the kicks.

Not sure why or how she did it, she reached out and grabbed a foot as it was about to connect with her face. She yanked the boy's foot with all her strength. This caused everyone to gasp and retreat as the boy came tumbling next to her. In a flash, she got on top of him and squeezed his throat with both hands.

As she squeezed harder, he wheezed and clutched at her hands, the whites of his eyes turning red.

"Get off him!" one of the girls screamed and reached for Eve's hands.

Eve knocked the girl aside, while keeping one hand around the boy's neck. The girl landed a foot or so away and hit the concrete with an audible thud. This elicited more gasps from the crowd. Paying no attention to the girl, Eve brought her other hand to the boy's neck once more and observed the tears streaming down his rosy cheeks.

"She's gonna kill him," another boy exclaimed.

The words struck Eve like a brick, and she loosened her grip on the boy's neck. Another boy lunged at her not a moment later and reached for her hands to pull her away. Waves of anger still crashing over her, she grasped the boy's wrists and turned to face him. She was staring into the face of the boy who'd started it all, the one who'd shoved her and called her a freak. Still gripping his wrists, she rose up and he had no choice but to rise with her. As she stood face to face with him now, she marveled that he seemed so small and frightened.

"You really are a freak," he managed, grimacing as she tightened her grip on his wrists. A cracking sound followed, and he released a piercing scream just as she let go of his now broken wrists.

Eve wiped her wet cheeks and glowered at him. "Don't call me that again." She looked at the other boy on the ground—he was coughing and struggling to sit up. Glimpsing the terrified faces of the other kids, Eve wanted nothing more than to disappear. Anything to escape their judgmental stares.

"Where'd she go?" one of the pigtailed girls asked.

"She was standing right there," a boy replied. "How did she—"

"Disappear," said the girl Eve had knocked to the ground. "How did she disappear?"

Confused, Eve hurried away toward the school building where she ducked into the nearest restroom. She stopped at the mirror, hoping her face wasn't too bruised. How would she explain to her mom that she'd gotten into a fight and almost killed a boy?

She covered her mouth to silence the scream that escaped when she looked in the mirror. There was no reflection. She held out her hands in front of her but saw nothing. "How...?"

Footsteps approached.

Eve ran into one of the stalls and locked the door. She sat

on the toilet, put her hands over her mouth, and cried silently.

As she opened her eyes and stared at the lake, she wondered about how different life might have been if she'd known other kids like her. Other kids with abilities. Kids who could disappear, who were stronger than other kids. What she'd have given to know she wasn't alone, a freak.

Soon she'd meet others like her, others who had probably spent their childhood feeling alien in a world not suited for their existence. Others who had been called freaks.

Eve stared out the window at the fields of corn, haphazardly placed billboards interrupting the monotony of the landscape here and there. Nibbling at her already chewed up nails, she tried not to think about the last time she'd passed through these bleak cornfields. To occupy herself and quiet her mind, she flipped through the radio stations in search of relaxing music that wouldn't remind her of home.

"So you're going to sit there and not say a word for the entire trip, huh?" asked Zoey, hastily merging into the left lane to pass a slow-moving minivan.

Eve stopped at a house music station and, bobbing her head, turned up the volume. "You know I've seen this DJ live? Just a year ago. He was amazing."

Without warning, Zoey turned off the radio. "Well, I'm glad to know you haven't gone mute."

Eve sighed. "What?"

"Look, I like a good weekend road trip, especially if it gives me a reason to spend more time with you."

"So what's the problem?" asked Eve.

"The problem is this isn't just a road trip, and you're being weird. Like, for instance, you haven't mentioned anything about how your last week at the school went. Did the kids cry? Did you cry? Are you scared about starting the new job?

And, yeah, why do you have me driving you out to Indiana?"

"I told you I need to pick up a few things," Eve said, biting the hangnail on her index finger.

Zoey chuckled. "The one thing you suck at is lying."

Eve gazed out the window. "You want the truth?"

"Um...obviously."

"Yes, I cried, and so did some of my kids. They even brought me cupcakes as a parting gift. And part of me is super scared that I fucked up and made a really bad decision because, honestly, what if all I'm good at is teaching? So, you want to know how my last week was? That's how it was. Bittersweet."

"Thanks for that. I don't know why you have to be so weird about sharing your feelings sometimes," Zoey replied. "Now, why are we driving to Valparaiso?"

"I don't know. I don't know why I asked you to drive me home. I was just—I was having a lot of thoughts last night, about when I was a kid, and I felt like I needed to come home. For some reason."

"So, this is a little trip down memory lane for you?" Zoey scoffed.

"No. Well, sort of. I want to pick up some of my belongings and Mom's old journals."

Zoey laughed. "Wait. You got me driving your ass all the way out here for journals? You're lucky I love you."

Eve turned to her. "Love...?"

Zoey kept her eyes on the road.

Grinning, Eve kissed her neck and rested her hand on Zoey's thigh. "All these years and that's the first time—"

"With age comes wisdom. Don't go getting all sentimental," she interjected. She kissed the back of Eve's hand and winked at her.

"You know, I would drive you back home to Philly if you ever needed your own trip down memory lane."

Zoey shook her head and laughed. "You don't even have a driver's license, and that's like twelve hours compared to this one-hour journey into corn country. Anyway, you don't have to worry about me ever wanting a trip back to *Nightmare on Elm Street*. No thanks."

"Didn't you tell me your mom was sick, though? Don't you plan to at least check on her before she croaks?"

"It was a mild stroke. I'm sure she's fine. Besides, she's got my aunt to terrorize, so no need for me to be there."

The venom in Zoey's tone caught Eve off guard. "I know she was pretty awful, but I think even if my dad were dying I might pay the old bastard a visit, if only to tell him a piece of my mind."

"Well, that's the difference between me and you, I guess."

"Damn. No offense, Zoey, but you should take some of your own advice as a therapist and deal with that anger."

"Exactly what Gabe says."

"Smart guy," Eve said and smiled. As she turned the radio on again, house music flooded the small space of the Toyota Prius. She spoke loudly over the music. "Oh, I should warn you that my dad will probably be home."

Zoey lowered the volume. "Are you serious?"

"Yeah. I'm letting you know because he'll try to hit on you. Just prepare yourself."

"Jesus, Eve. You couldn't have told me earlier. Look at what I'm wearing."

She surveyed Zoey's leggings and loose but low-cut shirt that accentuated her large breasts. "If we're lucky, he'll be gone with one of his women, and we can get my shit without having to see him."

"All the things you've told me about him..." Zoey shook her head.

"Yeah, that's the reason I've never bothered to introduce you to him."

"Shit, man. You sure you don't want me to turn around?"
Eve shrugged as they exited off the interstate. "It's fine."

For several minutes, they rode in silence while Eve stared
out the window, and Zoey cast her uncertain glances. At last,
she lifted Eve's hand and kissed it again. "I really do love you.
I'm sorry I never said it."

Eve's palms grew sweaty, and she closed her eyes. In
under ten minutes, they would arrive at her childhood home.
"I haven't been back since my mom passed. I wish you'd met
her."

"I'm sure I would've adored her."

"Yes, you would have," Eve replied as they turned down a
gravel road.

To their immense relief, Jackson Cooper wasn't home. But,
realizing he could arrive any minute, Eve hurried inside the
musky house and headed straight for the basement. "I'm
surprised he hasn't changed the locks," she remarked to Zoey,
who was trailing behind her. "Let's be quick."

Zoey had stopped in the hallway and was staring into the
living room. "When's the last time he cleaned anything? Jeez.
Does he do anything to keep the place livable?"

"Other than repairs here and there...no." Eve observed
the clothes strewn about the floor and the plates of half-eaten
food on the coffee table. "Well, that explains the smell. Come
on, Zoey." She proceeded to the basement door in the
kitchen. As they descended the rickety basement stairs, Eve
coughed from the swirl of dust and waved her hands in front
of her face. There was just enough light to illuminate the
room and prevent it from being pitch black. When they
reached the floor, she felt around for the light switch behind
the stairs and turned it on.

The first thing she noticed was all the dust coating
everything in the room—the washer and dryer, her old

bicycle, the railing of the staircase, and the boxes lining the walls. Cobwebs hung from the low ceiling. "Watch your head," she said to Zoey. "Last time I came down here, I was in college. I must've grown an inch or two because I don't think I ever realized how low the ceiling is, and with all these nails jutting out, just be careful. Look for a box that has two small X's on it, will you?"

For a while, the two of them scanned the boxes. Eve counted fifteen boxes, but none of them contained the X markings.

"Here are a couple of X's," said Zoey.

Eve hurried to her side, squatted, and tried to pull at the box, but it moved no more than an inch. With Zoey's help, they lifted the box and placed it on the floor next to the other one. Eve dusted off the box with one hand, while covering her nose and mouth with the other hand. She opened the box and stared at the old spiral-bound notebooks. "I packed up all my mom's valuables and mine and put them down here after the funeral. I planned on picking them up once I had an apartment. But after I got settled and so much time passed, I decided I'd never come back to this place while he was here. It's amazing he hasn't thrown all this stuff away." Eve stood and looked around.

"Doesn't look to me like he or anyone else has been down here in ages."

"Jackson Cooper is a superstitious man. He probably felt like there was too much of her down here. I wouldn't be shocked if he thinks this place is haunted or some nonsense." She shook her head. "Let's take these two boxes and put them in the car. I don't think I need anything else right now."

"Is that box just her journals?"

"Yeah."

"Wow. She must've written a lot."

"She did write a lot, even poetry." Eve smiled. "Come on,

help me lift this box, and let's see if we can get it up the stairs."

"Eve, what made you want to get these journals now?"

"Like I said, I was thinking about things, about my childhood lately. I guess. I don't know." They squatted to pick up the box but froze when a gruff voice came from the top of the stairs.

"Evelina? Is that you? What are you doing here?"

Eve closed her eyes for a second and inhaled before standing and turning her gaze to her father, a full-bellied man who was at least twenty pounds fatter than when she'd last seen him. "Yeah, it's me. I'm on my way out."

"Picking up a couple of your mom's things, I see." He descended the staircase, gripping the railing and fixing his light brown eyes on Zoey. "And you brought a friend," he said as he stopped near them. When he smiled, it didn't extend beyond his lips. Long ago, Eve had concluded that no one had a creepier smile than Jackson Cooper.

"Um, this is Zoey. Like I said, we were on our way out." Eve looked at Zoey's perturbed face and gestured toward the box. They both squatted again to lift it.

"I can grab that for you, young lady," said Jackson Cooper, looking at Zoey and winking.

Zoey and Eve took a step back, allowing him to pick up the box. They watched him make his way up the stairs, carrying the box on his shoulder. Anxious to get out of there, Eve picked up the lighter box containing clothes and mouthed to Zoey, "Let's go."

As she followed them up the stairs, Eve glanced over her shoulder at the cluttered basement. She thought about all the Saturday mornings she'd spent down there as a child, helping her mother do laundry and fold clothes. At times, they'd retreat to the basement and lock themselves inside to escape her father's drunken episodes. During those moments, the basement had served as their safe space where they talked or played board games, anything to pass the time until they could return upstairs. Eve wondered when she might see this place again and have time to go through the rest of her mother's belongings. She sighed. *Probably when he's six feet under.*

Soothing electronica music flooded the room as Eve sprawled across the bed, three journals lying in front of her. She briefly shut her eyes, falling into the music, and bobbing her head to every percussive beat. When she opened her eyes, she looked at the journals.

"Annie, can you find me a song?" asked Eve, looking at the digital clock hanging on the wall next to the door. The clock flashed green.

"Sure. What song would you like to hear?" came the calming voice of the virtual assistant. Zoey had gifted her with the virtual assistant, which doubled as a clock, for landing the SPI job.

Eve was still trying to get accustomed to the device. "Something peppy?"

"Okay. Check out this station," said Annie.

When the familiar tune started, Eve smiled. "Pat Benatar is a strange yet logical choice, I suppose." She began humming the song and turned her gaze to the journals again. Still humming and not wasting another moment, she opened the journal dated 1994, the year before Eve was born.

It turned out to be rather dry reading...entries about Marie Cooper helping her parents fix things around the house, gardening, and ushering at the church. After about fifty pages of the 1994 journal, Eve wondered if her mother had been the dullest woman on earth. The most interesting entries involved detailed descriptions of the physical sensation of being pregnant and her awe of it. Eve noted that she seemed elated about becoming a mother.

Sighing, Eve decided to forgo the remaining 1994 entries and skip to 1995. She hummed to the Melissa Etheridge song playing as she sped through the 1995 journal. Similar to 1994, many of the entries focused on mundane daily activities, and she began to skim and yawn.

Over the next half-hour she finished two of her mother's journals, yawning and fighting sleep. She wasn't sure what she'd hoped to glean from the journals other than some hint that her mother knew of her ability. *She had to have seen me use my abilities at least once. If she had, wouldn't she have written about it?* But the farther she read, the more she accepted that her mother never knew. *Or, if she did, she took that secret to her grave.*

With each entry she read, she could hear her mother's voice, the slow cadence, and the drawl. She figured that was all she needed from the journals. That was enough, perhaps.

When she glimpsed the clock and saw that it was past midnight, she closed the journal. Tomorrow was the big day—her first day at SPI—so a full night's sleep was of crucial importance. She gathered the journals and placed them in her nightstand drawer. Fluffing her pillow and tucking herself under the blanket, she stared at the ceiling. "Annie, set my alarm for seven tomorrow."

"You got it," replied Annie.

"Can you play music to help me relax and fall asleep?"

"Sure. Check out this station."

Classical piano music filled the room seconds later, and Eve turned off the lamplight.

Tomorrow her life would change. She still couldn't decide if that was good or bad.

3

Eve's leg shook as she sat alone in the meeting room. All manner of thoughts were zooming around her mind. Had she dressed appropriately for her first day of training? Was a blazer suit too much? Perhaps she should have ditched the jacket and heels. How many other people, others with abilities, would be participating in the training? Her heart raced, and her mind buzzed with possibilities.

When the door opened, a tall woman wearing a bright smile entered and sat, leaving one seat between herself and Eve. Not missing a beat, she turned to Eve and extended her hand. "Hi, I'm AJ Taylor."

Eve shook her hand, surprised by the firmness of her grip. "Eve Cooper. Are you a trainee?"

"Yeah, it's a pretty exciting opportunity, isn't it?"

Eve leaned closer and spoke in a hushed tone. "Do you mind if I ask...how did you find out about the job?"

"Oh, that hot agent contacted me with an offer. I mean, I thought she was full of shit at first, but when she told me more, it sounded like an awesome job. Like my destiny or whatnot, cheesy as it sounds."

Eve chuckled. "I know what you mean."

"That agent—"

"Agent Yu?"

"Yeah," AJ replied, "what do you think?"

"What do I—"

"I can't get a good read, but I'm thinking she's family."

"Oh," Eve said, smirking. "Yeah, I'd say so."

"Good."

"Huh?"

"Means I've got a shot," AJ replied, chuckling and punching Eve's upper arm. "Nah, I'm joking. She's not really my type."

Eve rubbed her arm and shook her head. "How old are you? I'm guessing this is your first job...look, let me give you some solid adult advice: avoid office romances. They only lead to awkwardness and sexual harassment accusations."

"You only live once," said AJ, glancing toward the door as it opened. "So how many trainees do you think there are?"

Eve shrugged. "No clue. I'm still trying to deal with the fact that there are others like me."

AJ moved into the seat next to Eve. "You didn't know there were others? I mean, I knew one other person with the ability—this loner kid in high school. I saw him go invisible once, and it blew my mind. It was a relief to know there was another person like me. He hid it from everyone, so I had to keep his secret. That's kind of how it was...you find out you can do this crazy thing and then you realize it's probably best to hide it from most people because you can't be sure how anyone will respond to it. So I guess I can understand how you never knew there were others. But...wow. Not one?"

Eve shook her head, suddenly overcome with embarrassment.

"My God. You've been in this world how long...thirty years?"

"Twenty-five. Twenty-five years."

"And you never met any others with abilities? Never even

knew there were others? How lonely."

"You have no idea."

The room filled up with seven more people as Eve and AJ continued talking. As Eve looked at all the people in the room, at all the others like her, she wondered how she'd ever believed she was alone.

When the door opened again, the room fell silent, and all eyes followed Agent Yu. She put her briefcase on the floor alongside the table centered in the front of the room and faced them. "Welcome to the Special Procurements Initiative," she said, a faint smile curling her lips. "You're officially our first class of trainees."

"First?" asked AJ. "Awesome."

Agent Yu nodded. "Yes. But you're not the first people with your skill that we've had here at SPI. It's taken us a while to find more of you and to put together an actual training curriculum suitable for your specific skillset. I've waited a long time for this moment, and I'm looking forward to helping you excel here."

She grabbed a remote off the table and pointed it at the ceiling. A screen projected on the wall behind her. "Mr. Kim, do you mind getting the lights?"

Seated near the door, an overdressed man—he was the only person wearing a full suit and blazer—rose and flipped the light switch.

"As you know, SPI has chosen you because of your unique skill, what we refer to as your 'cloaking' ability. As a refresher, let's walk through what SPI is and our role in keeping this country safe. I'll apologize upfront if this part and the next few minutes feel redundant, given the individual conversations I've already had with each of you before today," said Agent Yu turning to the next slide, which showed the official seal of the Central Intelligence Agency next to an aerial photo of the headquarters in Virginia. "SPI is an initiative within the CIA, and we focus on matters relating to the buying and selling of sensitive or dangerous defense materials."

AJ's hand shot up. "I'm sorry, but can you explain what that means again?"

A few people chuckled while others stared at Agent Yu for a response.

"In a nutshell, it means SPI is charged with interrupting weapons purchases and trade in dangerous items that could put our country at grave risk," Agent Yu replied.

Satisfied, AJ relaxed in her seat.

"As you can imagine, the work requires a high level of infiltration and stealth that, for years, has been undertaken by some of our best-trained field operatives. They're good at what they do. I should know, considering it's how I started my career at the agency." Large letters—Special Procurements Initiative—appeared on the screen above a photo of Agent Yu and a white man with thick blond hair and disarming green eyes. "When we discovered the existence of those with your cloaking ability, we knew we needed you. To be, in a sense, invisible is what any agent worth their salt desires most. But for you all, invisibility isn't a metaphor. It's a literal reality. We knew your skill would enable you to achieve what some of our regular field operatives couldn't. Total infiltration. In other words, a task that could take a regular operative months or years to complete, a cloaker could do within hours. This was a revelation."

During the presentation, Eve couldn't help but notice that the agent only spoke of the 'cloaking' ability. *Doesn't she know about the super strength? Or wait…do the others have super strength?* As she listened to the agent describe the early years of SPI, she puzzled over these questions. She wasn't sure why, but she felt it was best not to mention it for now.

For lunch, Agent Yu led the trainees down a wide but winding hallway that terminated at a large cafeteria already brimming with employees enjoying their lunch break. She directed them to a table in a far corner. "Lunch is complimentary. Grab what you like and mingle. In one hour, we'll return to the meeting room."

AJ nudged Eve. "The morning was awesome, huh? One month of classes, then we'll be in the field like real ass super spies."

"In field training, technically, since our entire training lasts for six months. So, in six months, we'll be real 'super spies'."

"All I know is I can't wait to kick ass in the field. It's like I was meant for this," AJ said, beaming.

"Yeah," Eve replied, distracted by the smell of food. "I'm just a teacher, so I'm pretty sure I'll suck at it. We'll see. Also, I think I smell tortillas or something. I wonder if they have tacos."

AJ pointed at a sign that read "El Paso Cantina."

Eve smiled. "Perfect. I'm starving."

"Miss Cooper," said Agent Yu, approaching her. "When you get your food, please join me at that table. There are a couple of people I'd like to introduce you to."

Eve's gaze followed her finger toward the table in the farthest corner and closest to the window. Two middle-aged people, a woman and a man, were engaged in what appeared to be a rather serious conversation. She recognized the blond-haired man as the one from the presentation slides. His green eyes flashed on her for a moment, and he smiled. His smile perturbed Eve for reasons she couldn't understand.

"Look at you, making an impression with the bosses already," AJ exclaimed to Eve, as Agent Yu departed.

She wished she shared AJ's enthusiasm. "Let's see if the tacos are any good."

"Well, we're not in Pilsen, so let's keep our expectations

low," AJ quipped.

Eve laughed. "True."

After she'd filled her tray with food—three tacos, chips and salsa, churros, and a Fanta—she headed to Agent Yu's table. She dreaded having to make small talk with strangers when all she wanted to do was gobble every morsel of food on her tray. When she reached the table, she pasted a smile on her face and sat her tray before her.

The two strangers introduced themselves as Doctor Catherine Thomas and Agent David Grobeck.

"Miss Cooper, how are you enjoying your first day?" asked Agent Grobeck with a Southern accent.

Eve ate a piece of the chicken and corn tortilla before responding. "Good so far. One of the trainees and I were talking about how ready we are to get to work."

"I'm glad to hear it." Agent Grobeck's voice was as cool as his eyes.

Eve noticed Agent Yu wasn't smiling but merely sipping her coffee. She looked at the woman who hadn't said more than a dozen words. "Doctor Thomas, what is it you do here?"

"I'm the staff psychiatrist," she answered.

"Technically not 'staff' since she's on contract from FordTech. But she's been with us for years, so she might as well be," said Agent Grobeck.

Agent Yu cleared her throat and coughed. "I'm sorry. Water went down wrong," she explained, covering her mouth.

Eve regarded her with increased curiosity.

"I've worked with a lot of gifted people over the years," said Doctor Thomas. "Some more gifted than others."

"All uniquely equipped to defend our freedoms in this era of widespread terrorism," Agent Grobeck noted.

Eve consumed the last of her taco and took a sip of Fanta.

"I don't think terrorism is any more widespread in this era than in previous eras. Just different weapons and, in some cases, different victims."

They were silent for a moment until Agent Grobeck spoke. "That's an interesting perspective."

She looked from him to Agent Yu to Doctor Thomas. "I'm honored to be part of something so important."

Agent Grobeck chuckled, cracking a smile for the first time since she'd sat. "It's our honor to have you here. Please let Agent Yu know if there's anything we can do to help ease the transition into SPI. The culture here can take some getting used to, and we're here to provide the necessary resources to make that shift as smooth as possible."

"Thank you. I appreciate the opportunity," Eve replied.

Agent Grobeck rose, buttoning his blazer jacket and extending his hand again.

Eve stood and shook his hand.

"We'll see you around, Miss Cooper," said Agent Grobeck before he and the doctor made their way toward the exit.

Eve resumed her seat and looked at Agent Yu who was wearing a stern expression and sipping her coffee. "Agent Grobeck and Doctor Thomas can be a little off-putting, I know. Anyway, eat up. You'll want the energy for the second half of today's orientation."

"What's the second half involve?"

"Hours of practicing your cloaking ability. I like to mix in some practice with the boring stuff, just to keep things interesting."

Eve's eyes widened. "Awesome."

Eve closed her eyes and all light and sound faded. She recoiled at the sensation of cool air brushing against her exposed arms. Her nose crinkled at the pungent smell of Lysol or another cleaning product, and she retreated further into her mind, shutting down all her senses until there was nothing. Just a dark, empty void.

"Miss Cooper, as you can see, has complete control over her cloaking," said Agent Yu, disturbing the silence that had enveloped Eve. "She moves in and out of it with incredible ease."

As Eve opened her eyes, she gazed at her peers seated around the room. Part of her felt like that little girl on the playground again, with all the kids staring at her, except they weren't laughing. They weren't staring at her because they couldn't see her. She was invisible.

"How often have you used your skill before now, Miss Cooper?" asked Agent Yu, standing next to an invisible Eve.

I'm pretty sure I shouldn't admit to shoplifting recently, or when I used my invisibility to sneak onto a party yacht with a bunch of rich white people. "I—well, not much. I was always afraid to," Eve answered, assuming a half-truth was the best response.

Agent Yu's gaze swept over the class. "What about others?"

Their answers ranged from "not much" to "just here and there" to AJ's enthusiastic "all the time!"

"I would sneak into department stores just before closing and swipe clothes," AJ explained. "At the beginning of eighth grade, I did it enough times that my mom didn't even have to buy me new clothes for the year. I'm talking good, quality stuff we could never afford to buy."

"Didn't your mom ever wonder where you were getting the clothes?" asked a chubby man near the front of the room.

"She already knew, found out about it when I accidentally went invisible at an arcade one time. I'd separated from her to go to the older kids' side of the arcade. She thought a pervert had snatched me or something, since I was only ten. I was on my last few tokens playing *Tekken* when she found me—told me she saw my disembodied head and almost fainted. Messed me up because I was so close to beating Kazuya for the first time."

Everyone laughed, and Agent Yu smiled.

AJ shrugged. "Anyway, she had me stealing stuff out of the grocery store sometimes after that. So she didn't care about me stealing clothes for myself. She figured I was a sign God was looking out for her, since she could barely afford to take care of me."

"Fascinating example. It's my hope that with your generous salary and benefits, you won't feel compelled to use your ability for criminal activities anymore," said Agent Yu. "Has anyone else been using their skill as often or as long as Miss Taylor? How old were you when you first used your skill?"

"I was five, according to my mom," said Samuel Kim, sitting at the farthest end of the table. He had pulled his dark hair into a ponytail.

Eve listened as they shouted out when they discovered they could be invisible. Five. Ten. Eight. Thirteen. *They were all young when they found out. I wish I had known these people when I was a kid. Do they have any other abilities?*

The chubby man's hand shot up.

"Yes, Mr. Rossi?"

"I was eleven. By high school, I was pretty good at it." Travis Rossi suppressed a giggle and averted his eyes for a moment. "I used it to scare one of my history teachers. I went to his class after school when he was packing up, and I got him to change my grade on the mid-term by…uh…pretending to be God. I don't even remember what I said, but it worked."

"Shit, why didn't I think of that?" AJ laughed.

"These are some hilarious examples, and I see you all are not scared to break the rules. You'll need that spirit here," said Agent Yu. "But I also see from these stories that many of you have gotten very comfortable with cloaking. I'm happy to know that because I'll be pairing you up soon based on your comfort and skill level, so be sure to turn in the questionnaire that you got at the beginning of this meeting. Now, let's return to Miss Cooper because I'm sure her legs are tired from standing here so long."

Eve shook her head, although no one could see it. "I'm fine."

Agent Yu instructed her to become visible again and cloak once more. She repeated this request two more times, and Eve performed on command.

"Notice that there's no struggle. Despite the fact that Miss Cooper hasn't spent much time using her ability, she's learned how to use it the way any of us use our limbs, with little to no conscious thought, as if it's impulse or instinct. Impressive. From what you all have told me, I assume many of you are as capable already. If you're not, this is how you have to become if you intend to be successful in the field."

The door squeaked open, and a few people turned to watch Agent Grobeck enter the room. He gestured for Agent Yu to continue and seated himself near the back.

"I want you all to understand that it doesn't matter how young you were when you first discovered or used your ability. It doesn't matter how often you've used it. You're all starting at pretty much the same point at SPI. Once I'm sure that you're comfortable with cloaking and able to do it instinctively, we will move on to technique." She turned to Eve—or where she imagined Eve was standing.

Eve stepped out of the dark void and reappeared.

"Thank you for demonstrating, Miss Cooper."

Heading to her seat, Eve looked at Agent Grobeck, who offered a half-smile and a nod. She sat next to AJ and turned her attention to Agent Yu.

"Now," said Agent Yu, "Let's—"

"Do you have the ability?" asked a blond woman with smeared freckles.

"No. I don't," said Agent Yu.

"Then, how can you teach us anything about our ability?"

This elicited grumbles and a "um-huh" from around the room, while others merely folded their arms across their chests and waited for Agent Yu to offer a valid response. But the question appeared to have rendered her temporarily speechless.

"That's a legitimate question," said Agent Grobeck, his voice low but commanding.

All eyes turned to him.

"I assure you that Agent Yu is a more than capable teacher, but I'll admit that what we're attempting here is a novel experiment. As such, it has its limitations. We're asking you all to take a giant leap and trust us in this endeavor. Might I suggest, Agent Yu, that we adjourn training for today a couple of hours early—it's just after three—so that you and I can discuss our trainees' concerns and adjust the training accordingly?"

Agent Yu nodded. "Let's call it a day, everyone. Training will begin again at eight tomorrow morning. You're dismissed."

AJ looked at Eve and shrugged. "You want to go for drinks?" she whispered.

Before Eve could answer, she heard Agent Grobeck calling her name. "Hold that thought, AJ," she replied. "Give me a second."

Agent Grobeck joined Agent Yu at the center of the room. As Eve approached, he smiled. "Miss Cooper, thank you for demonstrating. I was watching from outside and didn't want to interrupt your demonstration," said Agent Grobeck.

Eve smiled. "Thank you."

"Agent Yu and I have agreed that you, given your demonstrated control of your cloaking as well as your teaching background, would be the perfect co-instructor for this skills training."

"Are you asking me—"

"To co-teach the skills training alongside Agent Yu. Yes."

"I..." *How the hell did they come to this decision in less than a minute after dismissing the class?*

"Are you interested in taking on that role?" asked Agent Yu.

"We're sure the trainees would take well to having one of their own training them," Agent Grobeck added. "Because it'll require greater demands on your time, we'll increase your trainee salary by five percent."

Eve quickly did the math in her head and looked at the agents. "Okay. I'll do it."

He shook her hand. "Excellent. Agent Yu will have your revised salary agreement ready for you to sign tomorrow morning."

Once he departed, Eve turned to Agent Yu.

"I'll look forward to working with you tomorrow. I'm sure the class will appreciate it." She gathered her laptop and briefcase.

"Thank you, Agent," said Eve. "I didn't think I'd be teaching again so soon, but I'm excited."

Agent Yu nodded curtly and left Eve alone in the room with AJ, who was standing with her mouth hanging open.

"So it's the first day and they've already promoted you?" teased AJ.

Eve laughed. "What was that you were saying about drinks? I think this is a cause for celebration."

"Damn straight," AJ said, grinning. "We're getting tequila shots, and you're paying Miss-I-Got-A-Raise-On-My-First-Day. Come on."

Eve crossed her legs and reclined on the sofa as she sipped a cocktail. Sitting beside her, AJ hummed along to the soulful music coming from the speaker and chugged an IPA. Instead of talking, they soaked in the ambiance, watching the other customers. Throngs of people were lingering near the bar and slow dancing to the music or ordering drinks.

"How does it feel?" asked AJ.

"Huh?"

"Being the chosen one and all? I mean, I feel like SPI has big plans for you."

Eve smiled. "SPI knows my teaching background, so I guess Agent Grobeck figures this role would be a good fit for me."

AJ shook her head. "Nah, it's not just that. I think that guy Grobeck has his eye on you."

Eve scoffed. "Why?"

"Hell if I know," AJ said, shrugging. "I mean, look at how good you are at using your ability."

"I don't think I'm any better at it than anyone else—"

"Well, who cares. Cheers. You deserve it!"

Eve laughed. "You've known me for, like, a minute. How would you know I deserve anything?"

AJ guzzled the rest of her beer. "I read people well. Where are you from?"

"Indiana."

"I knew you weren't from Chi-Town," AJ replied, finishing off her beer. "Something too soft about you."

Eve grinned. "Soft? Whatever. So you grew up here?"

AJ nodded. "Lawndale. Then my mom got married, turned bougie, and moved to Oak Park right before I graduated high school. Anyway, don't worry. I like soft." She winked, standing up. "Now, you want to get to this game, or what?"

Eve looked from the VR headset in AJ's hand to the

television screen mounted to the wall. She took another sip of her cocktail. "I've never played a virtual reality game. I don't know how this works."

"Hey?" said a familiar voice.

When Eve looked at the door, she saw Zoey next to Gabriel. A wide smile spread across Eve's face, while Zoey appeared puzzled.

"Never figured you for one to come to a VR bar," Zoey said. She pushed some loose curls behind her ear and smiled. Without waiting for Eve to respond, she stepped forward and extended her hand to AJ. "Hi, I'm Zoey. And this is Gabriel."

"AJ. I love that dress, by the way." Barely disguising her flirtation, she looked Zoey up and down once and merely glanced at Gabriel.

"Zoey, this is a new colleague of mine," Eve said, approaching Zoey and planting a kiss on her cheek. "So, what are you two doing here? I figured real gamers wouldn't waste time with basic VR games like this...I mean, the reviews said the games are super basic."

"We like the vibe, and the cheap drinks," Gabriel chimed in.

AJ laughed. "A man of my own heart. You guys want to join us?"

Eve sighed. The last thing she needed was an awkward evening with Zoey, who was shooting AJ hostile looks every other second.

"Sure," said Gabriel, oblivious to the intense but silent exchange occurring between his wife and Eve.

"Awesome. Hey, Gabriel," said AJ, placing her hand on his shoulder. "Let me get you one of those cheap drinks."

Without hesitation, he accepted the offer and they headed to the bar, leaving Eve and Zoey alone in the room.

"She's cute," said Zoey, as Eve dropped onto the sofa.

"She's a colleague."

Zoey sat next to her and closed the space between them. "Hmm-huh."

"You know, jealousy isn't attractive on you, Zoey." *This is why our relationship didn't last in college. Well, that and you cheated on me with a law school girl and then married Gabe two years ago.* She sipped more of her cocktail.

"I'm sorry. You're right." She squeezed Eve's hand. "Seeing her with you made me feel like that lovesick college girl again, watching my girlfriend get hit on by girls way hipper and sexier than me."

"There was never anyone sexier than you. And, anyway, I'm not the one who ended up banging one of those girls and breaking us up."

"Touché." Zoey giggled, her face flushing pink. She held up Eve's hand and kissed it.

Eve brushed her lips against Zoey's neck. "Guess what happened to me today at work? I got a promotion."

"Damn, girl. That quick?"

Eve smiled.

"You are so sexy right now," she whispered, slipping her hand inside Eve's pants. "I could make love to you right here."

Gabriel and AJ returned with drinks. A look of confusion clouded AJ's face when Zoey kissed Eve with enough passion to make a sailor blush. After a moment, Zoey stood and approached her husband, who handed her a cocktail.

AJ surveyed them; her eyebrows raised. Smiling, she sat next to Eve and kicked her feet up on the table. "I think I've found my people," she said, toasting with her third IPA of the night. "Cheers to you, Eve. You're a luckier woman than I realized."

As the trainees gathered their belongings and filed out the meeting room, Eve lingered near the front desk. She stuffed her papers inside her large tote bag, shut down the computer, and checked the time. She had a one-hour break until the next session and wondered if she should run to the cafe next door to pick up a sandwich. When she saw Agent Grobeck approaching her, she wished she'd made a dash for the cafe. It would've spared her from having to interact with this man whose very presence irked her.

"Miss Cooper, how was your first class? I only caught the tail end, but from the looks of it, everyone seemed engaged."

She slung her bag over her shoulder. "Thanks. I tried to make it interactive by pairing people up to practice with each other. I don't know if it was effective, or what outcome I'm looking for. And it felt a bit weird because some of them are so good at cloaking that I'm not sure what I can teach them."

"Imagine how much weirder it would feel if you didn't have the skill and had to teach them," he said, smiling. "If it helps, think of yourself as a facilitator. Just like you, they already know how to use their skill. You're facilitating a class that allows them to practice and refine their skill."

She nodded. "It's mostly tricks I used with my high school kids to get everybody relaxed."

"Sounds like you're on the right track, and you have Agent Yu there to lean on for guidance," he said. "Do you have a moment?"

Eve groaned internally and smiled. "Yes. Sure."

"Great. I'd like to speak with you in my office." He motioned for her to follow him and continued to engage her in small talk until they arrived at his office.

It was a dim room, the only source of light provided by the floor-to-ceiling window that overlooked a cloudy, rainy Chicago skyline. A slender man about six feet tall stood in front of the window and peered out. Eve surveyed the stranger, his curly hair cropped above his ears and his hands in the pockets of his black pants. He turned around as Agent

Grobeck approached the desk. Light brown eyes that conveyed an unmistakable seriousness accented his cream-colored face.

"Miss Cooper, this is Mauricio Candela, an operative who joined SPI a while back."

The man remained silent and didn't come forward or extend his hand.

"Please close the door and have a seat, Miss Cooper."

She shut the door and sat in the chair opposite the desk. Agent Grobeck strolled to the bookshelf that lined one of the walls, while Mauricio resumed looking out the window. Eve watched in silence as the agent's hand swept over the spines of the books until he stopped and pulled out what looked like a worn mass market paperback book. He returned to his desk and laid the book down.

"I'm told this is one of your favorite books, and I believe you've taught it regularly?"

She looked at the book. *Fledgling* by Octavia Butler. "Yes. I've taught it for years. My students always enjoy it."

"I think you can tell a lot about someone if you know what they like to read. For instance, your love of this book—of this author—tells me that you have a strong sense of right and wrong, justice and injustice, that you're someone who understands the value of harmony among different types of people. It tells me that you recognize the need to right past wrongs and make the world better for everyone. Am I right?"

"Um...I suppose so," said Eve, trying not to look perturbed by the strangeness of the conversation. She looked from him to Mauricio, who was staring out the window with his back to them. Clearing her throat, she looked at Agent Grobeck and smiled. "I'm sorry, what is it you wanted to speak with me about?"

He sat behind the desk. "About you, the person. As you know, part of the purpose of this training is for SPI to learn more about the trainees."

"But SPI already knows everything there is to know about me."

"Not quite. We know basic facts that can be externally verified, sure. But do we know you, your feelings, and deeply-held worldview? Not really. We can only guess from the data. But because we want each of our operatives to be successful and comfortable with their duties, we need to get more insight about the person beyond the data. That's the only way to guarantee that we place you appropriately once this six-month FIO training concludes. Some of you will require additional weapons training, while others will be placed on more covert assignments. Your performance during this six-month period will enable us to make that determination. As I'm sure Agent Yu has explained, our goal is to ensure that you all become our elite team of counter-terrorism operatives, able to effectively disrupt trade and exchanges of items that present a danger to our national security."

"I see," she replied. "So you're going to be having a series of individual conversations like this with all the trainees?"

Agent Grobeck leaned forward and cupped his hands together on the desk. "Do you mind if I ask you some personal questions?"

"About?"

"Your family, your childhood."

"Oh, okay. Yes, that's fine."

"Great. Mauricio will join us, if that's okay. As I want him to take over these personal interviews with the new trainees, I'd like for him to observe. Is that okay with you, Miss Cooper?"

Eve looked at Mauricio, and he turned to face them now. For the first time, he smiled at her. She nodded to Agent Grobeck. "Sure."

AJ stretched out on the sofa and scrolled through Facebook on her phone. "It's probably just protocol."

"I don't know, AJ. This Grobeck guy is...off-putting. I've thought it since I met him that first day. And this meeting was so beyond awkward." Eve added olive oil and onions to the pan, turning up the heat. "I follow my instincts, and my instincts are screaming to me that something is wrong with this agency."

AJ smiled at something she was looking at on her phone. "Like what, Eve?"

"I don't know. I—"

"Look, they're trying to make sure they place us in suitable positions after the training. I'm sure that's what the meeting was about. Don't worry so much."

"I know. You're probably right." Eve added more onions to the pan, stirred in some tomatoes, and reduced the temperature to low. The fragrance of the rosemary, garlic, oregano, and a plethora of other herbs filled her nostrils. The water began boiling in the pot, and she added the linguine. "Annie, play Marvin Gaye's 'Got To Give It Up'," Eve told the virtual assistant.

"Good choice," AJ replied from the living room.

The upbeat kick, snare, and hi-hat melody flooded the room, and AJ rose from her seat, hips swinging and fingers snapping. Something about the synthesizer and Marvin Gaye's falsetto made Eve close her eyes and start singing along. She danced toward AJ, who had turned the living room into her own private dance floor. For five minutes, they laughed and danced and twirled about the room, letting the saxophone transport them to a 1970s dance hall full of the flyest, smoothest people they'd never met.

Then, the phone rang.

As if jolted awake from an all-engrossing dream, Eve stopped dancing and opened her eyes. The cell phone rang from the kitchen table. She hurried to get the phone while AJ continued dancing like there had been no interruption. She didn't recognize the number but answered it anyway.

"Miss Cooper? This is Agent Yu."

Eve quickly lowered the volume of the music.

"Hi, Agent Yu. This is Eve."

"Miss Cooper, I don't mean to call you at this hour after work, of course. So I'll be quick."

"It's fine." She turned off the heat under the pot of linguine and took it over to the sink to drain off the water.

"You met with Agent Grobeck today?"

"Yes, right after my class. He asked about my background, childhood stuff and—"

"Miss Cooper, I'm excited about your prospects at SPI. I think you're a natural for this work."

"Thank you, Agent. I'm...that means a lot."

"Because of that, I want to urge you to be careful with Agent Grobeck."

Eve was silent for a moment, not sure what to say. "I'm sorry? But what do you—"

"I won't say much right now other than to be careful. Take his kindness with a grain of salt."

Stumbling over her words, Eve replied, "What do you mean?"

"The truth is this training program was my idea because I think it's important that our operatives care about the work and feel a sense of purpose. Agent Grobeck had other ideas that...didn't go so well in the past. Just be careful, keep your head down, and do your job. I want to make sure that this training is successful so that your class becomes the first of many."

"I don't understand—"

"Miss Cooper, just take my advice."

Before Eve could say another word, there was a click, and

the call ended. She stared at the phone for a moment and laid it on the countertop. When a burning smell caught her attention, she rushed to the stove to turn off the heat under the frying pan. "Damn it. Why is it cooking so fast on low?" she groaned, stirring the tomatoes and thankful that most of it was salvageable.

"Who was that on the phone? You look like you saw a ghost," said AJ, coming into the kitchen. She sat at the table.

"Nobody. It's nothing."

AJ looked at her incredulously but shrugged. "Okay. Is the food done?"

"Yeah," said Eve, removing plates from the cabinet and puzzling over the strange call from Agent Yu.

4

Scrolling down the screen on her phone, Eve smiled at the beautiful numbers that represented her checking account balance, which included a signing bonus and her first month's salary. In her entire working life, she'd never seen that much money in her account at one time. As she sat at a lounge in Logan Square waiting for Zoey and Gabriel, she paid her bills online—the delinquent property tax bill, rent, electricity, credit card, student loan, phone, and internet—and thought about how much money she'd have left over to deposit into savings. *So this is what it feels like to not have to worry about money so much?*

"Miss, is there anything I can get you started with while you wait for the others? A drink or appetizer?" asked the server. Holding a small notepad and pin, he waited for her to respond.

"We're just getting drinks. I'll take a margarita with ice, sugar on the rim."

The man dashed to the bar, leaving Eve alone to continue daydreaming about her newfound financial security.

"Do you come here often?" Zoey whispered, her voice like silk. She brushed her lips against the back of Eve's neck.

Eve smiled at Zoey and Gabriel.

"My goodness, Eve, you look so fucking hot. Since when do you wear lipstick? And what in the world did you do to your hair? I love it," she exclaimed. "Just a month at that place, and you're already looking like a different person. Hell, maybe you should've changed careers a long time ago."

Grinning, Eve turned her head left and right so that they could take in her new haircut. "I thought I'd change things up a bit and go for a tapered look."

Zoey whispered, "If I could, I'd lay you on that table right now and—"

"Here's your margarita," said the server, placing a tall glass on the table and looking from Zoey to Gabriel. "Is there any drink I can get you started with?"

Not missing a beat, Gabriel replied, "She'll have a Strawberry Hennessey Island, and I'll take whatever hoppy beer you have on draft."

"Sounds good. And I'll bring waters as well," the server said.

They joined her on the sofa once the waiter departed.

"I paid the property tax bill on my family home," said Eve, beaming at them.

Zoey squealed and hugged her. "Oh my God, congrats."

"I can't imagine how relieved you are," said Gabriel.

Eve slurped the margarita. "I don't know what I would've done if I'd lost the house. My mom did everything in her power to keep it. It's the only thing I own, you know."

"It would've been like losing part of her, wouldn't it?" asked Zoey.

"I think so."

Zoey patted her thigh. "Well, cheers. Crisis averted. Meanwhile, you might want to think seriously about kicking your dad to the curb. I can't believe that asshole left you with the property tax bill."

"Don't ruin the mood by bringing him up. I wanted you

two here to celebrate and soak in the moment." She looked at Gabriel when he squeezed her hand.

Leaning against him, she gazed at Zoey. "I don't know what I'd do without you two sometimes."

The server returned with Zoey's and Gabriel's drinks, and they wasted no time raising their glasses to toast Eve.

"But that's not my only news," said Eve. "I go on my first field assignment tomorrow."

Zoey's eyebrows went up. "Like...on some *007* shit?"

"Nah, nothing that sexy." Eve laughed.

Lying on the hotel bed and enjoying plush pillows the next day, she closed her eyes and tried to settle her racing thoughts. What if she failed this first assignment? What if she screwed it up somehow?

"Hey, couldn't we have met somewhere else? Why was it necessary for us to check into this hotel? Not that I'm complaining—I love these pillows—but we're still in Chicago, so why couldn't we meet at the office or at a coffeehouse, or wherever?" asked Eve.

"This room offers more privacy than meeting in a public place. Plus, I wanted us to be as close as possible to the location of your assignment, which is why we didn't meet at the office." Agent Yu paused. "Here are the details." She placed a slender electronic tablet on the pillow next to Eve's head.

She grabbed the tablet and turned it over in her hands, searching for the power button. When she pressed her thumb against the dark screen, it lit up. "60.0" appeared at the center of a blue screen and began to count down in reverse. Once it reached "1.0," the screen went black and opened to an unfamiliar screen. Eve tapped on the document icon that read "Op. 21" and scanned the text.

Assignment: Retrieve item from location by any

available means. Draw no attention. Return item within 24 hours to nearest SPI branch and provide corresponding code.

Item: Drive 21 contains valuable information that could be weaponized and leave the US vulnerable to cyber and physical attack.

Location: 880 West Madison, Suite 2600, Room 18, Chicago, IL. Item believed to be in a safe box inside a desk drawer.

Subject: Carlos Manuel Padilla Salazar of Atkins and Salazar Solutions, Inc. Subject possesses Drive 21.

Background: Atkins and Salazar–US company founded in 1967 and headquartered in Chicago. Company provided government services and information technology support. Company recently purchased by and merged with Venezuelan company, Castillo Science Systems (CSS) for $5 billion. Atkins and Salazar still in the process of transitioning. No indication when transition will be complete. Drive 21 must be retrieved before transition is complete. If not retrieved, Drive 21 may fall into Venezuelan hands, leaving US vulnerable.

After reading the directions once more, she laid the tablet on the bed. "So how do we know the drive—I'm assuming it's a flash drive or external hard drive—is with this guy?"

"Our informant has confirmed that Salazar keeps the drive in his office at headquarters, specifically in a small safe box inside his desk," said Agent Yu. "Drive 21 is black, approximately two inches long and half an inch wide. We don't know what other items are in the safe. Or even the code to open the safe."

"Wait, so on top of sneaking into this place, I'm supposed to crack a safe as well?" she asked with a look of incredulity.

Agent Yu shook her head. "No, you leave that to us."

"I see. Okay." Eve was silent for a moment. "But what's so important on this drive?"

"That's classified."

"I understand. But I'm wondering...wouldn't it be helpful for me to at least know what I'm taking? Not knowing what's on the drive makes me feel like I'm stealing. And if that's all I'm doing, how are we any better than the people we're fighting? On our first day, you said SPI didn't condone—"

"There are times when the ends justify the means, Miss Cooper. The ends in this case being the safety of our country."

She sighed, assuming that Agent Yu had uttered that exact statement so often that it was almost instinctual for her. Eve rose and went to the bathroom where she stared at her reflection in the mirror.

"Well, we should get going," said Agent Yu, gathering Eve's jacket and handing it to her.

Still staring at her reflection, she slipped her arms through the sleeves, zipped it, and took three deep breaths. She made herself invisible and followed Agent Yu out the room. "Hey, can I ask you one more thing?"

They stopped at the elevator. "Go ahead."

"Has anyone ever failed their first assignment?"

Agent Yu barely moved her lips as she spoke. "Sure. But remember, this is still part of your training. The assignment is real—and we definitely need that flash drive—but you're still in training. Failure during training is a growth opportunity. Besides, you won't fail."

The elevator opened onto the first-floor lobby, and they hurried toward the exit where a car awaited them.

They rode in silence until the car stopped in front of an unremarkable high-rise building that housed Atkins and Salazar Solutions.

"Return to the hotel room by no later than five," said

Agent Yu, looking straight ahead. "The car will be waiting for you. That gives you eight hours to get the drive and get out. Don't be late."

"Agent Yu?"

"Yes?"

"What makes you so sure I won't fail?"

The agent smiled. "The fact that it worries you that you might."

"You've watched a lot of *The Matrix*, haven't you?"

Chuckling, she reached over Eve and opened the door. "See you at the hotel."

Stepping out the car, Eve looked at the towering building and then at Agent Yu. "See you soon," she replied and shut the door.

Like every other downtown office building, the floors were marble, and decadent chandeliers hung throughout the lobby. Two building attendants sat at a desk in the ground floor lobby and buzzed people through the turnstiles. Invisible, Eve rushed toward a turnstile and jumped over it.

Tapping her feet against the floor, she waited for the elevator and looked around to make sure she hadn't drawn any attention. As the moments wore on, she glanced at her smart watch and groaned. "Come on."

When she stepped inside the elevator and examined the buttons, she noticed something that looked like a key card slot beneath the up and down arrows. *Shit, I need an ID card or something.* She looked around, hoping to see someone approaching her, someone who could be her ticket up. But she was alone.

So Eve waited inside the elevator, quiet and invisible. Minutes passed and she looked at her watch, wondering how long she'd have to wait before someone arrived with a key card. *This is ridiculous. Why didn't they give me a card or a way to get up here?* Just when she was about to sit on the floor and get comfortable, the elevator opened and a woman entered. The woman slid a key card in the slot, which lit up. To Eve's relief, the woman pressed 26, and the elevator door closed.

When the door opened to Atkins and Salazar Solutions, the bright yellow and white walls of the office almost blinded her. Turning left toward the colorful cubicles, she swept her gaze over the numbers above the doors. As she crept along, it didn't take long to spot Salazar's office in a far corner.

She peeked through the hazy glass door to see if anyone was inside the office. *Empty. Good.* As quietly as possible, she opened the door and went in, making sure to close it behind her. The office was enormous, far too large for one person. That was the first thing she noticed. Next, she noticed the stunning view from the floor-to-ceiling window behind the large desk. Framed university degrees and certificates were strewn about the beige walls, along with framed photographs of serene landscapes.

Okay. Snap out of it. You're here for the drive. Where's the safe box?

Eve hurried to the desk, opened the drawers, and searched for a safe box. Nothing. She noticed the two locked drawers and sighed. After searching for a key and finding none, she groaned and sat. She thought back to the session when a senior operative demonstrated how to pick a lock. *Paperclip. I need a paperclip.* Her eyes scanned the desk and landed on a paper clip attached to a manila folder.

At once, she went to work with the paperclip, twisting it every which way. Yet, after a few minutes, she dropped the paperclip and threw her hands up in the air in exasperation. *Wait…oh my God, I'm such an idiot.* Breathing in, she clutched the handle of the locked drawer and applied the smallest amount of extra force to pull it open. It was the first time she'd used her super strength since that day on the playground.

She gasped when she saw it. A small safe box. Wasting no time, she slipped it inside her backpack.

As she stood, the door opened. Her heart dropped.

At once, Eve backed up and pressed herself against the window and tried not to breathe.

A man walked in, a middle-aged man who looked like the image of Salazar she'd seen in the assignment description. His wavy black hair hung over his ears. He wore an earpiece and was talking ninety miles per hour to someone. He didn't sound happy. When he ended the call, he removed the earpiece and sat behind the desk.

Eve inched away, tiptoeing toward a corner where she planted herself and held her breath. She looked at the door. It seemed so far away. Even if she reached it without being detected, wouldn't he notice the door opening and closing on its own? She had to find another way, without drawing attention to herself. *But how...?*

A soft whistling, popping sound, like a champagne bottle being uncorked cut through the silence. Salazar froze at his desk. *What the...?* She watched a small red dot appear on the breast pocket of his shirt. His eyes widened in shock then terror as he breathed in raggedly and clutched his chest before slumping forward against the desk.

Staring at Salazar's petrified eyes, Eve thrust her hand over her mouth to silence the scream before it came. Blood, more than she'd ever seen in all her life, dripped from the man and spilled onto the floor. The room seemed to spin a little as she leaned against the wall to steady herself. *No, no, no. This isn't happening. It can't be real.*

She closed her eyes while her brain wrestled with reality, only to be interrupted by a thud that came from somewhere near the desk. A desk drawer slid open, and she stepped away in sheer terror as her gaze stopped at Salazar's body on the floor. Lifeless. His eyes wide open just as they were before he'd fallen against the desk.

The reality hit her like a sack of bricks. *Wait. Someone else is here.*

"Stop," she whispered, "you're like me? Did they put two of us on the same assignment?" Why would Agent Yu not tell her that another trainee would be sent on the same assignment? It didn't make sense.

Next came the familiar whistling, popping sound, and she ran left to avoid the path of the bullet. Breathing hard and crouching, she rubbed her aching ribs and tried to approximate the location of the shooter. "Please, I have the drive." She covered her mouth with both hands. *Fool. Why would you say that?*

"Where are you?" said a deep male voice she didn't recognize.

She racked her brain, thinking about all the trainees and trying to match the voice with a face. When her eyes flashed on Salazar's dead body, she realized there was no time to hesitate. "I'm here." She approached the desk, following the sound of his breathing. He was standing somewhere behind the desk, she determined. "Someone's going to find him, and it won't take long. We need to get out of here."

"We?"

"I'm coming toward you now."

"Stay back."

Eve stopped. "Look, to be honest, I don't know what the fuck I'm doing right now. But we have to get out of here." She waited for him to say something, but he remained silent. "Just take my hand."

The door to the office opened, and she froze. She didn't dare move or turn around to see who had entered. When a woman let out a shrill, ear-piercing scream and ran out the room, Eve knew their time was up. She could hear the woman hollering in the distance, "Call an ambulance!"

Eve took her one chance. She reached out to grab the mysterious man.

After some awkward clasping at air, she gripped his clammy hand, and they bolted moments before several employees rushed toward Salazar's office. She ran to the elevator and cursed while they waited for it to open. "Come the fuck on," she groaned, tapping her feet and glancing over her shoulder.

As soon as the empty elevator opened, they ran in and exhaled as the door shut.

"Thank you for not shooting me, by the way. I mean, after missing the first time."

"I'm sorry to do this, Eve," said the man, still invisible.

"So you are one of the trainees? Why didn't Agent Yu tell me—"

In the next moment, a shattering pain ripped through her forehead as though she'd been hit with a hammer. Stunned, she stumbled to the floor as everything grew dark and quiet.

Eve squinted and shielded her eyes from the blinding light. She tried to sit up, but her head throbbed and her face felt hot. Lying against the pillow, she groaned. "What happened?"

Doctor Thomas and Agent Grobeck stared at her.

"Why does it feel like my head went through a grinder?"

"A guest found you unconscious and bleeding outside the hotel entrance and called the police. It seems you made it back to the hotel, although we're not sure how," said Agent Grobeck.

"The hotel? I was in the elevator at Salazar's building. I don't understand."

"Do you remember anything before you left Salazar's office?" asked Agent Grobeck.

Eve noticed Agent Yu was sitting in a chair near the door.

"I got the safe box that the drive is in. But then there was another cloaker, and Salazar..." Eve's eyes filled as the vivid image of Salazar's lifeless stare filled her head.

"He died, Miss Cooper," said Agent Grobeck. "We're aware. But we didn't recover a safe box on you."

"What are you talking about? The safe box was in my backpack."

"What backpack?" he asked.

"The one I was wearing. You don't have it?"

He shook his head.

"The other trainee, the shooter...he must've taken it," Eve muttered, sitting up and wincing through the pain.

Agent Grobeck shook his head. "Miss Cooper, I'm not sure I follow. We recovered the gun in your jacket pocket, but there was no backpack."

"Gun in my pocket? What are you—"

"While we'd hoped you could obtain the drive without harming the subject, we were prepared for that outcome. Your termination of the subject is not at issue here. The missing safe box, however, is," Agent Grobeck went on.

"My termination of the—I didn't shoot him. You guys didn't give me a gun. What's going on? Where's the other trainee? Where's my backpack?"

"Agent," said Doctor Thomas, "I think we need to let her rest."

Agent Grobeck softened his tone when he spoke to Eve again. "We'll check in on you in a couple of hours or so. Hopefully, we can help you retrace your steps then and get to the bottom of this. Okay? Get some sleep."

She was left alone with Agent Yu who hadn't stirred or moved from her seat during the entire exchange. She cleared her throat, her expression inscrutable as she observed Eve. "Do you care to tell me what the hell happened, Miss Cooper? You never struck me as the murdering type."

"I didn't kill anyone," Eve shouted, causing a sharp pain to dart through her head. "I didn't have a fucking gun. You know that."

"Keep your voice down," said Agent Yu, approaching Eve and lowering her voice to a whisper. "Look, I know you didn't have a gun, at least not when we separated. But that means something else is going on. We shouldn't talk here."

"Why not?"

"They should be discharging you today. What's a good location for you to meet me this evening?"

Eve ran her hands through her hair and rubbed her throbbing temples. "None of this makes sense anymore."

"Miss Cooper, what's a good place for you to meet me so that we can discuss this without being overheard?"

"The lake," whispered Eve, rolling her eyes. "At Foster Avenue."

Agent Yu stood and, before she exited the room, whispered, "Nine sharp. Not a minute later."

As Agent Yu approached, she glanced over her shoulder and looked left and right. The woman's nervous behavior unsettled Eve who was sitting alone under a veranda at the lake shore. Her head ached despite all the ibuprofen she'd taken, but she was relieved that the pain was subsiding.

"I'm going to make this quick, Miss Cooper," said Agent Yu, arriving at the veranda and not bothering to sit. She looked over her shoulder once more. "You need to be careful."

"Well, no shit," Eve mumbled. "I hope that's not all you've come here to tell me."

"No, it's not. I've begun reviewing CCTV footage of the day of the incident. It's twenty-four hours of footage, so it'll take me and my assistant a bit more time to wade through it. I think there's something Agent Grobeck isn't telling me, and

I think it explains what happened on your assignment."

"Where's the other trainee?" asked Eve. "He's the one who killed Salazar, who did something to me. He's the one who probably has the backpack and the drive."

"You were the only trainee assigned to Salazar."

Eve stared at her. "I'm confused. The person was like me, could cloak."

"Which is exactly what concerns me. From what you said earlier, this person likely had knowledge of the drive and was there for the same reason you were."

"He didn't just know about the drive. He knew about my assignment. Agent Yu, he said my name." *What the hell is going on?*

Agent Yu's gaze widened.

"I thought you all were keeping checks on people like us. Like how SPI watched me for years. How could you not know about this person, too?"

Agent Yu shook her head. "It's impossible for us to find all of you. Some of you are better at hiding than others."

Eve regarded the woman incredulously and folded her arms across her chest. She suddenly wondered why she should trust her. "Why are we meeting here instead of at the office? Come to think, why are you being so sneaky? I've wondered about it ever since that weird call when you warned me about Agent Grobeck."

Agent Yu met Eve's gaze but was silent. After a moment, she glanced over her shoulder.

"I've seen the way you interact with him. It's a little...hostile. I'm thinking you don't like him very much. Am I right?"

She stared at Eve with a look that was a cross between admiration and concern. "You're perceptive. It's a good skill for an operative to have."

"You didn't answer the question."

"I didn't answer the question because it's not relevant. The point is shady shit is going on, and I don't want you or any of the new trainees caught up in it. That's it."

"Right," replied Eve, studying the woman. "Have you found anything suspicious on the CCTV footage yet?"

"There's some strange activity right before you arrive at Salazar's floor. A man who seems to be, I guess you could say, lurking. He's there one minute and gone the next."

"The man who attacked me?"

"We don't know. My assistant is hoping to identify him soon."

"What does he look like?"

"We can't make out the details of his face yet. And he's wearing a hat, a fedora."

Eve laughed. "No way some hipster in a fedora attacked me."

"Like I said, we're reviewing the footage. I wanted you to know I may soon have a lead on this person you mistook for a trainee." She looked at her phone. "I have to go. My advice regarding Agent Grobeck is the same as it was before. Keep your guard up at all times with him. And don't mention a word of this meeting. Got it?"

Eve agreed. "Before you leave, I have one more question. Why couldn't you tell me this earlier, in the hospital?"

"Rooms can be bugged," said Agent Yu, not turning to face Eve. "Do yourself a favor and learn to think like the operative you're in training to become. It'll stop you from asking naive questions like that."

At once, the agent departed, and Eve watched her hurry to her car. Once she was gone, Eve sighed and leaned back on the bench. She gazed at the full moon casting a gray glow over the lake and giving the dark expanse a shiny shimmer. She closed her eyes, wondering why she'd agreed to meet with Agent Yu. The conversation had increased her anxiety and aroused more questions. What had she gotten herself mixed up in, she wondered?

Groaning and pushing aside these thoughts for a moment, she pulled out her cell phone and typed a text message to Zoey and Gabriel: "Hope you had a good day. Thinking about you. Xoxoxoxo!" She hit send and reread the text message a few times. The simplicity of it made her smile.

She wished everything was as simple.

If things were simple, she'd still be teaching a class of distracted high school kids instead of being embroiled in a situation that, in just twenty-four hours, had transformed into a murder mystery. Sitting there, invisible and quiet, she peered at the water and tried to hear the man's voice again. But all she could hear was the whistling sound of the bullet and the thump of Salazar's body falling against the desk as he expired. The image of his shocked face—his deep brown eyes wide with fear—froze in her mind.

"Who are you?" she whispered, pulling at her memory for the sound of the man's voice. It was a deep voice, not raspy, but smooth. Was there the faintest trace of an accent? She couldn't be sure.

As she stood and walked to the sand, her head tilted upward, and her gaze rested on the visible stars. The November air was cool but not cold. The warm spell that arrived yesterday was lingering, giving Chicagoans a couple of nice nights before the inevitable onslaught of snow. Her feet carried her toward the shore where she stopped and peered around. She was alone as far as she could see, just some cars in the distance behind her.

She unbuttoned her jacket and shivered as the cool air nipped at her neck. After removing her clothes and laying them on a patch of grass, she lurched into a sprint and gasped when she crashed into the cold water.

"Oh, fuck," Eve muttered, shaking at the shock of the ice-cold water. "Bad idea. Bad idea," she repeated, wondering if she'd catch hypothermia. The last time she'd gone for a nighttime dip was during July, a much saner time to enjoy the waters of Lake Michigan.

Eve steadied herself and closed her eyes, reaching for a happy image to replace the one of Salazar's dead body. She held her breath as if doing so might more readily elicit a welcome image. Zoey's bright face appeared, and Eve felt the warmth of Gabriel's body against her own. They were holding her and showering her with kisses, and she was laughing and running her fingers through their hair. "You know what's right," said Zoey when their eyes met.

"I don't know if I do," Eve replied, to which Zoey smiled. They held each other for a while, saying nothing.

When Eve opened her eyes, the sensation of the cold water snapped her back to reality, and she rushed to the sandy shore. Shaking all over, she put her clothes on and desperately wished her apartment wasn't three blocks away. *Fuck, I wish I were standing in my living room right now. Jesus, it's fucking cold.*

Not a moment later, she experienced a horrible tug in her navel region. Eve staggered and fell. But as she looked down, she noticed there was no sand. Warmth emanated from the surface...from her living room floor.

"What the...what?" She gazed around the room. *How...?* She sat up and collected herself, unable to understand what had happened. "Annie, what time is it?" she asked, wondering why on earth she cared about something as inconsequential as time right now.

"It is nine thirty-three," said the virtual assistant.

It clicked in her mind. *9:33 pm.* The same time her phone had shown when she looked at it on the beach, just as she'd thought about..."How much I wished I was in my living room," Eve said. Her mouth dropped open in wonderment.

"Holy shit." For only the second time in her life, she'd managed to teleport.

She fell against the floor and laughed.

"And you did it just like that?" asked AJ, snapping her fingers. She sat the bottle of beer on the coffee table and looked at Eve, who was changing the settings on Annie. "You thought it, and it happened?"

Eve nodded. "I bet you could, too." After she pressed the "reset" button, she turned to AJ and suppressed a laugh. AJ was sitting with her eyes closed and fists clenched on her lap. "What are you doing?"

"I'm concentrating. Trying to think about standing in the kitchen," said AJ.

"You look like you're trying to take a shit."

AJ burst into laughter as Eve rejoined her on the sofa. She punched Eve in the arm. "You messed up my whole vibe. I think I almost had it."

Eve took a swallow of beer and relaxed on the sofa.

"It's wild that you have other abilities. Teleporting and super strength—"

"Ew, you make it sound so cheesy."

"I'm just saying," AJ laughed. "It's awesome."

She shrugged and took another swig of beer. "I'm sure you have other abilities. You just haven't discovered them yet."

"Who knows. It would be kind of cool. I wonder what other abilities the trainees have," said AJ, kicking her feet up on the coffee table. But when Eve cast her a disdainful look, she quickly dropped her feet to the floor.

"AJ, I don't think you should say anything about it to other trainees. I haven't mentioned it to anyone because I'm not sure I feel comfortable with SPI finding out yet."

"Why?"

Eve paused, not sure how much she should say. "I think

we need to be careful with how much more information we give them about us. It seems they only know about the invisibility so far, and we should keep it that way for now."

AJ nodded. "I guess you're right. It's not like our employer has to know everything."

For a while, they sat in silence while reggae played softly, and AJ laid her head against Eve's shoulder. To have a friend who knew her secret...it was something Eve hadn't thought she'd ever experience. *Even if taking the job was a misguided decision, at least I got a friend out of it all.*

"Hey, AJ. Can I tell you something?"

"Yeah, what's up?"

"I'm thinking...maybe SPI isn't the right fit for me."

"What are you talking about? You've only had one field assignment. Shouldn't you give it more time before you start having second thoughts?" said AJ, a look of confusion shading her face as she looked at Eve. "I'm so excited about my first assignment next week. Agent Yu hasn't told me what it'll involve yet."

Eve nodded as AJ talked about the weapons training session she'd had last week and the thrill of learning how to disassemble a gun. "So, you're okay with the idea of having to shoot somebody?"

AJ shook her head. "Not really, but I knew taking a job like this might require it. Somebody has to do this job, right? To keep us safe."

"Keep us safe. Right." An image of Salazar's body sailed across Eve's mind. Hesitant to disclose too much, Eve launched into a lengthy monologue about her concerns with the work at SPI but left out crucial details—like the fact that she'd witnessed a man shot to death. *Maybe I should tell her. No, it might freak her out. But, then again, maybe it wouldn't bother her.* The last thought unsettled Eve.

AJ sat up. "Eve? What's going on?"

If I tell her, she might even be able to give me some advice. She wasn't sure if she wanted advice. Yet she knew she needed someone to understand the existential crisis that had been brewing since before she quit her job at the school. To her general surprise, she felt tears pooling, and her face grew hot. She averted her watery gaze and distracted herself by picking at her nails. "I saw a man die," she said, staring at her nails.

It wasn't long before she was crying and telling AJ about the day at Salazar's office, and AJ was holding her hand telling her everything would be all right.

When a knock came at the door, it startled them. "Are we expecting company?" asked AJ.

"Oh, damn, it's Friday. I can't believe I forgot. It's Zoey."

"You have a date with the boo and forgot about it?" She smiled, wiping Eve's wet cheeks.

Eve rose and composed herself. "We have movie nights on Fridays."

"Well, I'll scoot on out and let you two have your couple time." AJ gathered her jacket off the chair. "We can talk more later."

She gestured for AJ to resume her seat. "No. It's fine. Stay."

With a sigh and an incredulous look, AJ sat and reached for her bottle of beer.

Eve hurried to the door and calmed herself before opening it. Zoey greeted her with a bright smile and two paper bags.

"I got Thai food, your favorite up the street," she exclaimed. But after a glance over Eve's shoulder, Zoey's smile disappeared. "Am I interrupting something?"

"No. Come on in." Eve ushered her inside and closed the door. "You want a beer? I mean, wine? I have red and Moscato."

Zoey placed the bags on the kitchen table. "You know I

don't drink Moscato."

"Right. Sorry, I...long week." She turned to retrieve red wine from the cabinet and more beer from the refrigerator.

"Good to see you again, Zoey," said AJ, feigning nonchalance.

Zoey turned to Eve with a testy expression and leaned close to her. "Are you seeing her now?"

Eve laughed and shook her head. "No, Zoey. We're just—"

"Are you two dating?" Zoey asked AJ, not waiting for Eve to finish.

It was AJ's turn to laugh now. "Eve's like the opposite of my type, honey. I like my women more along the lines of Queen Latifah circa *Set It Off*. Feel me?"

Zoey stared at her blankly.

AJ cleared her throat. "No, we're not dating."

Eve covered her mouth to hide her laughter.

"Okay, whatever. Fine," Zoey replied, turning to Eve. "But it's our movie night, so I don't understand why—"

"Zoey, I'm sorry. I needed someone to talk to about things. Work. There's no one but you and Gabe. I promise." She reached for Zoey's hands and was surprised when she pulled away.

"I feel like you're hiding something from me. Ever since you took this new job you've been different," Zoey whispered. "Mostly in a good way, like happier. But other times I see a look in your eyes, like fear."

"I'm fine." She offered Zoey the glass of wine.

But Zoey folded her arms across her chest and frowned. "Come on, Eve. I'm a therapist. I'm paid to understand emotions, to know when people need help but don't know how to ask for it. Something is going on with you. Not to mention you look like you've been crying. Oh, and the big secret you were supposed to tell me. Still waiting."

Eve sat the wine glass on the countertop, grabbed two bottles of beer and headed to the living room. As she sat, she took a quick glance around and leaned back.

Zoey joined them, and they sat in silence, exchanging awkward glances for a while.

"Well, this is uncomfortable," AJ remarked.

Eve gulped some more beer and sat up, turning to Zoey. "AJ and I are friends for a very particular reason, because of something we have in common."

Zoey's head tilted to the right. "Besides the fact that you work together?"

"It's why we work together, why SPI hired us." Eve picked at her nails while trying to find the right words to avoid scaring away the most important person in her life. She searched for the perfect set of words but found nothing better than the straightforward truth. "We have abilities."

"Am I supposed to know what that means?"

"It's easier to understand if I show you." She grasped Zoey's hands and stared into her confused eyes. "Just keep looking at me."

"Eve, this is silly—" The rest of her sentence transformed into a scream when Eve disappeared. She would've fallen off her seat if Eve hadn't been holding her hand. Frantically, she looked left and right. AJ had disappeared as well.

"I'm still here," Eve said, squeezing Zoey's hands.

"Oh, okay. Wow. I really need to lay off the THC. I'm clearly going crazy." She blinked again and again. "Because, for some reason, it seems like you're not here."

"Zoey—"

She held up the empty wine glass and looked for Eve, blinking and staring into space. "There's nothing else in this, right?"

"You're not high or going crazy," Eve said, reappearing at once.

Zoey screamed and pulled her hands away. In a flash, she was on her feet, and the wine glass shattered on the floor. She pressed her spine against the wall as she gawked at Eve.

"I should've told you a long time ago, Zoey. I was scared of what you'd think."

AJ reappeared next to Eve, causing Zoey to clutch her chest in panic. Downing the rest of her beer, AJ stood and gathered her jacket. "I'm going to head out and let you two talk. You want me to sweep up this glass, Eve?"

Eve shook her head. "I'll get it."

With a nod at them, AJ made her way to the front door.

Eve and Zoey continued looking at one another, as if frozen in time. When the front door shut and they were alone, Eve got up to grab the broom. In silence, she swept up the shards of glass and dumped them in a plastic bag and dropped it in the trash. Once she stored the broom in the closet, she resumed her seat on the sofa.

"Eve..." Zoey was standing across the room and staring at her. "What is happening?"

"Can you come here? I wasn't trying to scare you. I'm sorry."

Zoey didn't move.

"Look, these abilities—"

"Abilities? Plural? There's more than just—uh—that thing you did?"

She's terrified of me. I never should've told her.

"What other abilities?"

Assuming she had nothing else to lose, Eve demonstrated her other two abilities by teleporting into the kitchen and then bending a cast iron skillet with her hands.

Still pressed against the wall, Zoey watched with wide-eyed disbelief as Eve proceeded to place the warped skillet on the table and sit.

"It's something I've hidden all my life. From everyone,"

said Eve, her eyes closed. Without warning, she teleported and reappeared less than a foot away from Zoey who jumped with fright. She stepped forward and caressed Zoey's rosy cheek. "I'm sorry I hid it from you. You know when I had you drive me home to Indiana? Well, I wanted to take a look at my old diaries because I'd been trying to remember all the details of what it was like when I first realized I could do these things. And I wondered if my mom had ever figured it out...that's why I took her diaries."

"Did your mom ever figure it out?"

Eve shook her head. "No. Or if she did, she never wrote about it."

"Where did these abilities come from?"

"I don't know. I wondered when I was a kid. But I was too busy trying to hide it from everyone to bother looking for an answer," said Eve, shrugging. "Even SPI doesn't seem to know. One of our meetings during the first month of training focused on when SPI first discovered people like me and how they spent years trying to determine the source of our invisibility."

"They never found the source?"

"No," Eve replied. "I think they sort of gave up on that and decided to focus on recruiting us to work for them."

After a moment, a smile spread across Zoey's lips, and she grasped Eve's hands. "My God, how the fuck did I get this lucky?"

"Wait...what? No. You're not afraid of me?" asked Eve.

"Why would I be? You're like a superhero."

Eve thought back to elementary school. She thought about the kids on the playground—the girl with the pigtails and the big boy who always picked on her—the way they'd all recoiled in terror the day she fought back. The day she discovered her abilities. None of them would look her in the eyes after that day. "No offense, but you're taking this better than I expected."

"How else should I take it?"

"I think most folks would run. Probably never come back. Just a minute ago you looked like you were about to run."

Zoey squeezed Eve's hands. "Do you want me to run?"

She shook her head.

"Good. Because I'm not most folks. You should know that by now."

Eve closed her eyes as Zoey kissed her lips. "You can't tell anyone. Okay? Promise me."

"Okay."

"Not even Gabe."

"I promise," she said, brushing her nose against Eve's neck.

While Zoey caressed her, Eve replayed AJ's simple words: "Everything's going to be fine. You'll see." *Maybe AJ's right, and I'm overthinking everything. Maybe it'll all be fine.*

If only she could get the image of the dead man out of her mind.

5

Eve stared out the window at the cityscape and fog concealing the tops of the buildings. She thought about how long it had been since the last sunny days. The worst thing about the colder months, besides the subzero temperatures, was the lack of sunlight. She wondered about how strange it must be to live in places farther north where the days are never sunny for long stretches of the year.

When the door opened, she turned around to watch Agent Grobeck enter. He was accompanied by the operative she'd seen during their first meeting.

"Thanks for waiting, Miss Cooper. You remember Mr. Candela?" said Agent Grobeck, shutting the door.

"Right." She smiled curtly at the operative. Just like the first time, the operative remained quiet. She was sure she'd never met a more stoic individual. For the first time, it struck her that she'd never seen him outside Agent Grobeck's office. Not once. He sat in the chair next to her, and Agent Grobeck sat behind the desk. "I'm assuming you wanted to hear about how the class is going—"

"Actually, Miss Cooper, that's not why I asked for this meeting. But I've heard great things about your instruction. It seems to be a great fit for you so far, and I hope you're enjoying it."

"I am. It's the best part of my week."

"I'm glad to hear that. Let's be honest, the work of SPI is unusual and not much can prepare you for it. I promoted you to that position because I thought being in the classroom would help you transition better."

She watched as he opened the laptop and pecked at the keyboard. "I do think being able to teach has helped a lot."

"And that brings me to why I wanted to speak with you. I have another opportunity for you that I think you'll be very suited for."

"Can I—before you get to that—can I ask a question?"

He looked up and gave her his full attention. "Sure. What's on your mind, Miss Cooper?"

"About the uh, incident, last week," she began. She glanced uncertainly at Mr. Candela, not sure if she was allowed to say much about the Salazar assignment in front of him. He stared straight ahead at Agent Grobeck. "The man who, you know, from my assignment. Do you have any leads on who he is?"

Agent Grobeck cracked an uncanny smile. "It's okay, Miss Cooper. Mr. Candela has been briefed on the Salazar matter. At this time, that case is closed, so there's no need for you to worry about it anymore."

"What do you mean 'closed'?"

"It's not a matter for you to concern yourself with at this time. We've handled it. You did a good job, and Agent Yu is looking forward to working with you to improve your field skills as we prepare your next assignment."

"I don't understand. You found out who killed him? Who was it? Did you get the drive?"

"Miss Cooper," said Agent Grobeck, still smiling. "How have you been feeling since the assignment? Has Agent Yu recommended visiting our staff counselors?"

A chill went through Eve as he spoke, and she peered into his eerie green eyes. *Why is he dodging the question?* She decided to play along and press a little harder. "I can't stop seeing Salazar's face, the moment he was shot. And I keep worrying. I keep worrying that the shooter might come after me."

"You have absolutely nothing to worry about, Miss Cooper. Trust me."

Her gaze averted, she sniffled. "I haven't been able to sleep well because...I keep thinking about it. How do you know he won't come for me?"

"Trust me. You are safe." He offered a reassuring nod and jotted notes on a Post-it. "I'll be sure to inform Doctor Thomas that you'd like to see a counselor."

"No, I'm fine," she replied, wiping away nonexistent tears. "I don't need that. I'm fine."

"Are you sure? We usually require it after an experience of this nature."

She sniffled once more. "Can I let you know if I want to see a counselor?"

"That's fine." He handed her a tissue. "For now, I'll have Doctor Thomas send you some materials we've compiled for trainees who experience trauma during an assignment."

She took it graciously and pretended to blow her nose. "Thank you."

Silence filled the room as she looked from him to Mr. Candela. She crumpled the tissue in her fist and met Agent Grobeck's gaze. He took it as his cue to speak again and proceeded to offer her another promotion that would include control over course design and a three percent salary increase. *A man is dead. I failed my assignment by not getting the drive...and he decides to promote me? This is not normal.*

During the entire conversation, she wanted nothing more than to get up and run. She ran through various scenarios in her mind as he spoke. If she took the promotion, she could save enough money to quit at the end of her training. Doing the math in her head, she figured it would be enough to keep her bills paid for at least a few months while she looked for a new job. Maybe Principal Gray would be happy to re-hire her, she thought. *I do miss my kids.* Or, perhaps, staying for the money wasn't worth it and she should quit now. After all, who knew what fresh horror might await her on her next assignment?

Once he finished, he leaned forward and smiled. "How does all that sound?"

I already paid the property tax on the house. It's the main reason I took this damn job. Just quit. Get out of this while you can, Eve.

"We can, of course, negotiate the salary increase if you'd like," he continued.

With a deep breath, she worked up the nerve to do what she knew needed to be done.

"Why would you do that?" AJ yelled.

Eve held the phone away from her face and waited for AJ to stop hollering.

"Is it too late to undo it? To—what do they call it—"

"'Nullify' it?"

"Yeah. That. Is it too late?"

"Probably not, but it doesn't matter. I'm not taking it back, AJ. It was a mistake accepting this job. I'm glad I realized it this early rather than, like, years from now." Eve sipped the latte and sat at the vacant table closest to the window.

"Eve! Come on, think about this for a minute. Are you sure—"

"Look, I've thought about this for a while, ever since I accepted the offer. I knew it didn't feel right, but I was desperate and wanted it to work out."

AJ groaned. "Are you at home? I'm coming over there. We need to talk about this."

"We're talking about it right now."

"You know what I mean."

"I'll be home in a couple of hours. But I'm telling you upfront you're wasting your time. And anyway, why do you care so much? We're still going to hang out, so what's the big deal?"

AJ fell silent.

"What's the big deal?"

"I feel like you're making this decision too fast. You could've at least waited until the new promotions took effect, see how you like it and all. But to announce your resignation not even a minute after the man gave you two more promotions? Come on."

"AJ—"

"And you're good at what you do at SPI."

"Well, I'll be good at the next thing, hopefully. At least all my bills are paid up. I've already submitted new CPS applications. I don't know, though, I may have to drive rideshare or sell homemade jewelry in the meantime to keep up with bills until I land a job. You know I make earrings and necklaces, right? Or maybe I never told you that."

"Eve, listen to yourself."

"I'm not worried about it. This all happened for a reason, and I think I'm going to end up right where I'm supposed to be."

"Stop. Just listen. I think you should give it a little bit longer. I don't get why you feel such an urgent need to quit out of the blue. What happened on your assignment...you knew something like that was possible. It's not like they didn't warn us. Why are you reacting like this?"

Eve closed her eyes briefly. But as soon as she saw Salazar's face, she opened her eyes, inhaled, and took another sip of the latte. Her voice was sterner when she spoke again. "I know what I'm doing, all right? Drop it." Before AJ could respond, Eve continued, "Look, that's only half the reason I called you anyway. The other reason is I'm having a post-Thanksgiving party at my house on Saturday. Just a few people—Zoey and Gabe, and a couple of history teachers I worked with before SPI. We'll be playing card games and drinking. I wanted to invite you."

"I guess I can't talk you out of this, can I?"

"No."

"And you're not going to tell me your real reason for quitting, are you?"

"No."

"But it definitely has something to do with Agent Grobeck and Agent Yu's warning about him, doesn't it? What did he say when you told him you were resigning?"

"He tried to get me to reconsider. He gave a whole speech about national security; you know the typical boilerplate stuff. It didn't work," Eve replied. She paused as Agent Grobeck's disappointed face and ominous words rang in her mind. "Miss Cooper," he'd said, his cold green eyes boring into her, "I don't think you're considering the repercussions of this decision." She couldn't explain why, but she'd had a distinct feeling he was hinting at something worse than the financial repercussions of being jobless.

"What about Agent Yu? Surely she tried to talk you out of it, right?"

Eve rolled her eyes. "Interestingly, she hasn't said a word to me about it. Look, are you going to come on Saturday or not?"

Sighing, AJ replied, "Sure. I'll be there."

When she ended the call a minute later, Eve pulled out her laptop. Try as she might, she struggled to shake off the image of Salazar's body. *Maybe I should've taken that offer to see a counselor.* For the first time, she wished her abilities included time travel so that she could undo the events of that day and erase the memory of Salazar's terrified face.

Focus, Eve. Focus.

After finishing off the lukewarm latte and emailing Principal Gray, she typed into the search bar on the computer screen and brought up the City of Chicago's job applicant portal.

Eve spread out at her kitchen table, drinking IPAs, listening to Ray Charles, and submitting online applications for teaching positions at CPS. After two hours, she was already feeling loopy from the beer and increasingly gloomy about her job prospects. She'd submitted dozens of applications to Chicago Public Schools, yet she knew it was all a shot in the dark. That was how this game went—apply to dozens of jobs in the hopes of getting one interview that still might not turn into a job offer. Few things crushed the ego into mush faster than the process of job hunting. If she were lucky, Principal Gray would respond to the email and welcome her back. Maybe she could even ask for a higher salary. But she dreaded having to explain why she'd impulsively quit teaching to take a job offer that she knew was too good to be true from the beginning.

She rubbed her temples as she stared at the screen. But, after five minutes of blank staring, she glanced at the cell phone next to her. At once, she picked up the phone and video-called Zoey, steadying the phone's camera so that she was looking directly at the viewfinder. "Hey," said Eve, blearily when Zoey's face appeared on the screen.

"Hey, you. What's up?"

"Just, you know, job hunting," said Eve, turning her phone's camera to show Zoey the laptop screen.

"Wait. What? When did you make this decision?"

"It's a long story. I'll tell you later. But, anyway, I'm—I was thinking about you. You busy?"

"No."

"Do you want to come over? You can bring Gabe, unless you want me all to yourself tonight."

"Eve, have you been drinking?"

Eve giggled. "Just a few beers. But, yeah, I'm not drunk."

"Which means you definitely are drunk, lightweight," said Zoey, laughing. "I can come over. But, first, I need you to cut yourself off. No more beer for you tonight."

"Yes, ma'am."

"I'm serious. I don't want to be cleaning up vomit when I get over there."

Grinning, Eve parodied a salute. "Sure thing, captain."

"Give me twenty minutes, silly. Love you."

"Love you, too."

When the call ended, the phone slipped from Eve's hand and hit the floor. She got on her knees to inspect the phone and was relieved to find it hadn't cracked.

As she prepared to stand again, she realized the floor was the place to be at the moment. She relaxed and exhaled. Lying on the hardwood floor of her hallway between the kitchen table and living room, a stupid smile settled on her face, and her head spun from booze. While staring at the ceiling, Eve saw the last couple of months of her life, from teaching at the school and tendering her resignation with the principal to her first day at SPI and the night she told Zoey about her ability.

The phone vibrated in her hand. "Hello?"

"Forgot to ask," said Zoey, "Do you want me to stop and pick up anything to eat?"

"No. I already ate. I just want you."

"You flirt." Zoey laughed. "I'll see you soon."

Eve looked at the window, at the bare tree branches visible through the sheer curtains. *Everything's going to be fine.* She pocketed the phone and closed her eyes. In the darkness, she saw only Zoey.

Eve picked at her nails and glanced at her peers around the room. They were gazing at Agent Yu, who had been leaning against the desk as she explained the importance of protecting the agency's relationship with a multinational company that specialized in intelligence research and 'disaster preparedness'.

Eve stifled a yawn and glimpsed the wall clock. *Oh, get me out of here. Why does this day feel so long?* She'd promised herself she'd finish out the week so that she could say goodbye to her peers and make sure she had their contact information. Leaving SPI didn't have to mean losing potential friendships with others like her.

As she looked around the room, she cursed herself for not making an effort to get to know anyone other than AJ.

"Yes, Mr. Kim?" said Agent Yu.

"Are you talking about FordTech International, the weapons contractor? The firm that Senator Abbott from Virginia used to sit on the board of before he was elected?" asked Samuel Kim. Eve noted a hint of disapproval in his tone.

"It's an intelligence and security firm, not a weapons contractor," replied Agent Yu. "But, yes, that's the firm. Senator Abbott resigned from his position to avoid a conflict of interest once elected."

Samuel Kim folded his arms across his chest.

"Mr. Kim, from your expression, it seems like this relationship bothers you."

He didn't respond beyond a barely audible grunt.

You don't trust this shit either, do you?

Looking as though something had startled him, he turned and stared at Eve.

Eve's eyes widened when she heard a voice in her head. His voice. "Did you say something?" she'd heard him say, yet his lips hadn't moved. *Okay, it's just the hangover talking.* She smiled at him, feigning nonchalance. *I have to stop at two beers from now on.*

"Why are her lips not moving?" came his voice again.

His voice was loud to her ears but, strangely, not drawing anyone else's attention. Indeed, why weren't his lips moving either? *Wait...can you hear me right now, Sam?*

He nodded.

Eve's mouth hung open. *Can—can you hear anyone else?*

He shook his head.

Has this ever happened to you before? Have you ever done this before?

"No, I don't think so," he said, his voice ringing in her head.

Your voice...it's like surround sound in my head. Not even like you're right next to me. It's louder. Louder and more...complex. Does that make sense?

"Not even a little," Sam replied, his brown eyes fixed on hers.

Who else can communicate like this? Eve looked at AJ sitting across the room. *AJ, can you hear me?*

AJ jumped and looked around; her eyebrows raised as she met Eve's gaze.

Oh, fuck. I'm doing this? You can hear me?

"Yes, I can," thought AJ, gaping at Eve. "What the hell? You're in my head, Eve. How is it even possible?"

I don't know. I've never...I just did it to Sam by accident somehow.

"How do you know it was you doing it and not Sam?"

Because I'm doing it to you right now, Einstein.

"Oh, right. Forget I asked that. I'm sorry, this is weird. Like I'm not talking, but we're talking. This is crazy."

Agent Yu cleared her throat. "All right. You're dismissed for today. See you here Monday morning." She closed the laptop, stuffed it inside the briefcase, and hurried to Eve. "I wanted to catch you before you leave. I know I haven't said anything about your resignation."

Eve nodded.

"Thank you for your service here. Take care of yourself," she said after a pause and extended her hand.

When Eve shook her hand, she felt a piece a paper. Before she could respond, the agent released her hand and headed for the exit. Eve looked at the piece of paper and read the words on it, two short sentences: *I haven't been able to identify the shooter. I'm sorry.*

She couldn't understand why Agent Yu had tried so much to help her, and she realized she no longer cared. After today, she wouldn't have to think about SPI anymore.

Smiling at that happy thought, Eve gathered her bag and hurried to AJ and Sam who were whispering to each other and casting furtive glances at everyone else. "Hearing each other's thoughts? How crazy was that?" she exclaimed in a high-pitched whisper when she reached them.

"On a scale of one to ten with ten being totally nuts, I'd give it a smooth eleven," said AJ.

Sam frowned. "It's creepy, actually."

"I'll say," said Eve, ushering them from the room. *Let's grab lunch at the pub next door. I need a drink.*

"Same," AJ and Sam responded in unison.

A lightness filled Eve when she left SPI after her last class that day. The cold wind beat at her exposed neck, and she pulled her scarf tighter while pulling the winter cap over her ears. As she crossed the street to Zoey and Gabriel's condo, she smiled, thinking about what was next for her. It was strange not to be afraid of uncertainty. She'd spent so much of her life trying to minimize uncertainty and avoid risk. Not having another job lined up before leaving her current job felt like the ultimate leap, one she wouldn't have taken even a month or so ago. Questions about bills and the real possibility of becoming homeless would've plagued her and stopped her from resigning so hastily. She didn't know why, but this time she didn't feel any fear. She just felt free. Unencumbered. She was ready, she told herself, for whatever journey lay ahead.

When she opened the door, Zoey pulled her into a fierce hug. "Congratulations, Eve! I can't believe you did it."

She ushered her inside the toasty apartment where Gabriel was busily preparing the dinner table. He beamed at her when she approached and planted a kiss on her cheek. "How you feeling?"

"Amazing." Eve handed her coat, scarf, and hat to Zoey.

"Well, you definitely set a record. I don't think anyone else in this room has quit a job so fast. Cheers to you." He handed her a wine glass. "It's not wine. Zoey found a beer she'd said you'd like."

Eve took a sip. "Hoppy. I like it."

"The food's ready, so you two can go ahead and have a seat." Zoey put a porcelain bowl of mashed potatoes on the table. She rushed to the kitchen and returned with a casserole dish holding steak and asparagus.

"That smells so good," said Eve, taking a seat next to Gabriel.

Zoey removed her apron, hung it on the chair, and sat. "All right. Let's dig in."

"Thank you for this. I know how much you hate cooking, Zoey."

She laughed. "We wanted to celebrate your transition. You've been through a lot lately, and I don't know how you've come through it so well."

"How do you mean?"

She reached for Eve's hand and squeezed it. "I mean, I've never seen you look like you're so at peace with things, like you're willing just to be you. I love it."

Eve flushed, not sure what to say.

"I think we should all take an extended weekend vacation soon. Just to unwind and celebrate the changes ahead. What do you think?" Gabriel asked, looking from Eve to Zoey.

"As long as it's somewhere warm," said Eve, grinning.

Zoey took a bite of steak. "My aunt has a condo in Aruba that she likes to rent out every winter. I can check with her."

"Aruba? Definitely count me in," Eve exclaimed.

They spent the rest of dinner talking about job prospects, the finicky weather, and vacation ideas for January. After dinner and two rounds of drinks, the three of them cleaned up the dining area and kitchen in relative silence. Eve welcomed the quiet, joyful atmosphere. She'd reached a point where she could enjoy their company in total silence, feeling no need to fill the silence with conversation.

Sitting in the living room later, she relaxed her feet on the ottoman. "I have to get home this evening to feed Mr. Pebbles, but I'll hang for a while."

Zoey and Gabriel joined her on the sofa. Eve rested her head against Gabriel's shoulder and closed her eyes.

"Eve," said Zoey. "Have you given any more thought to moving in here?"

She opened her eyes and looked at Zoey who was running her finger along the rim of the wine glass. "I thought about it this week, just in light of how tight things are going to be while I work on landing a job or getting my old job back at Martin Delaney. But not very seriously. Why?"

"It's still an option," Gabriel answered.

Zoey sat the wine glass on the side table. "Promise me you'll consider it."

"You guys are really gung-ho about me living here, aren't you? Like a cute little polyamorous family."

"Yeah," said Zoey, leaning forward and kissing Eve's lips.

Shaking her head, Eve smiled. "You know no one will understand our 'arrangement'. How will you explain it to other friends or family?"

"I don't care what anyone else thinks, as long as you and Zoey are happy." Gabriel sat his wine glass on the other end table and faced Eve. "Do you care?"

She shook her head. "Not really. Just saying folks will judge us."

"Let them," said Zoey, kissing Eve's shoulders as Gabriel unbuttoned her shirt.

Eve turned to Gabriel. "Do you love me?"

"Until a year ago, I didn't think I'd ever love anyone but Zoey." With one hand against her cheek, he stared into her eyes. "Yes, I do. I love you."

She brought his face to hers and kissed his lips gently. Her face a few inches from his, she turned to look at Zoey and smiled. "Okay, then. We can try living together."

Lost in daydreams about her future with Zoey and Gabriel, Eve hummed and bobbed her head. She imagined herself back inside a high school classroom, teaching a bunch of temperamental kids, and the normalcy of it warmed her heart. *Maybe I'll submit another application before bed tonight. I wonder if Don has responded to my email about coming back.* Humming and digging inside her purse for her keys, she came up the stairs and stopped at her apartment door.

She fell silent the moment she opened the door.

On the sofa sat a man wearing a black suit. His back was facing her.

"What the fuck?" was all she could say, as she managed to pull out her pepper spray. "Get out of my apartment," she yelled, pointing the pepper spray at him. But she lowered it when he turned around and fixed his green eyes on her. "Agent Grobeck? What is this?" A chill went through her as he stared at her.

He stood, buttoned his blazer, and cautiously approached her. "Miss Cooper, I'm sorry to barge in like this."

"This is totally inappropriate," said Eve, hanging back at the doorway instead of entering the apartment. Seeing him outside the office was disturbing enough. Thinking about how he'd broken in and probably gone through her personal things, both frightened and enraged her. "How did you get in?"

"Please calm down and lower your voice."

As something warm and furry brushed against her ankle, she jumped and screamed. A purr confirmed that it was Mr. Pebbles, and she exhaled. Not daring to take her eyes off Agent Grobeck, Eve used her foot to scoot the cat away.

"Look, if you've come to try to change my mind, let me save you some time. I'm not going back. I appreciated the opportunity. But, like I said before, SPI wasn't the right fit for me."

He stopped a foot or so away from her. "I'm willing to offer you a salary increase and further accommodations."

"You already tried that, and I rejected it. Remember? I'm not the one for the job."

"Miss Cooper—"

"You know, there's something I'd like to know. Why are you so interested in me? Why do all this to keep me at SPI when there are obviously others like me you can recruit? Others who are more qualified than me." This question elicited an eerie smile from him that sent shivers throughout her body. She fought the urge to run. Why did this man always make her feel the urge to flee? Eve wondered. She folded her arms across her chest. "Look, thank you for the opportunity, but I'd like for you to leave."

"Miss Cooper, please shut the door and let us talk privately. You can hear what I have to say, heed my advice, and come with me, or you can chance it on your own. It's up to you. I'm just asking that you let me make my pitch."

Chance it on my own? What the hell does that mean? Eve's eyes couldn't have been wider. Hot anger rose up, barely below the surface at this point. "Excuse me?"

"To be clear, I'm willing to make you an uncommonly generous offer not just because I know you'll excel at SPI. I care about your safety, Miss Cooper. Your safety means a great deal to me and many others."

"My safety?" She stared at him.

"May I have ten minutes of your time? That's all I ask."

She sighed and relented. "Fine. Five minutes, that's it. But the door stays open."

He flashed a smile that highlighted his pale, vacant eyes. "Thank you."

She took a couple of steps forward but kept space between them. "How did you manage to get inside my apartment anyway?" she asked, momentarily glancing down to usher Mr. Pebbles away from the entry.

At once, a nauseating odor that smelled vaguely like onions and gas fumes filled her nostrils. Black stars danced in front of her eyes, blurring everything around her as the room spun. She coughed and grabbed at her neck, struggling to breathe.

"I have her," she heard Agent Grobeck say. His words were followed by the sound of a thud and total blackness.

FADERS AND FUGITIVES

6

When Eve woke up, her head throbbed against the concrete floor of the empty room. She sat up and peered around, wondering if anyone was standing on the other side of the steel door. Was Agent Grobeck watching her? Sitting cross-legged and staring at the door, she tried to ignore the hunger pains in her stomach as she waited for his return.

After a while, Agent Yu showed up instead, and cool relief washed over Eve. She figured if there were anyone who might help her, that person would be Agent Yu. She struggled to stand as the agent approached.

"I'm here to take you to your session, Miss Cooper."

"Agent Yu, what's happening? Why is he doing this?"

She stared at Eve with a flat, emotionless gaze.

"This is torture. He's torturing me, Agent. I don't understand what I did to—"

"Miss Cooper, I warned you before. You brought this on yourself."

Eve stepped back, thunderstruck by the coldness of Agent Yu's dark brown eyes. Had the coldness always been there? *Did I just not see it before?*

"Come to me—slowly." Agent Yu tightened her fist

around the Taser hooked to her belt holster.

She reached the agent and whispered, "Can't you tell me what's going on? What I did?"

"Not another word," she said, roughly grabbing Eve's arm. *The room's bugged. That's probably why she won't tell anything. Maybe I can try the telepathy thing with her.* But she remembered she had no idea how she'd done it during class that day. Not sure what else to do, Eve kept quiet while the agent handcuffed her and led her out the room.

They walked down the hallway, passing only a few people—armed guards and other personnel. Like the room she'd been held in, the walls of the hallway were bare and imposing. Nothing about the place looked familiar. Was she still in Chicago? Were there others like her who were being tortured and starved in this place? *Or am I the only one here?*

At the end of the hallway, they went through a set of steel double doors and descended a short but steep staircase leading to another set of double doors. The sameness and repetition of the place made Eve's head spin. It felt like she was walking in circles.

After a while, Agent Yu stopped and dialed a code into a small touchscreen box on the wall. The doors opened into a space resembling a classroom—ten desks in the center of the room, and whiteboards on each of the four walls. It looked like the classrooms where she'd led training sessions.

In front of one board, Agent Grobeck sat hunched over a desk and flipping through a manila folder. Were it not for his formal business suit, he would've looked like a typical schoolteacher.

Agent Yu led Eve to a desk in the center of the room, handcuffed her right hand to the desk, and stepped aside.

"Good morning, Miss Cooper," said Agent Grobeck closing the folder and regarding her with feigned surprise.

Ignoring him, she studied the room and considered all the

ways she might make her escape.

He cleared his throat. "Let's try that again. Good morning, Miss Cooper."

"Good morning, Agent Grobeck," she replied through clenched teeth, visualizing herself punching his smiling face.

"That's better. I'd hoped this setting would make you feel right at home."

Eve rolled her eyes and glared at him.

"We have a lot to talk about, and I want you to be comfortable."

"Sure you do," she mumbled, not looking at him.

"What was that, Miss Cooper?" he asked.

She hesitated for a moment but then narrowed her eyes on him. "I was just saying that, you know, despite being abused and handcuffed to a desk, I feel as comfortable as ever. You're so kind."

He chuckled, standing up and buttoning his blazer jacket. "I knew from day one I liked this girl. She's got heart, doesn't she, Olivia?"

Agent Yu's impassive stare didn't falter. Eve studied her, wishing she could hear what she was thinking. What plan had Agent Yu devised to get her out of this situation? Agent Yu would protect her. Right?

As Agent Grobeck drew closer, Eve turned her attention to him. She stared at his face, noticing features she'd overlooked before. The slanted scar above his left eye appeared more prominent in the bright lighting, and there was a glint in his eyes that she'd seen only once before— during that moment in the hospital room after her mission. "Miss Cooper, there are some things I should've told you from the start."

"Such as?"

"Namely, you won't be returning to your regular life. That life is over. Among other things, a regular life would be a waste of your talents."

"What are y—"

"As you know, I wanted to do this the easy way, give you a nice salary and some perks. But it looks like that's not what you were destined for. Let's hope your little tantrum doesn't spark other resignations. But that's neither here nor there. The point is you're an SPI operative now, and you're going to start acting like it."

"You're forcing me to work for you."

"That's a somewhat crass way to put it, but yes, Miss Cooper. In a manner of speaking."

"You can't do this," said Eve, now struggling with the handcuffs and shackles. "What is wrong with you?"

Before he could respond, Agent Yu slapped Eve so hard the desk slid sideways.

"No more interruptions," she said.

Agent Grobeck rested a hand on his colleague's arm, but he never detached his gaze from Eve. "It's fine, Olivia."

Rubbing her stinging cheek with her free hand, Eve looked at Agent Yu in disbelief.

"I'm sorry, Miss Cooper. Agent Yu isn't accustomed to subjects being so engaged. Usually, our subjects are a lot less talkative...well, until they start begging us to let them go. But I get the sense you're not the begging type, are you?"

Eve's look of loathing was all the answer he needed.

"I didn't think so. You people tend to have an overabundance of pride."

"You people?" Eve's voice rang out in the room.

"You and those with your ability, yes. There's a certain arrogance I've observed among you. I suppose it comes with the territory if you're more powerful than regular humans. Who knows," he mused. "Now, as I was saying. You will resume your position as an operative. I know you have a lot of concerns, but I ask that you set aside your ego and consider the essential role you can play in protecting the security of your country."

"You know, I'm tired of this 'protecting the security of the country' line. You can't keep me here," said Eve, staring daggers at him.

He smiled. "Let me remind you that you were part of our first official class of trainees. Recruiting you by offering tempting incentives, like money and status, was Agent Yu's idea. In the past, we used more aggressive methods. But Agent Yu thought a softer, gentler model might be more ethical. I'm still on the fence about it, as you can see."

"You've kidnapped me, tortured me, and trapped me here to force me to work for you. There's a word for that. It starts with 's'." Her eyes skipped between both agents as she tried to determine which one she hated most.

Agent Grobeck scoffed. "That description is a tad dramatic, Miss Cooper."

As Eve looked at her shackled hand and considered her limited options for escape, she experienced an increasing sense of despair. She was stuck.

After a moment of observing her like a hawk, Grobeck launched into a brief monologue about the purpose of her upcoming work.

She noted key buzzwords sprinkled throughout his speech—words like "patriotism," "duty," "service," and "honor"—that echoed the speech Agent Yu had given during the first trainee meeting. While he droned on, Eve's thoughts lingered on scenarios of escape and stopped at one idea. Teleporting. She realized she'd been too dazed and confused in her cell to consider it until now. She replayed the time she'd teleported from the lake to her apartment. She hadn't teleported over such a distance since that night. Could she do it again? What would happen if she tried and only ended up across the room? *He'll know I have other abilities. If he figures that out, will I ever be free of him?*

Despair began to cloud her mind, but she tried to push it aside. There had to be a way out, and she was determined to find it.

Eve's legs were tired and her belly rumbled with hunger when Agent Grobeck stopped at a door near the end of the hallway. A nervous man in a white robe greeted them before hurrying away. Meanwhile, an automated voice prompted Agent Grobeck to state his full name and title into a black box at the doorknob. He dialed a code into the touchscreen. A click followed, and the door opened to a large room with several hospital beds. Doctor Thomas greeted them and took Agent Grobeck aside.

Standing next to Agent Yu near the door, Eve caught snippets of the exchange between Agent Grobeck and the austere doctor.

"The chip is ready?" he asked.

Doctor Thomas nodded. "But I need to check the battery one more time."

For a while, Agent Grobeck conversed with the doctor, periodically casting curious glances at Eve.

"We can't have another forest...?" said Doctor Thomas.

He tilted his head forward. "Yes. I'm trying to avoid that."

They stared at Eve before turning around and continuing their whispered conversation.

Forest? With a glance sideways at Agent Yu, Eve was tempted to ask the woman to clarify but stopped when she saw the expression on her face. A tinge of disgust had sailed over Agent Yu's face, her attention fixed on Agent Grobeck and Doctor Thomas.

When Agent Grobeck returned to them, the look of disgust on Agent Yu's face vanished. She gave him a half-smile.

"After the procedure is over, she's done for the day. Take her to her cell and come to my office. We have details to go over," he directed the agent. Without another word nor so much as a glance at Eve, Agent Grobeck headed to the door.

Agent Yu grabbed Eve's arm in a pinching grasp and led her toward one of the beds.

"Can you not squeeze so hard?" To Eve's surprise, Agent Yu loosened her grip and led her to the hospital bed.

"Lay back. This won't take long."

Eve hesitated at first. What were they about to do to her? Why shouldn't she make a run for it? Staring into Agent Yu's eyes, she searched for the woman she'd previously known, the woman who'd tried to help her. Her heart sank.

Agent Yu locked her wrists and ankles to the bed, while Doctor Thomas fiddled with an electronic tablet that wasn't much bigger than a phone.

Avoiding the gazes of both women, Eve stared at the ceiling and tried to visualize the best moments of her life. Why was it so difficult to fix her mind on a good moment?

The first blast of pain caught her by surprise. When it shot through her right forearm, she jerked and flailed in an attempt to free herself. At the next shot of pain, she was floating high away from everything, sailing away from herself, from the doctor and Agent Yu. She was staring at her unconscious body on the bed, watching the doctor carefully slice her open and insert something into her arm. Everything looked small and hazy from so far away.

There was serenity in this numbness. Peace. And was it just her eyes, or had someone dimmed the lights? She squinted, trying to make out the figures below. They were no more than dark shapes, growing smaller and smaller, as she lost consciousness.

When she woke, she was lying on the surgery room bed, her

wrists and ankles still strapped down. "What have you done to me?" she managed, thrashing and struggling with all her strength to get free.

"Be still," shouted Agent Yu. "Be still, or I'll leave you here and let you piss yourself some more."

But Eve persisted, thrusting her body up and down against the bed. "What have you done to me?"

"I said be still." Agent Yu slapped her hard enough to momentarily blur her vision. "And not another word."

Eve stopped moving and calmed herself, as Agent Yu undid the restraints. Her bandaged arm felt numb, as though it wasn't even attached to her body. The sensation was terrifying.

"Get up. Now."

As she sat up, sharp jolts of pain overwhelmed her, and stars danced before her eyes. She longed for the numb feeling again. "Agent Yu, please help me. You know this isn't right. Please," she murmured, her speech slurring as she tried to focus.

"Come on," barked Agent Yu. "Let's go."

Stepping onto the floor took effort, but Eve managed to avoid buckling. A lightheaded feeling paired with the piercing pain in her arm made walking almost unbearable.

Taking a deep breath, she walked alongside the agent. In silence, they proceeded into the hallway. Before long, she was back inside the empty room—her cell—and shaking all over. Alone. Too weak to hold herself up, she leaned against the wall and slid to the floor. An unpleasant odor caught her attention. She looked at her thighs and ran her hands over them, realizing she'd failed to notice the wetness earlier. She sniffed her wet hands. Urine.

Eve rested her hands on her thighs and stared at the bare walls. As the tears streamed down her cheeks and silence enveloped her, all she could see was her hand around Agent

Grobeck's pale neck and her other hand pointing a gun at Agent Yu's face.

Shaky from the cold and covered from the waist down in her own urine, Eve examined her bandaged arm. Blood had soaked through, and the bandage felt soggy at the touch. Wincing and looking away, she undid the bandage and dropped it on the floor. Hesitantly, she looked at her arm and stroked the three metal stitches covering the incision wound. To her surprise, the pain seemed to be subsiding with every passing moment.

Hungry and alone, Eve retreated into her mind and attempted to plot out every feasible escape plan. She figured she might stand a chance if she could get a good understanding of the building and swipe a key ring from one of the guards. But then what? Were there any other prisoners like her in the building? Could she figure out how to free them as well? Where would she go after escaping?

Her thoughts drifted to Mr. Pebbles and whether he was alive or had found a new mom. Maybe Zoey had stopped by the apartment and taken him home with her. Eve lay on her back and closed her eyes, wishing she could see Mr. Pebbles again and know he was safe. She wished she could feel Zoey's arms around her again.

Eve opened her eyes and looked around the room at the cameras in each corner. *If I even try to practice teleporting, they'll see. They can see everything.* Never before had she felt so trapped. She feared that despair was winning, that she lacked the physical and mental strength to fight it much longer. *No. No. You're stronger than them. Don't give up.* She closed her eyes and repeated this refrain until she believed it. She would find a way back to them, no matter what. With a smile on her face, Eve fell asleep.

Booted feet at the door jolted her awake after what

seemed like only a few minutes. She popped up and rose to her feet, ready to tackle whoever entered.

Agent Yu came in and approached her. At once, she covered her nose. "Here, take these and put them on," she said, handing Eve a pair of handcuffs.

Eve made no objection and, once she slipped the handcuffs on, followed the agent out the cell. She didn't dare speak or ask any questions anymore. What would be the point? Instead, she followed in silence as Agent Yu led her to the surgery room where Agent Grobeck awaited them. Once again, Agent Yu and Doctor Thomas strapped her to the bed.

She watched the doctor, whose merciless face and pale lips seemed to form a solid line whenever she smiled. The doctor's long, dark hair was pulled into the usual bun at the back of her head. There was something missing from Doctor Thomas, Eve surmised. Something essential. The same something Agent Grobeck lacked, she thought, watching him fold his arms across his chest and tap one foot against the floor. Between him and Doctor Thomas, Eve wasn't sure which one of them was more terrifying.

She'd heard of people lacking a conscience. But, to her knowledge, she hadn't met one until now.

Eve often had speculated about whether her father lacked a conscience or was merely a troubled man. She'd never reached a conclusion. Until now. Now she was certain. Her father was just a run of the mill asshole. Agent Grobeck and Doctor Thomas were psychopaths.

Before she could delve further into these thoughts, the first shock went through her body, snatching her undivided attention. The razor-sharp and burning-hot sensation pierced through her entire body and forced her chest and her hips upward. She writhed against the bed.

During a brief moment of relief, her gaze fell upon Agent Grobeck. He observed her while Doctor Thomas administered a second set of electric shocks. Another round of shocks followed, then another, until Eve was lost to the torment. More shocks came and, at last, Eve lay in a dark and soundless void.

When she regained consciousness, she was inside the cell. Sore all over, she balled up into a fetal position on the floor. She cried.

The sound of the door creaking open moments later caused her to scramble away, curl in a corner, and shield her eyes. "No, no. Please, no more. I can't—"

The door thundered shut, and she uncovered her eyes. Her visitor was gone but had left a tray next to the door. Like a weak and starved dog, she crawled to the tray. It contained a small bowl of oatmeal and a glass of water.

She picked up the bowl and stuffed her mouth with oatmeal until there was no more, licking the bowl to make sure she didn't miss a drop. Breathing hard, she turned up the glass of water and finished it in a few gulps. Her stomach growled for more, but she knew no more was coming any time soon.

This cycle—Agent Yu taking her to the surgery room, the shocks, Agent Yu leaving her in the cell afterward—would repeat several more times. It played like a scratched record. After the fourth time, Eve stopped counting and decided that something as abstract as time didn't matter. There was no time anymore. There was nothing, except pain and rage.

Doctor Thomas locked Eve's wrists and ankles to a bed. She stood next to the two agents and scrutinized Eve like she was nothing more than a lab rat. Accustomed to the routine now, Eve simply preoccupied herself with studying the white paint chipping off the walls. She expected more shocks, so she tried to ready herself by withdrawing into her mind.

"I'm going to ask you some questions, Miss Cooper," said

Agent Grobeck.

Caught off guard, Eve regarded him with suspicion.

"You'll answer each question, and if you refuse..." He cued the doctor.

Doctor Thomas pressed a button on the machine behind the bed, and Eve mustered all her strength to keep from screaming out when the shocks cut through her. She clenched her lips together, clasped her fists tight, and willed herself to endure the torture. Sweat beads glistened on her forehead and neck. It would be over soon, she told herself. *I'll be in my cell soon. I'll be fine. I've been through this. I'll be fine.*

"You'll get two to three shocks every time you refuse to answer. Is that clear?" he asked.

She frowned at him and nodded. "Agent?"

"Yes, Miss Cooper?"

"What day is it? Has Christmas passed?"

"Christmas was two days ago, Miss Cooper," he replied, not a hint of apology in his voice.

I've been here for weeks? She imagined Zoey, Gabe, and AJ probably had lost hope of ever seeing her again. The idea that she'd spent Christmas in this nightmare was almost more than she could bear.

"All right. Let's get started then. Tell me about your relationship with Jackson Cooper."

She blinked. "My father?"

"Yes."

"Why?"

Agent Grobeck signaled the doctor.

"Fine," Eve interjected before the doctor could push the button. "Jackson Cooper is a cheating, entitled, abusive piece of shit. If he died tomorrow, I'd feel sad but also relieved."

"Why?"

She sighed. "He beat my mom almost daily, and he beat me whenever he got tired of beating her. When he wasn't beating us, he was drinking all our money away or almost gambling away the house. The house my mom's parents built and left to her and to me." She paused, watching Doctor Thomas' finger twitch near the shock button.

"Go on," he said.

"The only time I saw my mom get mad and fight him was when we almost lost the house. She broke a vase over his head. He didn't like that, so she ended up in the hospital for a week. I thought she was going to die."

"Your mother did die later, correct?"

She paused. "Yes. Cancer. He came to her funeral drunk and left early, probably to be with one of his other women, came back, and then tried to start a fight with one of mom's friends. To this day, he lives in the house my mom's parents built. The county had a lien on it at one point, until I started footing the delinquent property tax and water bill."

"By law, it's your property. You could've sold the house and set yourself up financially by now. Why have you allowed him to stay there?"

"We've already talked about my childhood, Agent. What's the point of going over all this again?" she asked, frowning. "Why does it matter so much to you?"

"Because it's a window into your psyche, Miss Cooper. I want to know what drives you," he replied. "Now, answer the question."

She paused. "He's my father. You don't kick parents out on the street, no matter how shitty they are."

"Loyalty. I see. How does that make you feel?"

She sneered at him. "How does it make me feel that that piece of white trash is living free off the labor of my black ass mom and my black ass grandparents? I bet you can guess."

"Miss Cooper, may I remind you that if you refuse to answer—"

"If I thought I could get away with it and not feel any

guilt, I would've killed him a long time ago."

"Did you ever attempt to kill your father?"

"I considered it once—bought the rat poison and everything," she said, pausing and staring at him. "Unfortunately, I didn't go through with it."

"Interesting. So would it be accurate to say that you and your father are not on the best of terms?"

"Figured that one out all by yourself, huh?"

"Has your father or your mother ever exhibited any special ability like yours?"

"No." She glimpsed Agent Yu who was pecking away at the electronic tablet on her clipboard.

"So it would be accurate to say that you are the only one in your immediate family to exhibit your special ability?"

"Yes," she answered.

The questions went on in this fashion for a half-hour or longer, and she observed his expression go from bored to intrigued with every fresh answer. He appeared satisfied and even excited when she told him the story about the bully she'd stabbed in middle school. The kid, a large boulder of a boy, had recovered but never revealed who had attacked him.

"He was probably worried that everyone would find out a tiny girl defeated him in a fight and landed him in the hospital. He and his friends never bullied me again."

"Why did you choose that particular weapon, a knife?" asked Agent Grobeck.

Because I couldn't let anyone see how strong I was. She thought back to that playground fight in elementary school when she'd overpowered three kids and accidentally became invisible. "Why not?" she replied, smiling at him. "It was easier than getting a gun into the school."

"Tell me, how did you get him to follow you into the restroom?"

"How do you think? Like any other stupid middle school

boy, he couldn't say no to that offer."

"I see." He glanced over his shoulder at Agent Yu, who scribbled notes on her clipboard.

The questioning carried on, and Eve yawned.

When he stopped and turned to Agent Yu, Eve sighed and rested against the bed. Between the hunger and the pain in her temples, she wasn't sure she could take much more without passing out.

Agent Yu came forward and unlocked the restraints around Eve's wrists and ankles. "Stand up. Come on."

With a struggle, Eve pulled herself up and gripped the side of the bed for support. Her head spun as she stepped down.

Agent Yu gripped her hand to help her stand up straight.

Unsettled by the agent's thoughtful gesture, Eve pulled away. "I'm fine." She held her head high and followed the agents, a tall guard tailing them.

After taking her to shower, Agent Yu provided her a fresh set of clothes. Clean underwear, a plain white shirt, and matching white pants. Eve was relieved to be rid of the smell of urine and musk.

Agent Yu led her to another room guarded by two large men, both of them staring straight ahead with impassive expressions. One of the men nodded at Agent Yu and stepped aside to allow Eve to enter the room. At Agent Yu's orders, Eve stopped by a desk behind which sat a graying middle-aged man. Agent Grobeck, who was standing in the center of the room, leaned over the desk and whispered something to the man. They looked at Eve, both men displaying the same eager glint.

Agent Grobeck cleared his throat. "While it would be ideal to extend your training another couple of weeks, an urgent matter has been brought to our attention. As a result, you will be proceeding to the field to help SPI resolve this matter as fast as possible."

She blinked. *They're really going to send me out and expect me not to run? What am I missing?*

In the next moment, he launched into a long-winded explanation about the purpose of the mission. He spoke with conviction and excitement, like a football coach speaking to his star player before the big game. His voice boomed more than usual as he walked forward and regarded the player he'd mentored. A look of possessive pride mixed with an unsettling shade of violence lurked in his eyes.

Eve averted her eyes when something else caught her attention. Was she imagining it...or was she feeling warm air against her neck? Confused, she looked behind her, not listening as Agent Grobeck continued his speech.

"Don't move," came a whisper so low that Eve was sure only she could hear it. Her eyes widened as she watched Agent Yu, who was lingering at the door and talking to the guards. "I'm going to get you out of here," came the whisper again. *Wait.* She recognized that voice. *Oh, my God.*

"Is there a problem, Miss Cooper?" asked Agent Grobeck.

She shook her head. "No."

"Good. There's a bag at your feet. It contains new clothes and details about your assignment, just as before. Get dressed."

"Okay," she muttered, waiting for the men to look away so that she could change clothes. Seconds later, she realized they lacked any such courtesy. With a sigh, she pulled the new clothes from the bag and disrobed.

After changing into the jeans and sweater, she folded the clothes she'd removed and stuffed them inside the bag. Finished, she stood at attention and looked ahead at Agent Grobeck and the man sitting behind the desk. Her mind lingered on the other man in the room, the one who no one could see. Was he going to rescue her from this place? Was it a trick?

"Your assignment is straightforward, Miss Cooper, and Agent Yu will assist you," said Agent Grobeck. "It will be tempting to take this as your opportunity to run. Let me make it clear: running would be a waste of time. That little chip in your arm means we can find you wherever you are at any time. Running, tempting though it may be, will get you in big trouble, and we don't want that. Let me reiterate that what you've been selected to do is special and for no other purpose than the security of your country."

The mysterious man behind the desk stroked his bearded chin and surveyed her. He appeared anxious for this meeting to end. Indeed, he indicated as much by yawning and not bothering to cover his mouth. Then, he ran his hand through his gray-streaked dark hair and glanced at his wristwatch.

Agent Grobeck came closer to Eve. "Do you have any questions?"

She shook her head.

"Good. Pick up your bag and follow Agent Yu. She'll lead you to your car. Good luck."

Before she turned away, Eve met Agent Grobeck's gaze and held it. For a fleeting moment, she saw her hands around his neck and his eyes rolling in his head as he struggled to breathe. She smiled at him and then followed Agent Yu.

The invisible man's hand touched hers, and she inhaled, almost afraid of what he planned to do. Was she about to see another person shot dead? *Would it be Agent Yu this time?*

Outside the building at last, Eve sniffed the fresh air and looked at the cloudy sky. A part of her had wondered if she'd ever experience such small joys again. Peering around, she realized she was in a part of Chicago she hadn't seen before. Somewhere in the far southwest side, she imagined, noticing all the boarded-up industrial buildings and greystones.

When the black Impala pulled up, she slid in the back.

Agent Yu got in next to her and closed the door. The agent buckled her seat belt and instructed the driver to take them to Hotel Vertigo. She felt a hand brush against hers. *He must be sitting in the front passenger seat.* Eve tried to keep her expression as flat as possible, hoping to avoid giving away the presence of the invisible man who might be her salvation.

With an unhappy look, the agent shifted and stared out the window.

"Why are you doing this, Agent Yu?" asked Eve, as the car turned a corner onto a street lined with vacant and boarded-up homes.

The agent ignored her.

"Were you trying to help me before? Or were you just—"

A smacking sound stopped Eve mid-sentence, and she stared in confusion. The agent looked dazed all of a sudden. Another smacking sound. Spit came flying from the agent's mouth, and she passed out, her head leaning against the door.

Eve's heart raced when she saw the driver glance in the mirror, and concern spread across his face. He stopped the car and turned to her. But before he could reach his gun, there was another smacking noise, and he slumped over. Blood appeared at his temple.

"Open the door and push her out," the invisible man said.

Eve saw the front door open, and the driver fall out. At once, she reached over the unconscious agent to open the door. She pushed the agent out of the car, pulled the door shut, and locked it.

Her chest heaved in and out, while her brain ran laps the whole time. She clutched her chest as the car accelerated and haphazardly made a left turn onto a busy street.

When Eve finally looked up, she stared in disbelief at the man who was sitting in the driver's seat now and swerving the car through midday rush hour traffic. "You—you were the one who killed Salazar?"

"Yes," said Mauricio Candela.

"Wait…were you the one Agent Yu saw on the CCTV footage? Wearing a fedora?"

He nodded.

"But why wouldn't she have recognized you? You're always at the office building. I don't—"

"Agent Grobeck instructed me to interact with nobody but him. So I'm invisible when I'm not in his office. Ask yourself if you've ever seen me outside his office."

Silence elapsed between them as Eve's thoughts raced and her eyes widened with the sudden realization. *Agent Yu was right to distrust Agent Grobeck. Why would he want to hide the existence of Mauricio Candela from her and everyone else at SPI? Why was he okay with me seeing Mauricio? It doesn't make sense.* "I don't understand what's happening. Why were you at Salazar's office in the first place?"

He sped through a yellow light and made a left turn. "Because Agent Grobeck ordered me to observe you and report to him about your performance. He instructed me to interfere, if necessary, to retrieve the safe box."

"But I already had it. I already had the safe box before you killed that man. You didn't need to do anything else," she exclaimed. "I'm sorry, but none of this is making sense."

"It will. But, right now, we need to sneak into a hospital so that we can get that tracking chip out of you, Miss Cooper," he said.

7

They stopped at a hospital, ditched the car on a side street, and resumed invisibility. Once they found a quiet area in the joint and hip injury unit of the hospital, two floors up from the emergency unit, they ducked inside a tiny storage closet that smelled like ammonia.

"Where's the light switch?" Mauricio whispered, brushing his hand along the wall. "Hold on. I think I found it."

The light came on, illuminating a gray space stacked to the ceiling with transparent plastic tubs of latex gloves, wipes, Kleenex, hand sanitizer, and other sanitation items. Visible again, Eve and Mauricio regarded one another in silence. She surveyed his black suit and his thick black hair pulled into an untidy bun at the top of his head.

He dug inside one of the tubs on the shelf and pulled out latex gloves. "Here," he said, handing a pair to her.

"I still don't understand why you're doing this, Agent Candela." With her arms folded across her chest, she stared at him.

"You can call me Mauricio."

"Okay. But despite everything you said in the car, you still haven't answered the question. Why are you helping me?"

"Because of this," said Mauricio, holding up a small safe

box, the same one that had been in Salazar's office.

Her eyebrows went up. "You've had it all this time? If Agent Grobeck told you to retrieve it, why didn't you give it to him?"

"Miss Cooper, I wish we had time to talk more," he said, stuffing the box inside her backpack. "But we don't. We have to move quickly." He opened a pocketknife and reached for her arm.

"What...?"

"You first."

"First? You have a chip, too?"

He sighed. "Unfortunately. Hold out your arm."

She recoiled. "No. I'll do it myself."

"I can promise you it's easier if I do it."

She shook her head.

"Suit yourself," he said, sighing and handing her the knife. "Let's be quick. I guarantee you they're already on their way here."

"This is going to suck," she groaned, slipping on the gloves. After removing her jacket, she took the knife from him and placed the blade against her right forearm where Doctor Thomas had cut her open.

Although Doctor Thomas had applied a liquid sealant after inserting the chip, the wound was still fresh. The sight of it made Eve's stomach turn.

Sweat beads lining her forehead, she forced the blade through her skin. For a moment, she marveled at how easily it sliced through her skin. Yet all of the air seemed to leave her in the next moment, and she heard herself scream. Mauricio covered her mouth, and she squirmed.

As she forced the knife deeper, she screamed into the palm of his hand. Deeper and deeper she forced the blade until it hit a tiny pea-sized object.

Inhaling, she cut some skin to create an opening and

dizzily handed the knife to Mauricio. She dug her index finger inside her arm and searched for the chip, while he kept his hand over her mouth to silence her screams.

"I told you to let me do it," he muttered.

Soon she felt herself growing cold and wondering if she might pass out. But after a minute or so of digging, she pulled out a metal object that looked like a coin. "So small," she managed to say, staring at the chip and sinking to the floor in shock.

As Mauricio tied a bandage around her forearm, her eyes blinked and closed. "Stay with me," he pleaded.

"I'm good." She smiled weakly, struggling to keep her eyes open.

Once she was bandaged, he took the knife and wiped it with a towel and peroxide, spilling some on the floor as he poured it on the blade. All of this he did at rapid speed, hardly taking his eyes off Eve. Placing the blade's tip against his arm, he dug in and pressed his lips together to keep from crying out.

It didn't take him as long to find the chip. Once he removed the tiny metal object, he exhaled and examined his bloody arm. Hastily, he wrapped the chips in a cloth and dropped them in the trash bin. Blood dripped from his arm and spilled onto the floor as he looked around for the bandages. "Where did I put the box? Damn it, where's the box?"

"Mauricio," Eve mumbled, her voice low and trembling.

Surrendering the search for the box of bandages, he gathered Eve as she began slipping in and out of consciousness. She felt him cover her with her jacket and sling the backpack over his shoulders. Dimly, she heard him groaning as he stumbled from the closet with her in his arms.

The hallway was empty. He staggered toward the elevator, carrying Eve.

When the elevator opened to the emergency unit moments later, Mauricio headed to the help desk. "Help us," he called to the attendant at the desk.

The young attendant's gaze drifted from Mauricio's bleeding arm to the semi-conscious woman he was holding. "Sir, I'm going to need you to step back—"

"My girlfriend...we were stabbed," Mauricio panted.

Eve opened and shut her eyes, trying to stay conscious.

"Hold on," answered the attendant, picking up the phone.

Not a minute later, three nurses arrived with a couple of gurneys.

Eve's eyes focused on the thin strips of white light that looked like glowing ships sailing overhead. She sat up and looked around, spotting a heavily bandaged woman with a busted lip sound asleep on the only other bed in the room. Voices buzzed outside the door.

When she clutched her bandaged left arm, throbbing pain hit her like a shot of adrenaline. She jumped up, panicked. *They'll know I'm here. SPI will find me.* "Fuck," she yelled in a shrill whisper, grabbing the pack and jacket from the chair next to the bed. Making her way toward the door, she stopped and listened to the voices in the hallway.

Within five minutes, the voices grew distant, replaced by footsteps pattering against the linoleum floors. She cracked the door ajar and peeked out. A doctor and two nurses were walking down the hallway, away from her room. She watched until they turned to enter another room.

Eve tiptoed into the hallway. She proceeded to check the name tag on every door, searching for Mauricio's name as she made her way down the hallway. She opened a few doors and glanced inside, but Mauricio was nowhere to be found. Cursing under her breath, she wished she could remember everything that had happened before she lost consciousness.

As a nurse came near her, she averted her gaze and turned from him, hoping not to draw attention.

"Miss?" called the nurse. "You're not supposed to be here. Are you here to see a patient?"

After clearing her throat, Eve turned to the nurse. "My...um...my boyfriend, Mauricio."

"Mr. Candela?"

"Yes."

"Room two thirty-two, Miss." The nurse pointed ahead and repeated the number in Spanish. "Straight down and to your right."

Nodding and thanking him profusely, she hurried away and prayed the nurse would take no more interest in her. In room 232, she found Mauricio asleep in bed and another man lying awake in a second bed. The man's eyes followed her as she advanced toward Mauricio. *Why didn't I go invisible? So stupid.* She closed the curtains separating their beds.

"Agent Can—I mean, Mauricio," she whispered, leaning close to him and glancing at his bandaged arm. He didn't stir. She shook his shoulders and slapped his face. "Wake up. We need to go now."

At the second slap, his eyes opened and he squinted. Just as he was about to speak, she covered his mouth.

"We don't have time. For now, you're my boyfriend, okay?" She snatched up his blazer jacket and shoes from a chair and laid them on the bed. "Get dressed, and let's go."

He stared at her and didn't move. "Who are you?"

"Are you serious? Don't tell me you have amnesia or something?"

He drew away from her, his eyes wide.

She groaned. "Oh, for fuck's sake. It's me, Eve Cooper. The woman you rescued several hours ago?"

"Excuse me. But Eve Cooper is not a redheaded white woman." A look of incredulity mixed with fear clouded his face. "What's going on? Is this a trick by SPI?"

"Just call me Eve, all right? And...wait...what? I'm not a redhead..." She stopped when she saw her reflection in the wall mirror.

Her mouth dropped open. *What kind of crazy shit is this?* Staring in awe, she ran her hands over the pale white face and sandy red hair that hung to her shoulders.

But when she caught a glimpse of the clock on the wall, she turned to him. "Okay, I don't know what's going on, Mauricio. But we don't have time to figure it out. We have to go now." As she spoke, she heard a voice that didn't sound like her own. It was higher-pitched and somewhat shrill. How had she not noticed it before?

He gawked at her.

"Did you hear me? We have to go," she said in as loud of a whisper as she could manage.

He glanced at the clock and looked at the redheaded woman again. The frenzied look on her face seemed to settle his doubts. He put on the black blazer jacket, stepped into his shoes, and stood. "Let's go."

He took her hand, and they became invisible. They darted to the nearest elevator, passing the nurses Eve had seen outside her room earlier.

Once they exited the building, they slowed but kept a brisk pace and remained invisible.

"How did you change your appearance?" Mauricio asked as they turned onto East Huron Street and headed west.

"I have no idea."

"So you woke up as a white girl?"

"I guess. Look, right now we have to figure out what to do, where to go. There's no telling what'll happen if I come back looking like this. What was the rest of your plan?"

"I didn't actually have one."

She sighed. "We have to figure something out."

"Do you have any money?"

"I need to get to my apartment to get my purse and credit card," she said, tugging at him.

He didn't budge. "I mean cash. If you use your credit or debit card, they'll track you."

"Shit."

"Okay, how about we stop at an ATM and I can withdraw my savings? It's only a couple of thousand, but it'll help."

"That won't last us long. Will it?" Eve replied.

They stood there at the corner of East Huron Street and Michigan Avenue, thinking. Eve surveyed the crowded street. There was something peaceful about standing on the sideline and watching all the people move about with their lives. A man walking a basset hound and talking on his phone strolled by and stopped at the crosswalk.

Staring at Eve and Mauricio, the hound's tongue dangled from his mouth, and he pulled his owner toward them to get a closer sniff. She smiled at the dog.

The man stopped, turning to see what had grabbed his dog's attention.

"Nice basset hound, there. How old is he?" asked Eve.

The dog's ears perked up, and the man stepped back in alarm as his eyes searched left and right. As the dog pulled forward and sniffed Eve, she petted it on the head. With a rough yank on the dog's leash, the man hastened away, looking over his shoulder a few times.

"Why did you do that?" asked Mauricio. "You spooked the hell out of that guy."

"It's not like I meant to—I forgot we were invisible. Anyway, I always wanted a dog, a hound like that one. When I was a kid, we took in a stray basset hound for a week. My dad was out of town visiting his side of the family, so my mom let me keep the dog since she'd always wanted one too. When my dad got back, the first thing he did was yell about how there would be no dogs in his house. That same day, he dropped it off at the pound, and I never saw it again."

"I'm sorry. That's awful."

"Yeah, well. Life sucks," she replied and paused. "Look, there's an ATM over there. Let's withdraw all your money and then hop the first bus out of town."

"All right."

"But, first, I have to make a phone call."

"To who?"

"Agent Yu," said Eve. "I think she may be interested in Salazar's safe box. She suspects Agent Grobeck had something to do with my assignment going wrong. I bet that's piqued her interest about what's in the safe box."

"You can't think of turning it over to her or SPI. I didn't take it just for you to hand it over to them."

"Of course, I'm not going to hand it over to them. But they don't know that."

"I see."

"And after this call, you're going to tell me why you have it."

He sighed. "Fine."

Eve stared at the river as night began to fall. She whipped out the phone SPI had given her, checked the time—4:15—waited a few minutes, and then dialed Agent Yu.

"You know what you're doing is foolish, Miss Cooper," answered Agent Yu, skipping right over pleasantries.

"Yes. I'm sure it is."

"You sound different..."

Eve didn't respond.

"Look, you can fix this. I'm here at Hotel Vertigo as planned for your assignment. It's not too late for you to show up and fix this. Agent Grobeck doesn't know about your little escapade yet."

Eve smiled. "You're at Hotel Vertigo right now?"

"Yes, where your driver was taking us until you decided to take a detour."

"You're in the lobby, aren't you?"

"Yes. Are you here?"

Eve laughed. She could hear Agent Yu shifting around and moving, probably looking for her. "It's funny. I only guessed you'd be at the hotel, that an overly dedicated agent like you would insist on carrying out the mission no matter what. I mean, the smartest thing would've been for you to report to Agent Grobeck what had happened so that maybe you'd have some hope of finding me. But you have too much pride to fail, to have to ask your boss for help. And, honestly, who would want to ask that asshole for help anyway?"

"Are you going to do this the easy way or the hard way, Miss Cooper? It's up to you."

"You see that tiny red dot on your chest?" she asked, hoping that Mauricio was in position with his gun aimed at Agent Yu just the way he'd aimed it at Salazar.

Agent Yu's sharp intake of air followed by silence confirmed Mauricio was in position.

Eve exhaled and smiled. "Try to run or move a muscle, and the bullet will go in before you can blink."

"How do I know that's not a laser pen you have pointed at me?" Agent Yu asked.

"You don't know. But if you're feeling brave, go ahead and doubt me."

After seconds of silence, Agent Yu chuckled. "You're either stupider than I realized or smarter than I gave you credit for."

"You could say I'm very observant and a fast learner."

"What do you think you're going to achieve by—"

"I have the safe box with the flash drive in it," Eve interjected.

Agent Yu fell silent again.

"I'll destroy the drive before I ever turn it over to you people. But, then again, who knows. I may be inclined to turn it over to you depending on what you can do for me."

At this point, Agent Yu laughed. "I can appreciate that you've watched a lot of movies. But you're way out of your depth, honey."

"You're probably right. I mean, you know more about this shit than I do, and I bet you guys got a million ways to track me. But I don't have anything left, thanks to you assholes, so the way I see it, I have nothing to lose." She paused. "The others, are you torturing them too?"

"Torture is a harsh word. We prefer 'enhanced training'. And, no, it's reserved for difficult trainees."

"Where are the rest of the trainees right now?"

"They've all been sent on short-term field assignments as of yesterday. They're spread across the country and out-of-pocket at the moment."

"I need their phone numbers. Now."

"You don't already have that information?" asked Agent Yu.

"I'm a millennial. We don't memorize phone numbers. And I don't have my personal cell phone anymore. Thanks to you all."

Agent Yu snickered. "What does it matter to you where they are anyway?"

"They need to know what you people are doing."

"They do know."

"The facts. Not the lies you fed us during training," said Eve. "You're going to give me their contact information, phone numbers and locations."

"I don't have it, Miss Cooper. It's classified information."

"Bullshit."

"Actually, it's not. After your resignation, Agent Grobeck

decided to step in and take control of the training. The trainees report to him now. So, as far as their whereabouts, all I know is the cities they're in. Anything else about their specific assignments, he doesn't disclose to me. And I don't have access to their tracking chips. All that's above my pay grade now."

"So you got demoted. I don't care. Get access."

Agent Yu was quiet again.

"Let me clarify. If you refuse, that little dot on your chest will get painful for you. So, are you going to help me find them or not?"

Agent Yu breathed in. "Fine. I'll help you."

"Good choice. I'll call again soon, and you'll have information for me about the others. Understand?"

"Yes."

"If you get anyone else involved or in any way try to wiggle out of this arrangement, you'll get a bullet when you least expect it. Understand?"

"Yes," Agent Yu answered. "Can I ask where you got the gun?"

"Get the information," Eve repeated and hung up before Agent Yu could respond. After memorizing the agent's number, she tossed the phone into the river.

She looked at her watch and frowned. *That took longer than I expected.* She only had thirty minutes left to carry out the second part of her plan.

Eve stared at the sign that read "First Bank of the Midwest." Through the window, she could see a teller counting money and stuffing it inside something beneath the counter, the cash register. As she watched the teller count more bills and hand the bills to a customer, she thought her heart's pounding might break through her chest. *It's an insane idea. Stupid. Completely foolish.* But it was the only one she had at the moment.

She slung the backpack over her shoulders, pulled the straps tight, and puffed out her chest. *You got this.* She stared at the window of the bank and exhaled. The window reflected only the building and the cars behind her. She was still invisible.

Entering the bank felt akin to walking into the twilight zone. Eve couldn't believe what she was about to do. But she silenced any thoughts of hesitation and proceeded as lightly as possible toward the teller she'd watched from outside. The bank was approaching closing time, so there were only a half-dozen customers inside. She realized she couldn't have chosen a more strategic time. *Few witnesses.*

As she passed two tellers, she glanced at the cameras above each station.

"I'm thinking of taking a week off to go see my mom in Minnesota. I just...I need a break, you know?" said the younger teller who was absently drumming her fingers on the counter. "Can't even remember when I had more than a day off, do you?"

"Use your sick days. Tell Toni you have the stomach flu or something, not like she can stop you from using your paid sick time," her older colleague responded. "I have some vacation days I can donate to you."

Holding her breath, Eve slipped by the tellers who were too absorbed in their conversation to notice anything strange. She reached the teller whose station was in the farthest corner out of hearing range of the others. Standing behind the woman, Eve remained as quiet and still as possible. *Okay. Just do it. You got this.* She put her hand over the woman's mouth and, as soon as the woman screamed, Eve pinned her arm behind her back.

"Don't holler," Eve whispered, trying not to breathe in too much of the woman's raspberry cologne. The woman tried to scream some more, but Eve squeezed her arm. "Just be still and don't scream."

In the minute or so Eve had taken to reach the teller, more customers had queued at the teller stations. The room that had been mostly empty a couple of minutes ago was rather loud now, filled with chatter and soft music. All the other tellers were busy serving customers. Eve figured she had only a moment before one of the tellers looked in the direction of her hostage. She had to act quickly.

"I promise I'm not going to hurt you. I'm going to take my hand away and let your arm go. Then, I need you to open the drawer. Okay?"

Not saying a word, the woman nodded. When Eve released her, she opened the drawer and stood still.

"How much is in there?" asked Eve. "Don't say it. Write it on that pad."

The woman was staring straight ahead. She jotted a number on the pad above the register. $5000.

Eve sighed. She knew a bank wouldn't keep much cash at the registers, yet she'd hoped for a bigger haul than $5000. *There's likely a back area where they lock away larger amounts of money. In the movies, the large sums of money are always hidden somewhere in a vault.* For a moment, Eve combed her mind and tried to recall all the bank-heist films she'd ever watched.

"There's a customer coming," the teller exclaimed in a shrill whisper, looking straight ahead and barely moving her lips.

"Put it all in a bag under the counter, fast. But don't draw attention to yourself."

She stuffed the bills inside the bag, haphazardly dropping bills on the floor, and placed the small bag of cash on the counter. She pushed the bag toward Eve and continued staring ahead, still as a statue.

Eve forced the bag of money into the backpack and

zipped it shut.

"I...I have kids. Please don't hurt me," said the teller, trembling.

"I told you I'm not going to hurt you."

Fuck. She'll push the button before I can get away. In the movies, they always push the button. Frozen in place, she wondered what she could do to ensure she had time to get out of the place before the teller caused a scene. *I could try to teleport. No, too risky.* She chided herself and vowed to get a handle on teleporting. In the next moment, she decided it was best to just run as fast as possible.

An alarm sounded, and Eve knew her time was up. The teller had pushed the button.

"Help, she's taking off with the money!" the teller shouted.

Startled gasps and screams came from the other tellers and customers. An approaching customer, a well-groomed twenty-something in a business suit, stopped and threw his hands up.

Wasting no more time, Eve took this as her moment to run. She wove through the throng of terror-stricken tellers and the guards who were looking around for the robber, their weapons drawn.

When she bolted out the building, she broke into a sprint, turning corner after corner, glancing over her shoulders and swerving through crowds of people. As she reached a coffeehouse in the South Loop minutes later, she stopped and bent over. Her stomach and ribs ached, and she wheezed, gulping for air.

She wasn't sure how long it took to stop wheezing and feeling like she might faint. Standing up straight, she looked around.

No cops. No sirens.

Fuck me. I did it.

Inside the coffeehouse, an invisible Eve knocked twice at the restroom door. "It's me, Eve," she whispered. "Mauricio?"

He opened the door, grasped at the air until he found her hand, and pulled her inside. "What took you so long?" he asked, leaning against the door.

"I had to make a stop." As she became visible, she inhaled and exhaled. Her heart was still racing, and she wondered if she'd ever catch her breath again. But she rushed forward and hugged him tightly. "Thank you. Thank you for doing that. I think Agent Yu was scared shitless."

"It's all good." His tan cheeks flushed red. "Why are you so out of breath? What was your pit stop?"

Avoiding the question, she went to the mirror and checked out her reflection. *Ugh. Why do I still look like this?* Greenish-gray eyes set in a milky white face curtained by red hair looked back at her.

"Eve? Where did you go?"

"That's uh...yeah, I'll tell you later."

He regarded her with skepticism. "Fine. So what's next?"

"Let's hop a bus to Iowa," she answered, still examining her reflection.

"Why Iowa?"

"It's not Chicago. Better yet, it's the middle of nowhere."

He rubbed his head. "Makes sense."

"Probably best you stay invisible until we get there though."

"Do you think it'll work? Do you think she'll help you find the others?"

"No, not really," Eve replied, pushing her hair behind her ears. "But at least now she's scared of me, so I don't think she'll cross me. For now. Problem is, her boss is scarier than me."

"So we hide?"

She nodded. "Yes. For now."

8

A couple of hours before sunrise, the bus stopped at a gas station off Interstate 80 in Davenport, Iowa. Eve stepped off the bus, an invisible Mauricio alongside her. They headed down the dark road to a motel.

"You sure about this place?" asked Mauricio. "Small towns irk me."

"It's only for a few nights. Anyway, I doubt anyone will look for us here."

In the lobby of the rundown motel, a stale, moldy odor hung in the air, and peach-colored wallpaper lined the walls. With thinly veiled disgust, Eve surveyed the room—the dusty-looking navy-blue sofa and chair, and the plastic chandelier hanging over the entrance.

"How can I help you, Miss?" said a speckle-faced receptionist in his early twenties. He wore a big smile.

"I'd like your cheapest room for three nights." She put on her best rural, all-American girl accent to match her new face and red hair. It occurred to her that this face would benefit her.

The man pecked at his keyboard and stared at an outdated monitor screen. He quoted her the total. "What's your name, Miss?"

"Res Adler."

"Where'd you get that name?" Mauricio whispered.

A gloomy look sailed over her face. "Someone I used to know."

"What was that, Miss Adler?" asked the receptionist.

She cleared her throat and half-smiled. "Oh nothing, I just remembered I need to call a friend to let her know I'm in town. Haven't seen her in years."

He resumed typing, looking closely at the monitor screen. "Okay. We have a cleaned room in the renovated section. Usually the renovated section is an upgrade, but I'll waive the extra fee."

"Oh, wow. I appreciate that," she replied, smiling. *Damn, white girls really get the special treatment, don't they?* "Thank you."

"No problem, Miss. I'll need a card on record for any damages."

"All I have is cash. Is that okay?"

"Miss, we only accept—"

"I totally understand. It's just that...my wallet got stolen up in Minneapolis, and all my cards were in it. I can't get any replacement card until I get home." She paused, watching the young man's face twist into a sympathetic frown. "Would it be all right if I left the same amount in cash for you to hold for damages?"

He regarded her with suspicion.

From the silence and the look on his face, she knew he was about to break protocol because he felt sorry for her.

"I guess I could make a note here on your reservation. But I'm afraid you might have to hang around for a few hours after checkout, depending on when our housekeepers get to your room. Thing is we generally don't take reservations without a card—"

"In case someone damages the room and you need to charge the card, right? I totally understand," said Eve.

"Yes, that's right. But given your situation, I'll make an exception."

She flashed him a relieved smile. "Thanks, I appreciate that. I don't believe I caught your name...?"

"Dan." He smiled and handed her a receipt and key to the room. "And I'll tell you what. I'll put a note on the reservation that your room has housekeeping priority when you check out so that we don't hold you up too long."

"Thank you so much, Dan." She offered him a flirtatious smile before pocketing the receipt and key.

"Yeah, it's fine. We have a few long-term customers here who only pay in cash. We try to make it the exception, not the rule. You're in room one hundred and fifty-four. Let me know if you need anything, extra pillows, blankets, or whatever."

"I sure will," she replied, still smiling. "Thank you."

When Eve arrived at the elevator, Mauricio nudged her. "You know you're a little too good at the innocent act."

Smirking, she pressed the "up" button at the elevator. "Folks like a pretty white face with a cute Southern accent."

"I guess so. Oh, and I'm curious...Res Adler? Is there any reason you chose to represent yourself with that name?"

"First name that came to mind."

"That's it?"

"Sure."

They entered the room that smelled faintly of cigarette smoke, and Eve locked the door. When she flipped on the switch, Mauricio appeared. For a minute, they stood at the door and stared around the dank room. It reminded Eve of some of the hotel rooms they'd lived in for brief periods when she was a child before moving into the family home. With a long sigh, she went to the bed and dropped down.

"This is the renovated section?" Eve muttered.

"At least it's only a day or so," said Mauricio, kicking off his shoes at the door.

She removed her backpack and went to the bed. After opening the pack and looking inside, she poured the contents of the bag onto the bed. She stared in awe at the stacks of money, more money than she'd ever seen.

"Whoa," he exclaimed, hanging his jacket on the chair and ogling the cash. "Where did you get that?"

"Um, well," said Eve, turning red. "About that 'pit stop' I made before I met up with you at the coffeehouse...I sort of, maybe robbed a bank."

He gaped at her, at a loss for words.

When Eve woke up, she saw Agent Grobeck standing in her apartment. Her hands were around his neck and her knee pressing against his chest. Warm tears rolled down her cheeks, and she wiped them away.

"You all right?" asked Mauricio, lingering in the doorway of the bathroom. "What's wrong?"

"I just wish this were all a dream. But it's not, and I'm stuck here in this shitty motel with some strange man, and there's no way I can go home or call my friends. And I don't know if Mr. Pebbles is safe."

"Who's Mr. Pebbles?"

She thought about how Mr. Pebbles used to sit next to her on the sofa and paw at her, forcing her to pet him. If she didn't pet him right away, he'd whine and meow until she relented. Her smile faltered as she stared at the wall. "I'm so alone. Everything I ever knew and had is gone...because of this ability. Because I was stupid enough to think I could use it to make my life better." Tears dampened her pillow.

Mauricio shook his head. "It's not an 'ability'. It's your gift."

She scoffed.

"I'm serious. It's part of who you are, and it's your only

way to stop them. To get your life back." He paused, walking toward her. "Your gift is a blessing from God, Eve, not a burden."

"God?" she snorted. "My mom was on her knees every night praying to 'God'. And you know what? God never protected her."

"Eve—"

"Because he doesn't exist. And even if he does, I'd say he stopped caring about me a long time ago." She wiped her face and kept her eyes fixed on him.

"All right, all right. Well, how about we agree that you're not alone in this? And I'm your friend, not just a strange guy you're stuck with?"

"I barely know you," she replied, rolling her eyes.

"Okay then, so let's look at what you do know. We just threatened a federal agent together, and we're on the run from the government. Plus, you robbed a bank, and we killed a guy. I'd say we know each other pretty well at this point."

"*You* killed a guy. I had nothing to do with that."

"Fine. Fair point."

"And you tried to kill me."

"Also a fair point. For what's it worth, I wouldn't try it again. It was a spur of the moment mistake."

"That's...comforting. I guess," she replied.

He gave her a playful shove, and a smile curled her lips.

"There's that smile I saw the first time you were in Agent Grobeck's office."

His tender expression caught Eve off guard, and she flushed.

"Let's stay hopeful through this. Yeah?" he said, sitting on the bed and sighing.

She joined him and nodded. "Okay."

"Good. And let's talk about something lighter. Starting with why you've looked like a white girl since we left the hospital. You still haven't explained that to me."

Eve shrugged. "I don't know. It never happened before now. Are you capable of more than fading?"

"Not that I know of. But 'fading'...that's an interesting word choice. I never thought about it like that."

"Sounds better than 'cloaking'," Eve replied. "You really have no other abilities?"

"I'm pretty sure I don't."

She looked out the window. "Do you think SPI knows that some of us are capable of more? I mean, they don't even seem to know where the fading comes from, why some of us can do it and some can't."

He rubbed his chin. "I don't know. Do you think they know there's more?"

"My sense is they have no idea. It never came up in class. But if they don't, I bet they'll know soon, now that they have a whole class of trainees who probably have other abilities. No way SPI won't find out. And when they do—"

"*Ay, Dios mio.*"

"Yeah. We have to find the others. Fast. And warn them."

"Did you ever talk to other trainees about other abilities?" he asked.

Eve stared at him, thinking about her conversations with AJ regarding her abilities and her telepathy episode with Sam. Before she could say yes, it occurred to her that she didn't trust him. *He saved me from that place, but that doesn't mean I have to tell him everything yet. Agent Yu would tell me to play it safe, wouldn't she?* She shook her head. "Like I said, I didn't know I could do this until now."

She went to the bathroom and stared at her reflection in the mirror. Closing her eyes, she visualized her tight curls and freckles, the small mole on the left side of her chin, her wide nose, and bushy eyebrows. *I want to see my face again.*

When she opened her eyes and found a familiar darker

face staring at her in the mirror, she smiled. Her hands swept over her face, examining the shape of her eyes, lips, and ears, as if trying to memorize each detail. She ran her fingers over her tiny dark curls that were packed down to her head like wool.

"Oh no. Hey, come here. Hurry," said Mauricio, holding the remote and pointing it at the television.

She rushed to his side. "What's going on?"

He pointed at the television. "This is bad, Eve."

The same brown face she'd seen reflected in the bathroom mirror was now plastered across the television screen, while the *CNN* anchor mentioned a bank robbery that had occurred in Chicago. "This woman, believed to be Evelina Marie Cooper, a former high school teacher at Martin Delaney, was seen leaving the bank minutes after the robbery occurred. A spokesperson for Homeland Security stated that the department suspects she's involved in a Chicago-based terrorist cell they have been tracking. The department is pursuing multiple leads," said the anchor. The anchor was next shown walking through the hallway of a school that Eve immediately recognized. Her heart sank.

"She was always a bit aloof," said a familiar voice. The camera panned to two of her old colleagues, Kara and Rachel. They were sitting in the teachers' lounge.

"Kara Kowalski teaches ninth-grade history at the high school," the anchor explained.

"She never said much to me and mostly kept to herself," said Kara, looking concerned. "But I never would've thought she was capable of this."

Rachel, sitting across from her, nodded.

The camera turned to the anchor who went on to describe Eve's attire and to encourage anyone with information to call a hot-line number listed at the bottom of the screen. Mauricio switched off the television and looked at Eve.

"I swear there was no footage of me entering or leaving that bank. I was invisible the whole time and, besides, I was wearing the other face. There's no way I was seen." She groaned. "It was the weird nature of it all—you know, money disappearing into thin air. That's what put SPI on my scent. Now they're leaking lies to find me."

"Are you sure you were invisible the whole time?"

"Positive. And black spandex running pants? I don't own spandex running pants. Plus, you saw me yesterday. I wasn't wearing spandex!"

Mauricio surveyed her. "You'd look good in spandex."

"I should've seen this coming. I should've known they'd figure it out."

"Eve?"

"They've ruined me." *If I had just stopped myself from walking into that bank. If I'd just gone straight to the coffeehouse like planned.* Tears filled her eyes and rained down her cheeks as she stared at her silhouette reflected on the television screen. She slapped her face again and again.

"Eve?"

She struck her face over and over as if doing so would knock her back in time and undo what she'd done. "Stupid," she said, slapping her face so hard that it sounded like the cracking of a whip. "Stupid, stupid, stupid."

Mauricio grabbed her wrists before she could hit herself again. "Eve, look at me. It's going to be all right. We'll get through this. Okay?"

Sniffling, she snatched her hands away from him. As she wiped her face, she went to the bathroom and stared in the mirror. Deep brown eyes looked back at her, accented by long lashes.

"Eve?"

One at a time, she wished each of her features into nonexistence, picturing the redhead she'd seen in the mirror.

Mauricio stood at the bathroom door and watched her. "Eve, please."

Within moments, the redhead was staring back at her. The face of freedom. Frowning, she patted her rosy cheeks dry and turned to him. "I'm hungry. Let's get something to eat."

After lunch, they sprawled out on the bed and gazed at the cottage cheese ceiling. The muted television flashed now and then.

"I miss my family," he said, interrupting the silence.

"Are you married?"

"Fourteen years. Elisa and I were friends in high school. Not long after we started dating, she got pregnant. So we did what any good little Catholics would do—we got married. We were eighteen."

"Wow. Fourteen years?"

"Yeah. She used to drive me crazy. Nagging, picking fights. It was constant. She hadn't wanted to marry me, you see. But she couldn't say no to her parents. And she was pregnant—what would people think about her? Through all of it, we stayed together, and the babies kept coming. Three kids back to back, all girls. When my youngest was born, Elisa got herself fixed."

"How did SPI pull you in?"

"Just like they did you. Offered me a job with a salary I couldn't afford to turn down. But when I backed out of it after a year—"

"They came for you?"

He averted his gaze. "I had no chance to say goodbye or anything."

"They wouldn't let you see your family?"

"Agent Grobeck didn't trust me not to try to run with them. Probably thought I'd try to flee the country with them."

Eve nodded. "Well, who wouldn't do that?"

"Exactly," said Mauricio. "So they provided me an apartment, basically confined me to it when I wasn't working. He made sure to remind me that he'd harm my family if I tried to get away."

"Wow. So that's what was in store for me," she replied, shaking her head. "Grobeck said they didn't used to use soft recruiting methods, like these job offers. He said it was a new thing they were trying out because Agent Yu recommended it. But you said they offered you a job…"

"After me, Agent Grobeck switched back to harder methods. Capture, brainwash. That sort of thing."

"Did it work?" Eve stared at him, thinking about the horrors that others like her may have endured.

"Disappearing people and torturing is rarely a way to get people on your side. You'd think a man like Grobeck would be smart enough to know that, huh?"

She nodded. "Can I ask why you risked it now? Couldn't he still hurt your family now that you've gone AWOL?"

"My wife and kids are out of the country, out of his reach. It took me a while, keeping it off the radar, but I made sure of that."

She placed her hand on top of his, and he looked at her with watery eyes. "We'll figure out a way for you to get back to your wife and kids."

"I think about them every day."

As she nodded, she caught a glimpse of the clock. "We should get going before it gets dark. I saw a Walmart a mile or so north. We need to pick up a few things."

"You mean steal things? Like you stole all that money?" He gestured at the bag sitting next to the desk.

"I wasn't planning on it, but now that you mention it…" She stood. "Sure."

He shook his head in disappointment.

"What's the big deal?"

"It's illegal," he said, shooting her a reprimanding look.

"You're going to lecture me on legality?" Eve's forehead creased, and she crossed her arms over her chest. "You killed a guy recently, remember?"

He didn't look at her. "All right. What are we stealing?"

She grabbed her backpack and jacket off the chair and headed to the door. "Weapons, a change of clothes, among other things."

"I like the way you think."

"Good, because I know jack shit about guns or weapons in general. And seeing as how you shot and killed a man from at least twelve feet away, I'm assuming you know a lot about guns. So, I need you to teach me."

"You know I'm not proud of what I did."

"I spent my whole life doing the right thing, trying not to cause waves. Look at where I am." Eve shrugged, trying to be nonchalant. "You did what you had to do."

Stately white oaks, northern red oaks, and bur oaks crowded the dewy forest that lay just north of a narrow stream. Wind swept through the snow-covered branches. Mauricio and Eve had settled on a cozy spot deep in the forest, tucked far away from the road.

"Don't I need safety goggles and earplugs? Don't people usually wear that stuff for protection at gun ranges?" asked Eve, trying to remember the times her father had gone to the gun range. He never took her with him, but she recalled him packing up a lot of gear in a duffel bag.

He handed her the big *Men in Black* sunglasses he'd stolen from the store. "Sure. But we don't have any of that. So, you'll wear my sunglasses. And I'll cover your ears with my hands. You'll be fine. But, first, promise me something. After this, you'll tell me the real reason you chose to use the name

Res Adler."

"Why are you so hung up on that?"

"Because I may not know you very well, but I can tell when you're withholding something. Your left eye does a twitchy thing when you're not telling the truth. It's actually kind of cute." He smiled. "So? Do you promise?"

"Sure. Whatever."

"Great, then let's get started." He began by teaching her how to hold the GLOCK 26.

This task took longer than either of them expected.

"Now extend your finger straight and lay it flat on the side of the trigger guard. Just like that. You want to keep your finger outside the guard. Just relax." He watched her hand tremble. With a reassuring smile, he placed his hand over hers. "Whenever you handle a gun, make sure the barrel is pointed downward, clear of people. Keep it pointed downward unless you're ready to shoot. Do not point or fire upwards, ever. If you fire upwards, the bullet may injure someone when it comes down."

"Right. Okay."

"Now, let's work on the firing-ready position."

For hours, he trained her on how to hold the gun, how to lock and unlock it, load bullets into the chambers, aim, and shoot without losing her balance from the powerful kickback. They only went through one box of bullets, anxious to avoid arousing any unwanted attention. Although the forest was vacant, they were not terribly far from the road.

"I'll never be any good at this," she moaned, handing him the gun. "Maybe if SPI had put me in weapons training…"

"They have different tracks for the trainees. I'm guessing they didn't expect you to engage in direct combat of any sort. Although, I still think it's stupid not to make sure each operative has at least some basic comfort in weapons handling." He sighed. "But it's not exactly a bad thing to never be good at shooting." He aimed at a slender oak branch a few feet away. When he fired, the bullet pierced the branch, sending tiny flakes of bark flying this way and that. Slowly, the thin branch bent, snapped, and fell to the ground.

"That man wasn't the first person you killed, was he?"

"No."

She looked sideways at him. "How many?"

"Three," said Mauricio, after a short pause.

"You were ordered to kill them?"

"Yes, if necessary."

"It was necessary to kill Salazar?"

"Salazar was a monster. His company specializes in biological and chemical weapons manufacturing."

"Wait...what?" She turned to face him. "What are you talking about?"

"One of his weapons is called A2-10. Do you know what it does?"

"No."

"It melts flesh. It melts flesh from the inside out. I'm guessing SPI didn't tell you anything about this weapon or about the company."

She shook her head.

"I studied him and researched the company. Took me a while, but it wasn't hard to piece it all together."

"So is that what's on the flash drive? Information about that weapon?"

"I don't think so."

She stared at him blankly. "Then what's on the flash drive?"

"I wish I knew. I haven't been able to open the safe box."

"Okay. Just so I'm clear, you killed Salazar so that you could take the safe—i.e. the flash drive—and keep it from SPI? Because you didn't trust SPI anymore? But you don't know what's even on the flash drive?"

"Yeah, in a nutshell."

"Agent Grobeck never asked you about the safe?" she asked. "Weren't you supposed to give it to him?"

"I told him I'd failed to acquire it. That it wasn't in Salazar's office."

Eve nodded.

"Anyway, let's get back to what we're out here for," he said. He raised the gun and pointed it straight ahead. "Look at how I'm holding the gun. You want to hold it with both hands like this at all times—"

"How did you learn how to use a gun? Did SPI teach you?"

"My brother taught me. We hunted with my father when we were teenagers. He taught me how to use a hunting knife, a rifle, a shotgun. The three of us took a hunting trip every year."

"Sounds nice."

"It was," he said, smiling. "We were close. What about you and your family?"

"Only child. My dad was an abusive asshole, and my mom never left him. You know, the typical story."

"Oh," said Mauricio, pointing the gun downward and glancing at her. "Sorry to hear that."

She shrugged, watching him disassemble the gun and slip it inside the backpack before he removed the small green and silver pocketknife. "At least I learned how to fight and run when necessary. That's the one thing he taught me."

He snorted. "Glass half full, eh?"

"I guess so. Are you going to teach me how to use that thing?"

Mauricio looked at the pocketknife and turned it over in his hand. "This is a one-blade jackknife. Pretty simple. Handy for camping, fishing, that sort of thing. There's not much to teach you except how to open and close it." He opened the knife, and she stared at the blade until he closed the knife again. He repeated this a couple of times. "It's simple. But you have to be careful not to cut yourself, obviously. I can't say a pocketknife is the best weapon. Really, it's just a tool, and that's how you should view it. You never really want to be close enough to be able to use a knife, if you ask me. But, as far as weapons go, it's better than nothing. It'll be handy in a crisis if you ever need to cut some rope or MacGyver yourself out of a jam. Here, get a feel for it. You want this thing to be sort of an extension of yourself." He closed the knife and handed it to her.

Eve's fingers glided over the smooth green and silver handle.

"Tell me about this Res Adler. I'm guessing that's the name of someone you know. She meant a lot to you, didn't she?"

"How do you figure that?"

"I have a hunch."

"Oh, okay, Perry Mason."

"You're evading the question."

"We dated. That's all. Res is her middle name."

"I see. Your first love?"

"Something like that. We broke up in college, and she went and married a guy. You know, the typical story."

He chuckled. "I see. It must've been serious if you've taken to using her name."

Eve closed the knife and turned to Mauricio, her face bright red.

He threw his hands up in surrender. "All right. I won't press anymore."

"Good. Finish telling me about the uses of a knife."

With another lingering look at her, he cleared his throat once more and launched into a brief tutorial about how to use the knife.

After she opened and closed it a few times, an idea struck her. She pulled the tiny safe box from her backpack and, using the knife, tried to pick the lock.

"Here," said Mauricio, reaching for the box and knife. "Let me try." He sat on the tree stump next to her and picked at the lock.

"It's not going to work, is it?"

He groaned, closing the knife. "It was worth a shot. We'll figure it out later." He returned the knife and box to her bag. "Let's head back to the motel."

Lying on the bed and staring out the window, Eve figured she would've traded anything to remain in this position all day, relaxing and not worrying about anything. Yet her mind was preoccupied with thoughts about SPI, about what they might do if they found her. She was tired of thinking. Tired of worrying. Tired of everything. She just wanted to lie perfectly still in total silence.

Mauricio sat next to her. "Guess what? One of the faders was given an assignment in Philadelphia. We need to get to her before she finishes it and returns to them."

"Back up. A fader?"

He appeared confused. "What? You called it—the ability—'fading'. I assumed it only made sense to call those who have it 'faders'."

"Okay. But how'd you know one was assigned something in Philly? You didn't use the computers in the lobby to search, did you?"

"I was discreet," he replied.

An uncertain look highlighted her face, and she wondered why he was being so short with his words.

"Hopefully, she'll still be in Philadelphia when we get there. How we'll find her is anyone's guess, though."

"She's one of the trainees?"

"Yes. Last name Taylor. She goes by—"

"AJ?"

"Yeah."

Eve dug inside her pack for one of the cheap prepaid cell phones she'd bought at the Walmart. "I can call..." Trailing off, she closed her eyes and cursed herself. "Damn. I don't remember her number. It was saved in my old phone."

Oh God, do I remember Zoey's number? She closed her eyes and sighed with relief as the numbers appeared in her mind, etched there as if they'd always been there. Besides her own phone number, Zoey's was the only number she remembered. Shouldn't she call Zoey and Gabe? At least let them know she was fine? *But what would I say to them? How could I explain any of it without putting them in the middle of this shit? What if SPI is watching Zoey and Gabe?* She shook her head. No, she couldn't call them. Not yet.

"Eve? You all right?"

"Sorry, yeah, I'm fine. I think it's time for us to follow up with Agent Yu. She'll know more about AJ's whereabouts. After the call, we should head out."

"Right now?"

She nodded. "I know it's only been a couple of nights, but we need to get far away from here, meaning we might as well get started on our way to Philly. The next Greyhound is in a couple of hours. I checked yesterday."

He ran his hand through his hair. "I know I've asked before, but do you think Agent Yu will cooperate with us? I mean, it's not like we can actually make good on our threat since we're not in Chicago."

"The thing is she doesn't know we're not in Chicago."

He smiled. "Good point."

Rising from the bed, Eve yawned and stretched. She lumbered to the bathroom and turned on the shower to let the water warm up. "I'm going to get cleaned up, and then we can make the call and go. We'll have to wait a while so they can check the room and give us our deposit back." As she prepared to undress, she stopped and stared at herself in the mirror. The unfamiliar face slowly disappeared, replaced by her own. She swept her palms over her cheeks, through her hair, and gazed at her reflection.

"You spend a lot of time looking at yourself. It's not healthy," said Mauricio, lingering in the bathroom doorway.

"Thanks for the advice I totally didn't ask for."

"I'm saying you look fine to me. And if we make it through this, you won't have to wear the other face anymore. I can see how much it bothers you." He leaned against the doorframe. "Is this her face? Res Adler's?"

Eve laughed. "No. Quite the opposite, actually."

"Okay. Because that would've been extra weird," he said, smiling. "Do you have any contact with her?"

Eve exhaled and decided to tell the truth. "Yes, and more than anything I want to call her, hear her voice."

"Does that mean she divorced her husband?"

Eve shook her head.

"Oh, they separated."

She turned to him and smiled. "No."

"Wait. So then—"

"Mauricio, stop asking so many questions."

He chuckled. "All right. I'm fascinated that a woman like you would settle for being the 'other woman'. That's all."

"A woman like me?" asked Eve, her eyes wide.

"Well. Yeah. You're gorgeous. Surely there's no lack of single women or single men interested in you."

"Oh, I see what you're doing." His cheeks turned pink as she closed the space between them. The bathroom had steamed up from the shower running. "First of all, you've made a lot of assumptions with very little information, starting with me being the 'other' woman."

"That's not—I wasn't trying to—"

"Second of all," she said, pressing herself against him and speaking softly into his ear, "I need to hop in the shower. And seeing as how we're in a hurry to catch a bus, we'll have to resume this later."

"Resume...? Resume what?"

She placed her palms against his chest and forced him to step away. "If you'll excuse me." Before he could respond, she closed the door. Eve took one more glance at her reflection, slipped out of her clothes, and stepped into the hot shower.

After they checked out of the motel, they rushed to the bus station—Mauricio still invisible—and were the last passengers to board. Eve took an empty row near the back, and Mauricio plopped beside her. Not even ten minutes passed before they fell asleep, and the bus crossed the border into Illinois.

When the bus stopped at Union Station in Chicago hours later, Eve was jolted awake. She grabbed Mauricio's hand and whispered, "Hey, I need to get a prepaid credit card. For the next hotel. They sell prepaid credit cards at most places, right?"

"As far as I know. But I've never used one."

"Well, let's hurry," she replied, leading him off the bus. Looking to the left, she spotted a Walgreens at the end of the block, away from the crowd. "I imagine SPI has eyes everywhere around here. We need to be quick." She walked faster and squeezed his hand as they hurried toward the store. Her eyes darted left and right, checking for the presence of police or anyone who looked like an agent.

They arrived at the store and, to Eve's relief, there was no line at the checkout.

"How much would you like to put on it?" the cashier asked.

She handed him a wad of bills.

"Five hundred even?" asked the cashier.

"Yes," she answered, zipping up the backpack. She glanced over her shoulder and noticed a man in jogging clothes. Something about him worried her, and her heart raced. *Don't look paranoid. You're fine. They don't know this face.* But her concern intensified when he locked eyes with her and said something into a wireless earpiece.

"Your card, Miss," said the cashier.

She turned to the cashier, who proceeded to provide instructions about how to use the card. All the while, she squeezed Mauricio's clammy hand.

As she headed to the door, she looked back one more time, and the man in jogging pants met her gaze. He was approaching her while another similarly dressed man was walking behind him. *Stop worrying. There's no way they know it's me.* Yet the sudden presence of a policewoman coming up alongside the man dispelled any doubts that she'd been detected. All three of them looked straight at her as if daring her to run. *How did they—?*

Mauricio squeezed her hand, and at that moment, she did what was natural. She ran.

"You're you again," Mauricio exclaimed, breathing heavy. "You don't look like the redhead anymore. You must've changed before we walked into the store. It's the only way they could've—"

"Oh no. Oh no," Eve panicked. "I won't go back. I won't let them take me."

"Come on. This way," he yelled, tugging her as they reached the corner. They turned down an alleyway, rushed inside a small dive bar, and sprinted toward the restroom. It was unoccupied.

Inside the restroom, Mauricio locked the door and became visible.

As though frozen in a state of shock, Eve stared at her reflection. "I won't let them take me. I won't let them take me again. Not again."

"Eve, you have to change back. Or we'll never make it to the bus."

Frantic thoughts stampeded through her mind as she tried to concentrate on the image of the redhead.

"Eve, hurry."

"I'm trying."

"You can do it. You've done it before. Believe that you can do it again."

"I'm trying!"

"You have to relax, Eve."

"How the fuck am I supposed to relax right now?" she shot back.

In a flash, he gripped her arms and planted his lips firmly on hers. Stunned for a moment, she didn't move. Her eyes remained wide open, staring into his. It occurred to her how long it had been since she'd felt the warmth of another person. She parted her lips and allowed his tongue to dance against hers.

Loud knocks at the door interrupted them. "Police. Open up."

Mauricio released her.

"Why'd you do that?" she asked.

"To relax you. Did it help?"

When she turned to the mirror, she saw her own brown face and tapered dark hair.

More banging at the door. "We need you to come out Miss Cooper."

He squeezed her arm gently. "Relax," he whispered, fading. "You can do this."

Eve fixed her gaze on her reflection and concentrated on an image of red hair and greenish-gray eyes. No change.

Sharp pains like knives shot through her chest.

"Miss Cooper, come out right now. This is the last time I'm asking."

Still concentrating on changing and losing hope with every passing second, she heard a key turn in the door. Taking five deep breaths, she pressed her palms against the sides of her face and closed her eyes until there was total silence and darkness.

When the door opened, the policewoman from the store had her gun drawn and pointed at Eve's chest. She lowered her gun as the red-haired woman turned to face her. Tears glistened on Eve's rosy cheeks.

"What's happening?" Eve managed, surprised by how believable her confusion sounded. She stared at the cop and her partner, standing alongside the two men in jogging clothes. Invisible, Mauricio remained still.

"I'm sorry, Miss. There was a mistake," the policewoman said, holstering her gun. She sounded angry rather than apologetic. "We were looking for someone else." Without another word, the cops and the two men glanced around the back of the bar and ran out the front door.

All the bar patrons were staring at Eve in bewilderment. She wiped her face, caught her breath, and with an air of nonchalance exited the bar. Seeing no sign of the cops or the two men, she took Mauricio's hand and sprinted to the bus stop, still looking over her shoulders now and then.

They took an empty row near the rear of the half-empty bus.

"I think I figured something out," said Mauricio, breathing raggedly.

Before she responded, she slipped in the earplugs they'd gotten in Iowa and connected them to the cell phone. The last thing she needed was for people to think she was talking to herself. "What? And keep your voice down so people just think I'm on a call," she asked, her eyes closed as she inhaled and exhaled in rapid succession.

"I think when you panic, you lose control of your ability. I think it's why you changed back." He paused, and she felt him move closer to her.

"No shit, Sherlock."

"Eve, I'm serious. We can't let what happened tonight happen again. We won't get away next time."

She massaged her aching ribs.

"And another thing. We know for sure they have no idea that we—or you—can change your appearance."

"They might figure it out after tonight."

"No. I doubt it. From what I can tell, they don't have a clue. But we need to stay one step ahead of them."

She opened her eyes and looked around to make sure no one was watching or hearing them. "How?"

"That's what we have to figure out."

9

After passing out of Chicago, the bus rolled along the busy interstate, stopping several hours later in Cleveland. Hesitant after the incident in Chicago, Eve and Mauricio made a quick dash to the Wendy's, used the restroom, grabbed combo meals to-go, and rushed back to the bus. They ate in silence as people piled onto the bus.

"It's been a month since I was in my apartment, reading and petting Mr. Pebbles," she said, swallowing the last bit of the dry burger. "As much as I don't want to endanger my friends, maybe I should contact them." It wasn't too late to contact Zoey and Gabe. They could at least make sure Mr. Pebbles was okay and maybe pay up her rent. She was sure the landlord had already served an eviction notice. All her valuables, her music, her clothes, would be tossed out—if not already—or claimed by whoever was charged with emptying out her apartment. Her books, a collection she'd spent years building. All of it would be gone. A surge of anger shook her.

"It's unwise, Eve. Trust me. You don't know if SPI is watching them," said Mauricio.

The bus started moving again, and Eve sighed. "You're probably right."

She got up and discarded the Wendy's bag in the trashcan.

Once she returned to her seat, Eve tried not to think about the life she was missing in Chicago. But she couldn't help but wonder where Mr. Pebbles was, if the ornery cat was alive, and who was feeding him. She'd given Zoey a key to the apartment, she remembered. *Hopefully, he's with Zoey and Gabe. They'll look after him for sure.* She consoled herself with this thought, thankful that at least Mr. Pebbles might be fine. Did she tell Zoey that Mr. Pebbles liked a bit of milk mixed with his water, or that he liked to nibble on crackers?

Lost in these miserable thoughts, she fell asleep, slumped against the window.

When she woke, the mountains of Appalachia had replaced the snowy Midwest fields. As the bus traveled along the empty Pennsylvania highway, her mind drifted back to Chicago. An image of Zoey centered in her mind, and she closed her eyes. She saw Zoey's honey brown eyes, and that big, dimply smile of hers. Her fingers ran through Zoey's tight curls and down her back. The warmth of Zoey's arms enveloped her, and she smiled, lost in the sweet fragrance of cocoa butter.

Unable to hold it in anymore, Eve let the tears gush. But she silenced her sobs, careful not to draw attention. Overwhelmed by the realization of all that she'd lost, she cried quietly, looking out the window and watching the sun set over the valley. After a while, she rested her head against Mauricio who was sound asleep.

When the bus arrived at Union Station in Philadelphia later, she'd cried so much that she felt almost numb. Not speaking, she took Mauricio's invisible hand, and they scuffled toward Rittenhouse Square. The streets were teeming with people leaving offices and heading to bars or else home.

"I hate bus rides," said Mauricio. "Maybe we need to think about buying a cheap car."

"Yeah, I hate bus rides, too. But our money will only

stretch so far, and we don't know how long we'll have to be on the run like this. Not to mention, I'd hate to get pulled over by the cops for speeding or something and land back in SPI's hands."

"Good point. Well, all I know is I've been looking forward to the hotel pillows, to be honest. Why do hotels always have the best pillows?"

"These are life's important questions."

"Indeed," he chuckled. "I've never been to Philly. Have you?"

"Nope."

"Well, let's hope we find Miss Taylor."

"AJ."

"Yeah. I wish we could've talked more about a plan before we got here. But it's not like we could do that on the bus," he replied. "Anyway, let's hope we find her quick so we can keep moving."

Keep moving where? We don't know what the fuck we're doing. What's our plan besides finding the faders? But just as that question occurred, an answer popped into her head. For the first time all day, she smiled. "I need a laptop."

"Why?"

"I'm going to write about what SPI did to me, what they've done to others like us. And then shop it around to the media to see if anyone will run it. I have a friend with media contacts."

"Do you really think it's a good idea to broadcast this?"

She stopped and turned to him, although she couldn't see him. "People need to know, Mauricio. The world needs to know what they're doing to us. You really think Americans will stand for having their own people kidnapped, tortured, and turned into...super soldiers or some shit?"

"If most of those people look like you and me, then yeah. They'll stand for it because, you know, history."

"I just think if people know, they'll want to —"

"You have way too much faith in people," he interjected. "Also, you know you should put in your earplugs. You look like you're talking to yourself right now."

She looked around, noticing the wary glances and stares of the pedestrians. She lowered her head, put in the earplugs, and continued walking.

As they reached an intersection, the light turned red, and she stopped at the crosswalk. She could feel Mauricio staring at her. Barely moving her lips, she mumbled, "The point is publicizing this might scare the shit out of SPI. And, if we're lucky, it might get some human rights groups and NGOs breathing down their necks to keep them distracted while we find the other faders."

"Assuming the other faders will even care about what happened to you. Let's face it, if SPI is paying them well enough, they're not going to give up the cushy job."

"You gave it up."

"So did you. But look at the price we paid." He paused. "I'm just saying we should keep our expectations low. But I'm with you. All the way."

She squeezed his hand.

The light at the crosswalk changed, and they resumed walking, eventually stopping at two hotels and inquiring about room rates. After ten minutes, they settled on one at the corner of Rittenhouse Square and Walnut Street and booked a room for three nights.

Eve gazed around the bathroom at the white marble floors, the sink and floor-to-ceiling mirror, the gray stone tiles in the shower enclosed with a glass door. *I could live in this bathroom.* Mauricio stretched out on the bed while she ran a warm bath and prepared for a nice, long soak. How long had it been since she'd had a relaxing bath? She'd lounged in the Jacuzzi one Saturday afternoon with Zoey and Gabriel not too long ago, although it felt like a whole other lifetime.

Examining her reflection, she caressed her cropped red hair. This face wasn't hers, and she knew she'd never get accustomed to it. The smeared freckles on the bridge of her nose would always seem foreign and somehow wrong. The bright-colored eyes would never be familiar to her. She longed for this whole ordeal to be over, so she could change out of what had begun to feel like some sort of unnatural mask. But she had to admit she adored her new bangs.

As she disrobed, she studied her body. Flatter breasts and wider hips, thighs bigger than her own. She'd always wanted fuller thighs. She turned to the side, stared at her ass, and frowned. *Figures. All these thighs and no ass.* When she faced the mirror again, Eve closed her eyes and imagined her own face and body.

She opened her eyes and, to her surprise, was staring at a brown face. Her face. She turned to the side and smiled. "That's more like it."

"Did you say something?" asked Mauricio.

"No." She heard some shuffling in the room beyond the bathroom door.

"All right. I'm going to run out for a bit and look for a laptop," he said. "Do you need anything else?"

At once, Eve turned away from the mirror and opened the bathroom door. "Actually, yes."

Mauricio was standing near the bed and zipping up his jacket. He looked at her and froze, his eyes traveling from her thighs to her breasts. Meeting her gaze as she approached, he replied, "I was going to also, um, get us some sandwiches..."

She unzipped his jacket, slid it off, and let it fall to the floor, before fussing with the buttons on his shirt. Her eyes were fixed on him, their faces mere inches apart, as she unsnapped his jeans. Zoey's face floated to the forefront of her mind, but she pushed the image aside and focused only on Mauricio.

"Eve, are you sure we should—"

"Yes. With all this stress, we could both use a release. Don't worry, I have an IUD."

Squatting, she slid his pants down and then his boxers but kept her eyes fixed on his. When she rose again, she took his hand and led him to the bathroom. There she pressed him against the wall and nuzzled her nose against his neck. "That kiss at the cafe in Chicago...it's not the kind of thing a woman forgets. But I am a little fuzzy on the details. Why don't you refresh my memory?"

Steam rose from the Jacuzzi tub filled with hot water and bubbles. Mauricio brushed his palms against her cheeks and brought her face closer to his. As their lips met this time, she put her arms around him, and when he lifted her, she wrapped her legs around his waist. She'd needed this—the raw exhilaration of being close to someone, even if it were empty and temporary.

She wasn't sure how long she'd soaked in the tub after Mauricio left, but by the time she stepped out, her skin was paler and wrinkled. After moisturizing her hair and drying off, she exited the bathroom and turned on the television.

No sooner had she slipped into a T-shirt and sat on the bed, Mauricio appeared in front of the door with shopping bags in both hands. She noticed the door had not opened. "Did you just literally walk through the door?"

"Yeah, I did it in Cleveland. When we stopped at the Wendy's, I went through the restroom door. But I thought I was going crazy."

"Wait. You never mentioned this. Why didn't you say something? You can go through solid walls?"

"Yeah. I think I have the hang of it now. I have to

concentrate on what I'm trying to walk through and then hold my breath and walk through. It's kind of fun, after a while." He grinned. "You're not the only one with more than one gift, as it turns out."

"I see," she said, regarding him with curiosity. "What's in the bags?"

"Food, a laptop computer, and other necessities—snacks, washing detergent, a couple of spare flash drives." He sat next to her, dropped the bags on the bed, and pulled out the laptop box. "I took some of the cash and got the cheapest laptop I could find."

She stared at him with a testy expression as he pried the box open. "Why didn't you just steal it?"

"Because I'm not a criminal," he answered, casting her a disdainful look.

"You've killed people. Multiple people."

"For SPI."

"Murder is murder."

"Not when it's for the government."

Eve sighed. "Look, it's not like I like having to steal. But I'm trying to look out for myself, for us. We have to be strategic. This money won't last us forever."

"Eve, you can't let them turn you into this person."

"What person?"

"A person with no code," he replied.

She rolled her eyes. "I do have a code. Live. Survive. That's my code, and it means I can't always play nice. You should understand that."

"Fine. Next time I'll send you to the store. Computer name?" he said when a text box appeared on the screen and prompted him to enter a name.

She stared at him blankly.

"What login name do you want for the computer?"

"MisterPebbles," she offered.

He typed in the name and continued pecking at the computer. "All right." He turned to her. "It's all yours now. Password is 'Indiana_Eve'. Get it?"

The blank expression sailed over her face again.

"Since we're on this mission to find precious items— faders—and stop SPI from getting weapons. And you're from Indiana."

"But we're not archaeologists. Anyway, I never liked that movie."

"Loser."

She stuck her tongue out at him.

"Well, keep the wireless turned off. I'm sure they have other ways of tracking us, but let's not make it easy. Your sandwich is in that bag—I got you a southwestern chicken hoagie. You're welcome." He winked at her, before pulling out a disposable phone he'd purchased. He inserted a SIM card and excused himself to the bathroom.

She closed her eyes and took a bite of the hoagie. For the next five minutes, she savored every bite. Nothing had made her appreciate food more than being practically starved by SPI. After finishing the final bite, she gulped the lemonade and turned to the computer screen.

"How are we going to find AJ Taylor?" Mauricio asked, emerging from the bathroom. He stood near the window.

"I don't have a clue."

"Do you have any hacking skills?"

Eve shot him an amused look. "Do people still use that word...'hacking'? Seems a little outdated."

"Yes, they do. Hand me the computer," he said.

She did as told and watched him bring up the command prompt and then proceed to type in some code she didn't understand.

After a few minutes, he cleared his throat and turned to her. "Uh, just so we're using our time wisely, while I'm doing this, you can work on the story, yeah? The one that's going to win you a Pulitzer for journalism? I bought pens and a notebook. They're in the other bag over there." He pointed toward the desk next to the window.

She laughed and took this as her cue. "Sure thing, boss. I'll get out of your hair."

"I know I said you'd look good in spandex," he said, watching her walk to the desk. "But I have to say, this T-shirt and panties look is even better."

She glanced over her shoulder and winked at him.

It was almost sunrise, and Eve was passed out on the bed—pen and notebook on her chest—when Mauricio exclaimed, "Got her!"

She sat up and looked left and right until her gaze landed on Mauricio. He was sitting at the desk with the light of the computer illuminating his face.

"I know where she's staying. We got her."

"Oh. Right," said Eve, registering the import of his words but failing to care at this early hour of the morning.

"She's staying only ten minutes from here. I can walk it."

"Hmm-huh," Eve murmured.

"I'll go to her this afternoon. See if she's willing to join us." He saved the document and turned off the computer before joining her on the bed. "While I'm gone, maybe you can use the quiet time to write."

"Awesome," she managed to say, not registering anything he said and too sleepy to muster up an ounce of genuine enthusiasm. She fell against her pillow and, in mere seconds, was asleep once more.

Marie Cooper removed pink and blue rollers from her hair and combed through the bouncy curls. Eve stared at her mother, admiring the way her curls and dark skin seemed to shine in the sunlight. "Isn't sand interesting, Eve? Millions of tiny grains of minerals and rocks and shells. But mostly it just sort of looks like one big sheet to us, huh?" She smiled, squatting to meet her daughter at eye level. "Until you try to pick it up. See?" She grabbed a handful of golden sand, and it poured through her fingers.

Eve reached down to grab a handful yet gasped when she saw her feet. They were sinking into warm sand.

"Here, try it," said Marie Cooper, smiling a big smile. She grasped Eve's hands and lowered them to the sand.

In a panic and struggling to move her feet as the sand rose to her calves, Eve snatched her hands away. "Mom, I'm sinking," she screamed. "What's happening?"

From a distance, a strange woman approached, running toward her but looking back at the shore as though she was being pursued. As the woman drew closer, Eve squinted to get a clearer view of her. "Mom, we have to—" Eve began but stopped. "Mom?" she shouted, looking around as the sand reached her waist.

Marie Cooper was gone.

The strange woman was still approaching, and now Eve could see that she was limping.

"Help me," Eve screamed, reaching for the woman.

For a moment, her fearful brown eyes swept over Eve. She glanced over her shoulder before pulling Eve up and dragging her to the nearest patch of grass several feet away. "This...forest. I can't save," the woman said, taking a step back and stumbling.

"Forest?" said Eve, looking at the sandy beach. "What forest?"

The woman's mouth opened wide and her face contorted, as though she was crying out in pain. But there was no sound.

Still lying on the grass, Eve watched in terror as the woman's face changed from pale to tan, and a familiar set of features materialized.

"Agent Yu?"

The woman paced, mumbling something to herself. Her eyes narrowed on Eve all of a sudden, and she stopped.

Just as Eve started to speak, everything went dark.

When she blinked, she found herself staring at the ceiling of the hotel room. It took her seconds to realize there was no beach, no sand.

"You all right?" Mauricio mumbled, lying next to her. "You were shaking."

A glance at the clock next to the bed informed her that it was morning. "Yeah. Just a weird dream."

He turned over and, not a minute later, was snoring again.

With a long yawn, she got up, grabbed the laptop off the desk, and went to the bathroom. Sitting on the floor and leaning against the bathtub, she stared at the blank document on the computer screen.

As she closed her eyes, she began typing. Images of the dank, empty cell flashed in her mind only to be replaced by images of herself chained to a hospital bed while Doctor Thomas and Agent Grobeck hovered over her. She pressed her eyes shut, not wanting to erase the images. She needed these images.

Submerging herself in this quicksand of painful memories, she cried as she typed at rapid speed. She was afraid she'd lose the courage to write the story if she didn't get all the words out at this moment.

About one thousand words and several cramped fingers later, she closed the laptop and cleaned up, trying her best to suppress the terrible memories she'd dredged up. After putting on a sweater and jeans, she stared in the mirror at her face. *I need the other face.* She let this thought replay until the rosy cheeks replaced brown ones and thin lips replaced fuller ones.

She pushed the red hair behind her ears and headed downstairs for breakfast.

The cafe was already filling up with hotel guests and people in suits on their way to work in the office buildings nearby. One bored-looking bartender was staring at a television above the bar. Eve passed the large booths and sturdy wooden tables covered in white cloths. The deep red fabric of the booth seats gave the place a 1920s vibe. It reminded her of her favorite buildings in Chicago.

As she took a seat at the bar, the bartender tore his gaze from the television for a moment and turned to her. He flashed her a fleeting smile. "I'll go get you a menu. Just a mo—"

"No worries. I'll take French toast, scrambled eggs, and coffee," she said.

He nodded and hurried to the espresso machine at the other end of the bar. In a moment, he returned with coffee and milk. "Sugars are there," he pointed and left to greet the second customer who had sat at the other end of the bar.

Eve sipped coffee and looked out the window. She'd give anything to hear Zoey's voice. On mornings when they were not together, Zoey always sent her a voice text that usually consisted of a simple "Morning, lovely" or "Morning, Eve, you were the first thing on my mind. Love you." She smiled at the thought of how much it would comfort her to see one of those messages again. *I can't keep this up—I have to call her.*

"Is anyone sitting here?"

She looked at the tall, dark-haired man standing next to her and smiling. Like so many other patrons in the cafe, he looked like he was on his way to work—somewhere particularly snazzy, she decided, given that he was wearing a three-piece suit. She admired the pink-striped tie. "No. Help yourself."

He sat next to her.

Meanwhile, Eve retreated to her thoughts of Zoey until the bartender arrived with her food. As she commenced eating, she felt the man glance at her.

"I'm sorry, Miss?" he said.

This time she noticed his thick English accent. *I am not in the mood for small talk, not even with an attractive British man.* She inhaled and glanced at him.

"If you don't mind, I'd like to buy you another coffee."

"I think it's free refills," she replied, not looking at him.

"Perhaps a mimosa?"

Here we go. She took a deep breath. "Sure."

As he flagged the server, Eve drained the cup of coffee and did her best to put on her friendliest face.

He extended his hand. "I'm Orson."

She wasn't surprised by his firm grip. This was a man who took himself very seriously; she'd concluded that the moment he approached her. "Nice to meet you, Orson. I'm Res."

"Res. That's a beautiful name."

She smiled.

Not waiting for her to respond, Orson proceeded to explain that he was in town "on business" from London. She could sense that a nagging loneliness plagued him. There was a certain sadness in his eyes. Even if she wasn't in the mood for conversations with strangers, she had to admit that there was something magnetic about him. She listened to him talk about the science and research firm he'd started with his brother and how he was hoping to expand its reach.

When he got up to leave later, she accepted his phone number on a napkin, knowing that she'd never contact him again. But she supposed it was nice to have a normal conversation with a normal person, for a change.

She pulled the prepaid phone from her jacket pocket and dialed Zoey's number from memory. As the phone rang, she laid twenty dollars on the bar and made her way to the hotel lobby.

"Hello?"

Eve was quiet, her eyes wide. *What do I say? Shit, why didn't I think this through?*

"Hello?"

"Hi-hi. Zoey, it's me."

"Eve?"

Struggling not to cry or draw attention to herself, she swallowed. "Yeah. I—"

"Gabe, oh my God, come here! It's Eve. I'm putting you on speaker," she hollered. A pause and some loud shuffling followed.

"Eve?" said Gabriel. "Where are you?"

"Where have you been? I thought you were dead. Everything was still normal in your apartment, all your clothes still there. But you were gone. I tried calling you and even visiting your dad and calling that friend of yours, AJ, but I didn't have her number," Zoey exclaimed, sobbing and sniffling.

"Look, I don't have much time."

"What do you mean?" asked Zoey. "What's going on? And why do you sound...weird?"

"Zoey, just let me finish. I don't have much time. I don't know if this call is being traced."

"Traced?"

"I'm okay. I mean, well, not really. I'm just...things are very difficult right now. But I'm safe here in Philly."

"Philly? You're in Philadelphia?" asked Zoey.

"Yeah. It's a long story that—"

"We're in Philly."

"What? Why?" Eve's mind was racing.

"Mom died."

"Oh, shit. I'm sorry, Zoey."

"Where are you staying? We're heading back to Chicago

on an early morning flight tomorrow, but we have to see you."

Eve sighed. "I can't say. Just meet me at the City Hall, in the Big Circle, at six."

"Eve?"

"Six," she repeated and ended the call before Zoey could respond.

Her heart nearly dropped out of her chest, and she leaned against the sofa. Fear, worry, relief, excitement. An array of feelings crashed over her in one massive wave. She thought about her normal conversation with the normal man named Orson, about the story draft she'd written just over an hour ago, and about whether Mauricio would be able to find AJ today. But none of those things mattered right now.

She was going to see Zoey and Gabriel again.

After spending the rest of the morning and part of the afternoon at a coffeehouse two blocks from the hotel, Eve returned to the room. Thoughts of Zoey and Gabriel swam around her mind as she walked along the quiet hallway. How much she longed to feel their arms around her, how much she needed to tell them, how much she couldn't tell them. She'd have to figure out how to tell them enough to explain her disappearance but to not endanger them. *Tell them only what they need to know.*

When she opened the door to the room, she froze.

AJ was pacing and mumbling to herself, while Mauricio was sitting on the bed. At once, he turned to Eve and smiled.

AJ surveyed Eve and glanced at Mauricio in confusion. "Who's she?"

Eve stepped in and shut the door, her eyes glued to AJ.

"Stop pacing, Miss Taylor," he said.

She looked at Eve. "Are you another fader?"

"AJ...it's me," replied Eve, approaching her.

She backed away, her mouth hanging open and her gaze shifting from Eve to Mauricio.

He offered AJ a reassuring nod. "It's her."

Eve met AJ's huge brown eyes that conveyed surprise. "It's a new ability I have. To look like other people."

She moved away from them and reached for her coat hanging on the desk chair. "I don't know what kind of games you're playing, man, but this ain't my kink. I'm out of here."

I need my face. Eve closed her eyes for a moment and opened them.

That's when AJ screamed and dropped the coat. Covering her mouth, she staggered backward.

"A lot has happened, as you can see," said Eve, taking a couple of steps toward AJ. "I was so worried about you, about whether you were safe. I uh—"

AJ thrust her arms around Eve and squeezed the air out of her. "Eve," she cried. "I thought you were dead."

"I'm sorry I didn't call. I couldn't risk it. And I sort of forgot your number."

AJ stared at Eve with watery eyes. "I didn't think I'd see you again." She wiped her face with the sleeve of her shirt and sniffled.

Eve noticed her bandaged arm. "They chipped you, too?"

"Yeah, but I took it out. We flushed it down the toilet to throw them off my trail."

Mauricio cleared his throat and stood. "Right after we left Miss Taylor's hotel, we went to a pharmacy and took bandages and first aid stuff."

"Took? I guess that means you're getting used to stealing shit now?" Eve smirked at him.

"You're a bad influence," he teased. "Anyway, she's agreed to join us and help find the other trainees. And she has a flash drive."

Eve caught the flash drive when he tossed it to her. She

turned it over in her hand.

"My assignment here was to get that and turn it over to SPI," said AJ. "I don't have a fucking clue what's on it."

Eve pocketed the flash drive. "Who cares right now? I have so much to tell you, AJ."

"You can start by telling us where you were all day," said Mauricio.

"I finished the story," Eve declared, beaming.

He looked impressed. "Already?"

Nodding, she pulled the laptop from her backpack and went to the desk.

"Story?" said AJ. "Also, you can shape shift now?"

"Yeah. I'll fill you in later. And we're meeting someone this evening," Eve replied, turning on the computer and typing in her password.

"Someone who can help us?" Mauricio asked.

She smiled. "I hope so."

Wearing red-framed glasses and a thick pea coat, Zoey stood under the archway of the City Hall. As the icy wind beat against her coat, she pulled the winter cap over her ears and folded her arms across her chest. She scanned the area. Aside from a redheaded woman in a black jacket walking toward her, she was alone in the courtyard.

Eve slowed as she approached Zoey who cast her a fleeting disinterested look. She stopped a couple of feet away, met her gaze, and watched an apprehensive expression settle on her face. Of course, this pale face and red hair made Eve a stranger to Zoey. She smiled as she thought about a quote that had never meant much to her until this moment. "Remember when we read *Another Country* together in college? 'Strangers' faces hold no secrets because the imagination does not invest them with any'..." She paused, trying and failing to remember the rest of the line. "Well, something about lover's faces being mysteries. I think Baldwin was on to something with that."

Zoey stepped back. "I'm sorry? Do I know you?"

"You always liked that quote."

"I'm sorry," said Zoey, walking away. "I don't have any money or drugs."

"Zoey, it's me. Eve."

She stopped at once, her back to Eve. When she turned around, she surveyed the strange woman and shook her head. "Look, I don't know who you—"

"Zoey Res Ellis. It's me."

AJ and Mauricio stood at Eve's side, invisible and silent. He gripped her hand and whispered so that only she could hear, "This is Res?"

"How do you know my name?"

"The same way I know raspberry-flavored lip gloss was your favorite in college. I always liked the taste of it when we kissed."

Zoey covered her mouth and clutched her scarf with her free hand. Her head tilted to the side, and she looked Eve over. When her hands dropped to her sides again, she stumbled over her words. "How—what—I don't understand."

"I'll explain everything. But I can't risk being seen out here," said Eve. "Where's Gabe?"

"Waiting for us at the house. I came alone."

At the house?

"The car's right this way." Zoey pointed beyond the archway where a red Volkswagen Jetta was parked with the emergency lights on. "Let's uh...we should go before I get booted." She kept her distance from Eve, staring at her with a look of confusion, distrust, and fear.

Eve's heart sank. It was the same look she'd seen in the faces of those kids on the playground in elementary school.

She'd spent years hiding, hoping she never would give anyone a reason to look at her that way again.

"Eve?" said Zoey. "We should go."

"AJ and another friend are with me. Is that okay?"

"With you? Where?" Zoey asked, looking left and right.

"They're standing next to me. Invisible."

"Right. Okay," she said, still regarding Eve with a wary expression. "Yes, it's fine. Let's hurry."

Eve grasped AJ's hand and, with Mauricio flanking her on the other side, they followed Zoey to the car.

"Eve," he whispered, "why didn't you tell me we were meeting up with your girlfriend?"

"She's not my girlfriend," Eve shot back in a shrill whisper that drew a sideways glance from Zoey. "I mean, sort of. It's complicated."

Once they seated themselves inside the car and buckled up, Zoey peeled into the rush hour traffic. She almost clipped a moving van on her right side as she switched lanes and made a hasty turn.

They sat in silence for a while as she weaved through traffic along the narrow streets, jamming on her brakes here and there or otherwise honking at slow drivers. Realizing she'd forgotten about Zoey's erratic driving style, Eve held onto the door and tried not to look terrified.

"I'm sorry," Zoey began. "I can't process...with you looking like this."

"I should've warned you."

She erupted in nervous laughter. "What could you have said? 'Hey, I have a slight case of Caucasian, don't be alarmed'?"

"I know this is a lot."

"Understatement of the fucking century. I don't even...how is any of this possible? There are invisible people in my backseat. And you went from looking like Erykah fucking Badu to Amy fucking Adams. None of this makes sense," she yelled, speeding up to pass a slow-moving SUV.

It was Eve's turn to laugh now. She bent over, holding her stomach as the laughter convulsed her body. She laughed so hard she coughed and choked a bit. "I've missed you. I've missed you so much. I think about you every day."

Zoey swerved to change lanes again and turned down a neighborhood street, away from heavy traffic. "Don't."

"What?"

"Don't say that. Not looking like this. It's too—it's weird, Eve."

No longer laughing, Eve fell silent and looked out the window. This was going to be more difficult than she'd anticipated.

"I'm sorry. I missed you, too, Eve." Zoey paused and glanced at her. "Are you...stuck...like this? Looking like this? Or is it some kind of temporary disguise?"

"It's temporary." Eve continued staring out the window as Zoey cruised along a quiet neighborhood street. Bare tree branches canopied the street, and all the houses sat on expansive lawns.

Zoey pulled into a driveway of a modest two-story home with a wraparound porch, decorated with two comfortable looking rocking chairs. It reminded Eve of a more decadent version of her family home in Indiana.

"This place is beautiful, Zoey."

She frowned, turning off the car and unlocking the doors. "It wasn't so beautiful to grow up in."

As they got out the car and headed to the porch, she recognized the house from photos Zoey had shown her in college. "Why are we stopping at your—"

Before she could finish, the front door swung open, and out came Gabriel wearing faded jeans and a leather jacket. He stopped at the steps and waved at them but paused when he saw Eve. A familiar look of confusion settled on his face, and Eve was amused by his attempt to try to play it off with an awkward smile.

"I thought you were picking up Eve," he said, kissing Zoey on the cheek.

"Yeah. I did," Zoey said.

"Wait...huh?" His gaze swept from her to Eve.

Zoey stepped nearer to him. "Let's get inside."

Seated on the bar stool in the kitchen, Gabriel downed a glass of water as though he'd run a marathon. Eve stood next to Mauricio and AJ, both of them now visible. She exchanged glances with Zoey who was standing beside Gabriel and scrutinizing the three of them. Gabriel looked at them and shook his head before taking another gulp of water.

"Babe, I think something extra was in those gummies we got from Landrien," he remarked, massaging his temples.

Eve closed her eyes for a moment, fixated on her normal appearance, and opened her eyes when she heard gasps from Zoey and Gabriel. She looked at her hand and was relieved to see it had returned to its soft brown.

"I need to sit," said Gabriel, staring transfixed at Eve.

"You are sitting," Eve replied.

Zoey's eyes were wide with disbelief as she cautiously approached Eve. "How...?"

"I don't know how. It's just something I can do," Eve replied, closing the space between her and Zoey. In a flash, they were enveloped in one another's arms and sobbing uncontrollably, smothering one another with kisses.

Gabriel hadn't moved and merely watched in silent amazement.

Eve met his gaze and extended her hand for him to join them. Within moments, Gabriel's kisses replaced Zoey's, and tears dampened his face. As she held them, she realized she'd forgotten the safety and peace of being in their arms. This was home.

"Um..." said AJ, clearing her throat. "Can I ask why the hell you two are in Philly?"

They wiped their faces and turned to AJ.

"We're wrapping up my mom's estate," said Zoey, drying her face and sniffling.

"When did she pass?"

"The day after Christmas."

"Oh, Zoey. I really am sorry," said Eve.

Zoey shrugged with a nonchalance that raised eyebrows. "I wish she'd just gotten the dying over with years ago. Would've saved me a lot of time and money."

"Come on. That's pretty harsh," Gabriel said, casting her a patient look.

"It is what it is."

Eve regarded Zoey with pity and empathy. She reckoned she'd feel the same way once her own father finally died, and she hoped it would be sooner rather than later. "Well, anyway," said Eve, remembering her manners. "This is Mauricio, a...colleague of mine."

Mauricio shook their hands and introduced himself. Gabriel used this as an opportunity to lead them from the kitchen and into the den.

As they arrived at the den, Mauricio nudged Eve and whispered, "Complicated, huh?"

She smiled. "The official term is 'polyamory'. Technically," she said. Her next words caught in her throat, however, when she saw a woman with short-cropped dark hair sitting near the sofa. She turned to Zoey and Gabriel. "Zoey, I didn't think I needed to tell you not to involve anyone else. I don't know what SPI is willing to do to keep this under wraps. I don't want anyone getting hurt."

"I know. I should've mentioned she would be here. I

asked her to come and listen because I thought she might be able to help."

"Help how?"

The woman came forward and locked eyes with Eve. "I'm a civil rights attorney," she said.

Eve frowned at Zoey. "You invited an attorney?"

"I had a strong feeling you might want one, and Landrien Moriset is one of the best. Believe me."

Eve ran her hand over her head and looked from Zoey to Landrien. "Wait. Did you say *Landrien?* As in the same Landrien who, when we were dating senior year, you decided to—"

"Yeah," Zoey mumbled, turning red and glancing at Gabriel. "That Landrien."

Eve chuckled, feeling a rush of jealousy. "Any of your other exes here I should know about?"

"Look," said Zoey, rolling her eyes. "I'm worried about your safety, Eve. They literally kidnapped you. I mean, lucky I stopped by the next day or Mr. Pebbles—"

Oh my God, how did I forget to ask about Mr. Pebbles? "What happened to him? Is he okay?" asked Eve, leaning forward.

"He's fine, Eve. We have him. Well, he's with our neighbors while we're here. But he would've been in your apartment for days without food and water if I hadn't dropped by the next day to check with you before the party. And I only dropped by because you weren't returning my calls and texts, which is totally unlike you."

Eve sat on the sofa, while AJ and Mauricio sat opposite her in two lounge chairs. "Thank you for taking care of Mr. Pebbles."

"He's a good kitty. Although he's pissed on all of our throw pillows so far," said Gabriel, smiling. He sat next to Eve, and Zoey sat on the other side of her.

That sounds like Mr. Pebbles.

"If I may interrupt again?"

Everyone turned to Landrien Moriset, who was still standing.

"My understanding is that you have some extraordinary abilities. Is that right?" asked Landrien.

"Yeah..."

"You're not the first person I've met with abilities. I've seen some interesting things in my time, so I'm inclined to believe almost anything is possible. That said, I would simply like to offer my observations about your legal options here. If I may?"

Eve locked eyes with the woman, not sure why she felt an impulse to trust her. "Sure. Go on."

"If you don't mind telling me what's happened to you, I'd be happy to help you."

"Help me sue them?" asked Eve, amused. "What good is suing when these people literally have the power to do whatever they want to us?"

"First of all, I don't know who 'these people' are—Zoey didn't give me all the details. But if these people violated your civil liberties—"

"My civil liberties? That's cute. I guess you could call torture by a rogue federal agency a 'violation of my civil liberties'."

"Torture?" Zoey looked at Eve with wide, shocked eyes. "SPI tortured you?"

"Based on what you've said, Eve, what happened to you is likely illegal under current law, and the agency needs to be held accountable for its actions. As I said, I'd be happy to help you."

"And what's your fee?" asked Mauricio.

"Fee?" Landrien smiled. "No fee, other than the attorney's fees I'd receive from opposing counsel if I win, assuming this even turns into a case. This would be pro bono for you, as a favor to Zoey."

Eve scoffed. "So, because Zoey is a friend of yours, you're willing to take a case completely free of charge?"

"Yes, she is, Eve," Zoey replied. "Just like her husband is helping me wrap up my mom's estate, free of charge. That's what friends do."

Eve shifted in her seat. "Friends, right."

"And from what I understand," said Landrien, "you engaged in minor criminal conduct at some point. Is that right?"

Eve gave a slight nod and averted her gaze. "Yeah, I mean I don't know if bank robbery is considered 'minor'."

"So you actually did it?" exclaimed Gabriel. "We read about it in the *Tribune* and didn't believe for a minute that it was true."

"I can explain..." Again, Eve shifted in her seat and looked at her hands.

"No need to explain right now. But you're right, bank robbery's not minor," Landrien said and paused. "Can they prove you did it?"

Eve looked at the attorney, not sure she understood the question. "Excuse me?"

"Is there any evidence they have or could obtain connecting you to the alleged robbery?"

"Um," Eve began, combing her brain. "No."

"How sure are you?" she pressed.

"Ninety-nine percent sure," said Eve.

"Then I know a criminal defense lawyer who could help you with that if and when it becomes an issue. Because," explained Landrien, looking at the whole group now, "if you do sue, every nasty, illegal, or nearly illegal thing you've ever done will be used against you. Make no mistake: nothing about this lawsuit would be easy. It might even put your life and freedom at greater risk. So you need to decide if the greater good is worth the potential cost to yourself or the loss of your own freedom."

Silence swept over them, and they all exchanged uncertain glances with one another.

Landrien handed each of them a small business card that said Moriset & Granger, LLP. "You can reach me anytime at that cell number. It's up to you the course you decide to take. I'll hold no hard feelings if you decide not to call me."

Eve offered a halfhearted smile. "Thank you, Landrien. I'll hang onto your information."

Slinging her purse over her shoulder, Landrien gave the three of them a nod before turning to Zoey and Gabriel. "Zoey, Jordan will call you tomorrow, since he has a few more questions regarding your mom's will."

"Sure," Zoey said. "I'll be glad when it's all over."

Gabriel rose. "Let me walk you to the door."

Once Landrien and Gabriel departed, Eve turned to Zoey. "Look, my bad for not warning you about Lan—"

"Yeah, I'm sorry for getting jealous."

Zoey grinned and touched her nose against Eve's nose. "I kind of like when you're jealous."

"You always did like a little drama." Eve planted a kiss on Zoey's lips. "Speaking of, I need you to do me a big favor."

"Sure. What?"

"I wrote an account of what happened to me," said Eve, taking a deep breath. "I need you to use your old journalist contacts to get it published. Can you do that?"

She held Eve's hands between hers. "You bet your ass I can."

10

When Agent Olivia Yu parked, she shut off the engine and stared at her hands on the steering wheel. She closed her eyes and did the breathing exercises that her therapist had recommended for stressful moments. "All right, Liv. You'll be fine."

After brushing her hair behind her ears and checking herself in the mirror, she stepped out of the car. "You're going to be fine," she muttered. "You've dealt with this douchebag for years. This is just another day."

Olivia Yu wasn't the type of woman to cower in the face of conflict. Part of her welcomed conflict. A little conflict kept things from becoming too boring. Yet Agent David Grobeck represented more than a pleasant bit of conflict to spice things up. He was something else, she'd concluded.

In the time she'd been working directly under him, she'd realized that there was something wrong with the man, something missing. The terrors she'd watched him inflict upon other people haunted her, and so she spent most of her time blocking out and trying to forget what she'd witnessed on the job with him.

Of course, she admitted, some things, no matter how terrible, had to be done for the sake of national security and the safety of everyone. If one person had to be tortured to protect a million, then so be it. Torture, she told herself, was a necessary evil sometimes and should be reserved for extraordinary circumstances.

David Grobeck, it seemed, had other ideas.

"Agent Yu," he greeted her as she walked into his office. "Shut the door behind you." On his desk, there were four folders neatly stacked one on top of the other, a cup holding pens, a stapler, and a bottle of hand sanitizer. Staring at his computer monitor, he spared only a glance at her.

She watched him rub sanitizer on his palms. Leaning back in his chair, he crossed his arms over his chest. "I've been informed that Eve Cooper is in the Philadelphia area at this time. Is that right?"

"Yes, sir," she replied, sitting in the chair in front of the desk. "That's right."

"But we don't know precisely where. Correct?"

"Correct, sir."

"Once she escaped, it was your idea that we hold off on aggressively pursuing her. Correct?"

"Yes, sir."

"Because you assumed she would keep you in the loop and perhaps, inadvertently, become a more useful asset to us. Is that right?"

She held his gaze. "Yes. We want to help other trainees learn how to manage their ability, but it's been a struggle. Why? Because we're not one of them. But she is, and she has a gift for teaching. That's why I recruited her. It's why we promoted her to instructor immediately."

"She's rejected that path, Agent."

"Yes, sir. But I believe that if she thinks she's doing it— teaching the trainees—to resist us, she's more likely to embrace it as a...calling. Imagine a team of fully trained individuals with their abilities working for us."

"Yes, but there's a question I should've asked before I ever accepted this little proposal of yours—your proposal to let them all fall into her clutches. What's to say they'd be willing to return to SPI? What makes you think they'd come back to work for us?"

She smiled. "Most of them are young and not from money, sir. To a poor person, nothing is more tempting than money and job security. If that weren't the case, we'd have no military."

"Touché," he said, nodding.

She waited for him to go on, but he merely stared at her with an inscrutable expression. "As I was saying, we need her. You've seen it yourself, she's a good teacher, and her cloaking ability is quite evolved. Furthermore, the trainees trust her because she's one of them. If we give her time to—"

"They're calling it 'fading' now."

"Sir?"

"They're referring to the ability not as 'cloaking' but as 'fading'."

"Oh. Right." Although somewhat confused, she didn't bother asking him about the source of this information. "As I was saying, if we give her time to train them and then we can bring her back in—"

"I don't disagree that we need her. And your proposal was...novel. But I'm shutting it down, effective now."

"Sir?"

"Your current assignment is to bring her in. So the question, Agent, is do you feel you have control of the assignment?" He stared at her with icy eyes.

She lifted her head higher and replied, "Yes. Yes, sir, I do."

"Interesting." He placed his elbows on the desk. "You see, I know you're not being honest with me. You're trying to save face and save your professional reputation. Because your reputation is on thin ice right now. Very thin."

Agent Yu responded with an unblinking stare.

"You've lost control of your assignment, Agent. You don't know her exact whereabouts, and you have no workable plan for how to apprehend her. Do you?"

"Sir—" she began but stopped when he held up his hand.

"Would you care to explain to me how this operative has eluded you for weeks now?"

"I am sure that if given a little more time, I can—"

"This is not the first time you've lost control of an assignment."

"Sir?"

"But Miss Cooper was a special assignment, Agent. I explained this to you before giving you the assignment. And you insisted you were capable of handling her, that you would not fail as you did before with Special Operative Forest Sherman. You remember Sherman?"

Her hands balled into fists on her lap, but she remained quiet and held his gaze. "What happened to Sherman was not my fault. You know that."

"You're aware that I didn't have to take another chance on you, that I could have assigned Miss Cooper to a more capable agent but that I believed in your skill and vision. Clearly, I overestimated you. So, I have a question. If you were me, what would you do in this situation?"

Agent Yu's shoulders drooped, but she held her head high. "I'm sorry, sir. She removed the chip and, whatever she's doing, she's making sure not to leave a trail. I have had no call from her since a couple of days after her escape."

"You haven't answered my question, Agent. What would you do if you were in this situation?"

She cleared her throat. "I don't know, sir."

"Well, let me help you out. For example, I could assume that you assisted Miss Cooper in her escape and that you are continuing to assist her in some naive attempt to subvert me. How else could she evade our notice so well for this long? How else could she have known about the tracking chip?"

"Sir?" She blinked. "As I've informed you, someone else helped her escape. I believe the person is likely still with her. I'm working on identifying the person. But I'm not assisting her."

"Aiding and abetting a terrorist is an extremely serious crime," Agent Grobeck went on and stopped to allow this sentence to simmer. "But if you're not helping her, then I can safely assume you're grossly incompetent and fire you right now. There goes your pension and your career. No amount of CPR would ever resuscitate your reputation. You'd never get another job in the federal government. I'd make sure of it." He sighed as though this conversation was draining him of energy.

"Sir, I have not assisted her, nor am I incompetent. I have more years—" She hesitated, reconsidering her words. "My years of recruiting experience and successful assignments in this department speak for itself. I assure you that I can and will complete this assignment if you give me more time. If you can give me more time, a couple more weeks perhaps, I promise you I can deliver her to you. This doesn't have to get any worse than it already is."

"Well, considering what hit the news today, you sure as hell better hope it doesn't get worse." He turned his computer screen to face her.

Agent Yu pulled her chair closer to read the article on the screen. A large headline read— "A secret black site in Chicago?" She scanned past the headline and stopped after the fourth paragraph. Her heart sank when she saw her name and Grobeck's name. She sat up straight and looked at him.

"Congratulations, we're both trending. Thanks to your incompetence."

"I—"

"If you're helping her, I can't imagine why you'd let her smear your name. Although, I can only assume from your expression that you had no idea she intended to do so, meaning you're more incompetent than I realized."

Her body stiffened. She stood, narrowed her gaze on him, and his eyes widened in surprise.

"Resume your seat, Agent Yu."

"I can't prove to you my innocence or my competence, David." It had slipped out. His name. She couldn't recall ever referring to him by his first name, and she took pleasure in the look of shock on his cruel face. "So I see no reason to sit here and let you continue to demean me."

"Excuse me?"

"I have far more years of experience at SPI than you have, and I'm better at this job than you are. But they made you, a good old boy with connections, my superior."

"Agent, you are out of line."

She ignored his interruption. "For years, I accepted that. Not anymore. You can fire me right now if you'd like, but know this: you'll never find her without me, and she'll undo everything SPI has worked to accomplish. I'm willing to own my mistake in this and to try to rectify the damage. You can do that as well—admit your mistake and try to fix this shit show. But if you choose not to, believe me when I say I'm not going to go down with you. When the shit really hits the fan, it'll be on you."

"Until now, word has never gotten out about these individuals. I've worked with Charlie Ford and Senator Abbott to make sure of that. What mistake did I make this time, agent, besides putting you on this assignment?"

"You overestimated yourself. And just like I did, you underestimated her."

His eyes flashed with a level of fury she hadn't seen him

exhibit before. There was something feral about his expression, but just behind it, there was the shadow of a smile.

For a moment, she pondered that smile lurking beneath the mask of rage. That smile frightened her more than anything he'd said in the last ten minutes. Was he hiding something, something he'd use against her eventually?

"I have an idea about how to find her," said Agent Yu. "You can either let me do my job now, or you can fire me. It's up to you. What's it going to be?"

A knock at the door interrupted the moment, but neither of them moved.

"Yes?" he said.

A timid-looking assistant ducked her head in. "Mr. Grobeck, the meeting on the Cooper matter is starting in conference room one in ten minutes. Charlie Ford of FordTech International is waiting there, and Senator Orval Abbott is on his way. He may be a little late."

"Thanks, Jen. I'll be out soon."

The assistant nodded and shut the door.

Agent Grobeck sat back in his chair. "Find her. And don't come back to me until you have news."

"Thank you." She didn't smile or show any other signs of relief. Instead, she turned to leave. But before she exited, she faced him. "One more thing. That is the first and the last time you'll refer to me as incompetent."

He glared at her, and now it was her turn to smile.

After she exited his office, she hurried through the cubicles of young interns, all of them staring at her. When she reached the empty hallway, she leaned against the wall and exhaled.

Olivia Yu sat at the kitchen table and peered out the window at the rain pouring on the patio. As a child, she'd liked to walk outside in the rain during thunderstorms. None of the adults at the group home took much notice whenever she drifted away from the house. On some occasions, she walked around and stayed gone for hours, enough to give her some hope that one day she'd leave for good.

Listening to the thunder pound against the roof, she had an urge to go for a walk. Yet now there was nothing to run away from, nothing that the outside could bring her that she didn't have already in her home—safety, freedom, comfort. So she stayed put, forced her thoughts on Eve Cooper, and reread an email she'd received from an operative with information regarding her whereabouts. A photograph was attached to the email. She'd spent at least thirty minutes studying it.

"He's one of us," the operative had said about the dark-haired man in the photo. "I've seen what he can do."

"What he can do?" she'd asked, curious about the operative's choice of words. The operative was silent. "You understand that the agency's top priority is to prevent dangerous and deadly weapons from falling into the hands of terrorist groups, groups that seek to destroy this country and our way of life? SPI is trying to protect the American people. If you have information that the agency should know, I implore you to share it."

"I understand."

Something about the operative's reticence had left Agent Yu wondering if there was more that she and the agency didn't know about these operatives. Were they capable of things other than invisibility?

She'd seen evidence to suggest so years ago, but that was just...no, Sherman was a special case. She never should have let Agent Grobeck and Doctor Thomas near him. He'd be alive if she'd known earlier, if she hadn't doubted her eyes, if she'd shielded him from those maniacs. Someone that gifted in the hands of Agent Grobeck and Doctor Thomas...she should have known what would happen. She should have known better.

It occurred to her that Agent Grobeck's mention of Sherman's name during the meeting was a threat. He'd pin the whole Forest Sherman debacle on her if she failed to complete this assignment and apprehend Cooper—that much was clear to her now. But if she completed this assignment, what about the next assignment? Would he wield Forest Sherman as a weapon against her again if she hit a rough patch in the next assignment? She knew the answer. As these thoughts raced through her mind, a cold reality set in.

She needed to destroy Agent Grobeck. But how?

"Who is he?" she'd asked the operative about the man in the photograph.

The operative had offered no response other than silence.

"Okay, that's fine. Can you at least tell me your name? I'd like to know who's helping me."

"I'm not helping you," said the operative.

Before Agent Yu could respond, the operative hung up.

Staring at the photograph now, she tried to recall the faces of all the trainee operatives. The man in the photo resembled none of them. She got up, poured herself a glass of water, and studied the photograph on her phone. "Maybe he's one the agency hasn't found yet. That's the only reasonable answer." She drained the glass of water and dialed her assistant.

"I need you to run a face for me. I'm sending the image to you now." She hit send and the photograph disappeared.

"Sure. What information do you need?" said Owen Creekmur.

"Any file we have on him. Any criminal records, financial statements, newspaper clippings, anything you can find on him. When can you get that information to me?"

"Right now," he answered. She could hear him pecking at a keyboard. "The man's name is Mauricio Candela. A few weeks ago, he checked into the ER downtown. According to the report, he had a deep knife wound in his right arm."

Agent Yu stood. "His right arm?"

"Yes. The report states that he was accompanied by a young woman, no name, and they both were treated for similar wounds. The young woman's wound was on the right forearm as well. Treatment was terminated due to the patients' unavailability."

"So they both took off, in other words?"

"It seems so. The record ends there."

Agent Yu sat once again. "A wound in his right arm," she mumbled to herself.

"Just a moment, I'm searching for more information. It looks like he has no bank records, no property records, and there's no criminal records that match his name. Wait...there's a Mauricio Candela whose passport was scanned at an airport in Calgary five years ago."

"Canada? He's a Canadian operative."

"Possibly, Agent. I'm still looking...but presumably these individuals are not unique to our country, and we were prepared for the likelihood that other governments would have similar individuals in their intelligence agencies."

"Yes," she replied. "I remember Agent Grobeck saying that we needed to be ready for that reality. But for the Canadians to send them into our country to spy on or steal information from us...they're our allies."

"Agent Yu?"

"It doesn't make sense. And if they didn't send him, how did he happen to meet Cooper? It's too coincidental."

"Agent Yu, it's an American passport."

She leaped to her feet. "He's one of ours?"

"It appears so. And, oh, this is unusual..."

"What is it? What's unusual?"

"I'm seeing footage here from our cameras. The image is fuzzy, but the system is giving me a face match, so it's definitely him..."

"Get to the point, Creekmur."

"It's a match with the unidentified man in the CCTV footage from Salazar's office. And from another match...it also appears that he's met with Agent Grobeck at least once."

Agent Yu closed her eyes and sighed. "That motherfucker."

"Agent, may I ask why you didn't have me run his face the day Miss Cooper fled? You knew she was being assisted by someone, a man—you said you heard a male voice in the car that day. We already had the CCTV footage from Salazar's office. Why didn't you have me run the man's face then?"

"Is it foolish that I wanted to wait? To see how far they would go first?"

"May I be frank, Agent Yu?"

"Of course."

"Yes, it was foolish."

Sighing, she went to her patio and stared out the window. The rain had stopped, and the wind was blowing with enough force to bend the trees. "Don't say anything about any of this to anyone. This conversation is between you and me, you understand?"

"I understand."

"And Creekmur, do me a favor and look up everything you can find on Zoey and Gabriel Ellis," she said, remembering the call her assistant had traced.

"Yes, ma'am. You got it."

Agent Yu stood at the gate, pulling her scarf tighter to protect her neck from the ice-cold wind. She opened the call box, dialed the number Creekmur had provided, and waited as the phone rang.

"Hi, how may I help you?" said a woman with a voice like silk.

"I'd like to speak with you about Eve Cooper."

There was silence.

"Miss?"

"I don't know an Eve Cooper. I'm sorry."

"I only want a couple of minutes to talk," said Agent Yu.

"Look, I don't know—"

"I think she's in trouble, Miss Ellis. I only need a couple of minutes of your time."

Silence again. Agent Yu waited, careful not to press too hard. For this to work, she had to apply just the right amount of pressure and that required restraint. "Miss?"

A moment later, there was a buzz, and the gate opened.

When Agent Yu entered the greystone apartment, she looked at the narrow stairs and watched as a tall woman and a man of similar height descended. They stopped on the last stair and regarded her with suspicion.

Agent Yu softened her expression and furrowed her brow in concern. "I'm so sorry to show up like this. I'm a former colleague of Eve's."

They remained quiet and watchful.

She took this as an opportunity to launch into the cover story she'd practiced, lacing her voice with urgency. "I...there've been whispers at SPI about something big. Something involving Eve, and I just...I didn't know who else to turn to...to warn her." She kept her voice low and looked around frantically.

Zoey took a step forward, but Gabriel placed his hand on her shoulder. She backed up. "Warn her about what?" asked Zoey.

"SPI is coming for her," said Agent Yu, pleased to see the fresh fear on the woman's face.

Gabriel folded his arms across his chest. "Coming for her how? When?"

Agent Yu looked around and shook her head. "I don't know. I'm not sure. But there's a man with her that they're—"

"That guy...Mauricio," Zoey muttered to Gabriel, "I knew I didn't trust him—"

Gabriel immediately shushed her.

This exchange piqued Agent Yu's interest. "I think it's him they want, not her. But I don't know. I'm just guessing." She fidgeted and looked at her phone. "I'm sorry. I have to go."

"Hey," said Zoey, coming forward as if to urge the agent to stay longer.

With her hand on the doorknob, Agent Yu looked over her shoulder at the couple. "If you have any way of getting in contact with her, please warn her. Tell her if she's smart, she'll get out of the country."

Not waiting for the couple to say anything else, she pulled her scarf tight and rushed out the door.

"Look, I don't have time for a meeting right now. I'm still in the process of trying to clean up the shit you made," said Agent Grobeck as Agent Yu stopped him in the hallway outside his office. "Which is why I have a call with a reporter from *The Chicago Sun-Times* in less than ten minutes." He opened the door, and she followed him inside.

"Sir, I have an update on—" she began, but he held up his hand dismissively.

"Agent Yu, now is not the time. Unless you've managed to somehow make this media blitz disappear, and I seriously doubt you'd be capable of that given you can't even keep up with one operative, nothing you have to say is important right now. We can meet later. I'm sure Jen can find some space on my calendar." He sat behind his desk, opened the laptop, and shooed her away. "Shut the door on your way out."

Smiling, she merely stared at him.

He groaned. "How many fucking times do I have to—"

"Sir. I've got her," said Agent Yu.

His eyes widened. "Where?"

She sat in the chair across from his desk and crossed her legs, still smiling at him. "If you want to save yourself and win this, I suggest you stop being a tool for five minutes and allow me to explain my plan that, by the way, involves how you should handle this reporter."

He shifted in the leather chair. "Fine. I'm listening."

"First of all, we need an extraction unit ready to deploy in Philadelphia as soon as possible."

"How soon?"

"This week."

"Oh, my God. I can't believe it," Eve murmured, sitting on the bed and staring at the computer screen. "Mauricio!"

"What? What's going on?" He emerged from the bathroom.

AJ, who was standing at the closet door and admiring her reflection in the mirror, turned to Eve.

"Zoey came through. She did it. First *The Chicago Sun-Times* and now *The Washington Post* is running stories based on my leak," she exclaimed, staring at the screen. "I didn't even think the *Sun-Times* would run the story, and now this."

"Doesn't it usually take longer for newspapers to run a story?" asked AJ. "It all seems really fast."

"I think they like the sensationalism of it all," said Mauricio. "This *is* an election year and an insane story like this looks terrible on the current administration."

"No, it looks like they're tying the abuse of the faders to a larger issue. The second paragraph here talks about black sites that have been discovered around the country where regular people—not faders—have been taken," she said, leaning close and reading the screen, "This reporter is claiming it shows a general pattern of the federal government engaging in constitutional violations against Americans. There's some stuff here about habeas corpus and so forth. This *Post* reporter just connected it to a wider issue she'd been reporting on about this administration for the past several months. Interesting. The article went up a half-hour ago, and it already has sixty-five comments. Not all of them are nice comments. Some folks think I might be paranoid or schizophrenic."

Mauricio sat beside her and skimmed the first paragraphs. He threw his arms around her and planted a kiss right on her lips. "This is incredible, Eve."

"Just think...other faders will read these articles or hear about them. Imagine how many of them might quit SPI once they hear about others quitting, once they learn about what SPI is really doing."

"Yeah," AJ said. "I don't know. Most of the trainees in our group were kind of desperate for a job, to be honest. I know I was. I don't know if this would be enough for them to quit."

"Maybe not all of them but some of them," Mauricio insisted, beaming at Eve. "And then there are the faders that SPI hasn't found yet...and the fact that most people don't know we exist. This story getting out there—"

"Changes everything," said Eve. She looked from AJ to Mauricio. "No matter what, we changed the world! This requires drinks. Should we go down to the hotel bar?"

"No," said AJ, shaking her head. "We can't risk it."

"Okay. Well, I can go grab drinks, and we can celebrate here...?" Eve offered.

"Let's be careful not to celebrate too soon," said AJ. "We don't know what SPI will do, or if this will even make them back off us."

Mauricio rubbed his head as he often did whenever he was

dissecting a problem. "AJ's right. We shouldn't get too happy yet."

"And we still haven't found the other trainees...faders. I know Sam is also somewhere here in Philly, but—"

"Why would he be here, too?" asked Eve.

"He was sent here before me, but then something happened and they had to bring him back in. So they sent me to finish his assignment. Before Mauricio showed up at my hotel, Agent Grobeck had called to tell me Sam would be joining me to finish the assignment," said AJ.

Eve looked confused. "I thought they weren't putting more than one operative on an assignment."

"Maybe Agent Grobeck made an exception so that Sam could finish the job," AJ replied, shrugging.

"Well, all right then. Let's celebrate here," said Mauricio. "There's a liquor store a couple of blocks west."

Eve closed the computer. She got up, gathered her coat, and slipped on her sneakers. "I'll get some wine."

As she opened the door, the phone rang on the nightstand. They all turned and stared at it as though they'd never seen a phone ring.

"Who would be calling the room phone?" asked AJ.

Without thinking, Eve shut the door and rushed to answer it.

A fearful look sailed across AJ's face. "No, don't answer it, Eve. What if it's SPI or somebody?"

"Nobody even knows we're here or who I am. It's probably just the front desk. The only person I gave this number to was Zoey," she said and picked up the phone. Before she could say "hello," a woman spoke in a panicked voice. Eve sunk onto the bed and pressed the phone against her ear. "Zoey?"

"Eve, I'm so glad I caught you. I was worried you might've checked out," she said, breathlessly.

"What's going on? Are you all right?"

"I'm fine. We're in Philly. Can you come to my mom's house now? This can't wait."

"Why? What can't wait?"

"I can't say over the phone," said Zoey.

"Eve, you're not safe," Gabriel added.

"What's happened—"

"Eve," Zoey shouted. "Stop asking so many goddamn questions. I don't want to meet you out in the open this time, so I need you to come to my mom's house. Write down this address now, and get your ass over here as soon as you can."

She reached for the pen and notepad, wrote down the address Zoey rattled off, and hung up. Her mind racing and her heart thudding against her chest, she looked at the worried faces of Mauricio and AJ. "Hand me that backpack," she said to AJ. "We have to go meet Zoey and Gabe."

"What?" asked AJ. "Is something wrong?"

Eve stood. "Yes, and I have a feeling we're not coming back to this room. So get all your shit, and let's go."

Gabriel opened the door and surveyed the empty neighborhood street. "Come in," he whispered to the three invisible people standing in front of him. He shut the door and locked it. When he turned around, Eve was looking at him, AJ and Mauricio standing next to her no longer invisible.

"Where's Zoey?" she asked.

He kissed her cheek and gestured past the kitchen. "She's in the den." They followed him, and he cast a dubious glance at Mauricio but said nothing.

As they arrived in the den, they found Zoey standing near the window and rubbing her temples.

Eve rushed to her and pulled her into a tight hug. "You scared me when you called. I've never heard you sound like that. What's going on?"

"We got a visit from a woman claiming to be your colleague at SPI," said Gabriel, standing next to Zoey. "Scared Zoey so much that she insisted we hop a flight back to Philly right away."

"What woman?" Terror gripped Eve, and she looked at AJ and Mauricio.

"Oh, God," AJ murmured.

Eve turned to Zoey and Gabriel. "Was this woman thin, average height, Asian?"

"Yeah," they said in unison.

"It was Agent Yu."

"Oh, God, Eve. If they're visiting Zoey and Gabe now, my mom—" AJ began.

"Hold on," Mauricio interjected, stepping forward. "What did the woman say?"

Zoey regarded him with caution. "Just that something's about to go down. And that...that she thinks they're particularly interested in you."

Everyone stared at Mauricio's bewildered face. "Me?" he asked.

Zoey nodded. "Yeah."

"But look," said Gabriel, "we might have a way to get you out of the country safely. I have a friend who can get you passports, and we can help out a little with money, between the two of us."

"Get us out of the country?" asked Eve.

Mauricio slumped onto the sofa. "We're not trying to get out of the country."

"Yeah, and what about that lawyer friend of yours? Landrien Moriset? If all else fails, we can call her up and file a lawsuit against SPI. If we have to, we'll call the goddamn ACLU," Eve said.

Zoey clasped her hands together. "We read an article in the *Sun-Times*, not your article but one that was quoting you.

Folks are already talking about it, Eve, about the 'faders', the people who can hide in plain sight. There are at least a dozen articles at this point. It's all anyone's talking about."

"To be fair, a lot of people think you're nuts and that the president would never authorize torture of citizens on US soil," Gabriel added. "But a lot of people believe you, too."

"Why wouldn't they believe me? It's not like this country doesn't have a history of—"

"Eve, you accused a secret federal agency of illegal torture on US soil no less, and raised the possibility of special super-powered people. As bogus as your story might sound to some folks, it's just plausible enough for other folks to believe. Which makes you a threat to some enormously powerful people." She grasped Eve's hand and looked into her eyes. "They'll come for you."

"And they'll kill you when they find you." Panic accented every syllable of Gabriel's words.

Eve shook her head. "No, they won't. They need us."

"Oh, don't be foolish," AJ burst out, stepping forward. "None of us are that important to these people. Don't be naive."

The teapot whistled, and Gabriel hurried to turn off the stove.

"Let's sit," said Zoey, leading Eve to the sofa.

He returned with a tray carrying five teacups and a teapot. He sat it on the coffee table and poured everyone a cup of green tea. "Eve, there's already a lot of fear out there. Imagine how that fear is going to set in over the next few days. We're talking about a hidden group of people, a new type of human. That's what your story has exposed, not just SPI."

"If you all stay," said Zoey, "SPI will find you, and God only knows what they'll do to you."

"They'll find us if we leave, too," Mauricio replied.

Eve slammed down the teacup, spilling some of it.

"Mauricio's right. What good will it do us to run if there are other agencies like this all over the world? I bet you good money there are more like us all over the world, being used the same way. Stopping SPI is the only chance we have to get our lives back. And I want my life back, even if it did suck sometimes. I had you and Gabe. I had us. I miss us," she said, holding in her tears. *Why does it have to be like this?* "Living in hotels, always wondering how they'll torture me if they find me, or if one day I'll just kill myself to get free from it all— that's not a way to live. I don't want to spend the rest of my life living like this. Hiding."

Mauricio frowned. "I say we call up Landrien Moriset and start a lawsuit. It's time to stop running."

"Fuck that. I'll take the passport and money," said AJ, standing with her eyes fixed on Gabriel.

Eve stared at her, not sure if she was feeling disappointment or empathy for her friend. "AJ..."

"I'm not like you, Eve. I'm not a fighter," she said, briefly looking at her hands. "Gabe?"

"Yeah?" he answered.

"What does your friend need from me to get started on a passport?" asked AJ.

A thud came from the living room. Glass shattered, followed by more thuds that sounded like booted footsteps. Mauricio and Eve sprang up and turned toward the living room. Zoey and Gabriel were on their feet and staring in horror as the noise grew louder.

The lights flickered out.

"What's...what's happening?" Eve whispered, looking at the door leading to the living room. She reached for Zoey's and Gabriel's hands but grasped only air. "Zoey? Gabe...where—?"

Three low cracking sounds came from the room. A moment later, screams from Zoey pierced the eerie quiet.

"Stop right there!" a man yelled.

"Zoey!" Eve screamed, searching the darkness for any sign of her or Gabriel. A moment later, a man brushed by her, and it kicked her into action.

She took off running through the pitch-black house, the sound of several pairs of booted feet against hardwood floors reverberating around the room. She ran as fast as her legs would allow, keeping her arms spread out in front of her to avoid running face-first into a wall. Panting and running with all her strength, she followed the vertical sliver of light ahead. *Please be the front door. Please be the front door.*

Just as she reached the light, her feet hit something solid, and she stumbled before losing balance. When her face hit the floor, her teeth chattered, and a metallic taste filled her mouth. An object burst into pieces near her, and she instinctively shielded her face.

Spitting out blood and wiping her eyes, she looked around, trying to see through the impenetrable blackness. *Get up, you idiot, and run!*

As she pulled herself up, a cold hand grabbed her wrist. Kicking like a wild woman in a futile attempt to free herself, she started to scream but another cold hand covered her mouth.

"Quiet," a man whispered. "And be still."

She continued to struggle but to no avail as the man's thick arms encircled her. "Let me go," she shouted into the palm of his hand. "Let go of me!"

Cold air slapped against her face, and when she blinked, she was staring at rowhouses lining an empty street. Before she could register what had happened, there was a sharp, familiar tug inside her stomach. Suddenly, she was standing in the middle of Center City. Staring at the iconic "LOVE" sign, she opened her mouth to scream, but a second sharp tug in her stomach silenced her. This time she found herself in the middle of a cluttered room in a dim apartment and gazing into the eyes of a man she'd never seen before.

THE SPECIAL PROJECT

11

The man released her and she spun around, backing up against the wall and staring wide-eyed at him. Terror surged through her as she looked around. How had she gotten here? Where was here? Where were her friends? "Zoey, Gabe, where are they?"

The lanky, dark-skinned man with locs stood at a safe distance and watched her. He wore an apologetic expression. "You mean the other people who were with you? I'm sorry, I don't know. I didn't have time to help them. I had to get us out of there."

She pulled out the pocketknife and pointed it at his chest. "Don't come any closer, or I swear to God I'll use it."

"Be cool. I'm not going to hurt you," he said, staring at the knife.

"I'm not going back to that cell. I'll die first." Her free hand dug inside the backpack dangling from her shoulder. She retrieved the GLOCK she hadn't touched since Iowa, dropped the knife, and held the gun in both shaky hands. She raised it until it was level with his face.

He threw his hands up in surrender. "Easy. Easy. My name is Niles Woodard."

"Stay back," she barked, squeezing the trigger.

"Um...the safety's still on."

Fuck. Where is Mauricio when I need him? She kept the gun pointed at the strange man and didn't move. "Where are they? Where did SPI take them?"

"Please put the gun away. I'm not going to hurt you. I'm a fader, too," he pleaded, his voice lowering.

She lowered the gun, and his shoulders drooped as he exhaled.

"I've followed you for a few days. You know the coffeehouse you went to on Tuesday? I saw you disappear when you left. You came out of the coffeehouse, turned down the alleyway next to it, and looked around to make sure nobody else was watching. I wondered if you were running from someone at first. Then, you just disappeared." He stopped and watched the realization hit her. "Yeah, you didn't know I was there because I was invisible, too. I sometimes take that alleyway as a shortcut on my way to work. And that was one of those times.

"To be honest, I didn't believe what I was seeing. I'd never met anybody else like me. But I was curious, so I followed you to your hotel and waited, but you never came down again that day. I came back the next morning and saw you in the hotel cafe getting breakfast by yourself. You looked kind of sad like before. I hung out there and waited to see if you'd do it again, disappear. But you didn't. I even returned a couple more times. I started to wonder if I'd imagined it because I wanted to feel like I wasn't the only one. The only one who could do...things. You know, I considered going up to you and introducing myself and asking you flat out if you had the ability, but then I thought that might be weird.

"Today, I'd promised myself if I didn't see you disappear that I'd drop it. I mean, I'm not some sort of creepy stalker. But when you left the hotel this evening, I noticed you mumbling to yourself, which was weird. Then, you did it. You disappeared again. I really hadn't imagined it! Needless to say, I was obsessed with the idea of meeting you, talking to you. So, yeah, I followed you to that uppity neighborhood." He paused. "And...oh, you can also change how you look, too? I saw you change in that house. It's incredible."

Eve dropped the gun, dizzily surveying the room. The walls seemed to tilt a bit and blur. Her stomach did somersaults that rose up to her chest and throat. In the next moment, she bent over, and her lunch spilled forth in a chunky, pink mess.

Niles ran his hand over the top of his head, standing back and observing her dry heave. "Oh, man. That was my favorite rug."

She pressed herself against the wall, and sunk to the floor. The walls tilted as she struggled to focus her eyes on the man whose voice sounded muffled. The room grew dimmer until there was no light and no sound.

Eve rolled over on the hard bed and opened her eyes. Her head throbbed, and a stench of vomit clung to her nose. "Where am I?"

Niles brushed his hair behind his ears. "You're in Germantown. My apartment was the only place I could think of when everything happened."

"You're not with SPI?"

He shook his head.

"You had nothing to do with the attack?" She sat up, rubbing her eyes.

"No. Like I said, I followed you and your friends. I was standing in the kitchen, listening to you all talk when the lights went out, and these men in military fatigues showed up pointing guns. They couldn't see me, obviously."

"Then?"

"Then, you—your skin—started changing colors from brown to white. Like you were trying to change back to the white girl again or something. Your hair kept changing. It was the most amazing thing—"

"What about the others? What about Mauricio?"

"They went one way, and you went the other. I grabbed you before anybody could shoot you. And I brought you here."

"How did you bring me here?"

"I learned how to hop a few months ago."

"Hop?"

"Through space, like teleporting," he clarified. "The first time I did it, it sort of happened by accident. I was thinking about visiting my mom in Virginia, and the next minute I was there in her living room. It was seriously weird."

"You can teleport?"

"Well, I prefer 'hop'. It just sounds less...silly. Can you do it, too?"

Her mouth hung open in disbelief. "Yeah, but I've never met anybody else who could. And I'm not good at it."

"The trick is you have to—"

"Before I fell, I heard shots or something," Eve muttered, her mind running over the events at the house. She recalled the sound of Zoey screaming and Mauricio hollering. "Did the others get away?"

"I don't know. It was dark. I think they were running to the back door the last I saw. All of it happened so fast. Maybe they faded eventually. Why didn't you fade?"

She shook her head, tears streaming as she stared at her hands. "I panicked."

"What did those people want with you and your friends?"

She wiped her eyes. "'Those people' are SPI agents. They track down faders, people like us."

Niles stood, staring at her. "They know about your

abilities?"

"About my ability to fade, singular. Yes, they do. And, more importantly, they know I'm the woman who exposed their sorry asses." The walls began moving once more, and she pressed her hands against the sides of her head.

"Exposed them? Wait a minute. You're the woman, the whistleblower who was tortured? Are you for real?"

She got to her feet, stretched, and wiped her face dry.

"Wow. I saw that article in the *Post* yesterday."

"Part of me thinks I never should've leaked information about SPI. Maybe all it did was make things worse." She dusted herself off and grabbed the backpack off the floor next to the gun and knife. After sliding both weapons inside the bag, she checked to make sure the safe box, AJ's flash drive, and the money were still there. Slinging the backpack over her shoulders, she proceeded to the door and looked at Niles. "Are there any hotels near here?"

"You're leaving?"

"Yes."

"Wait," he said, hurrying to her. "Stay here. There's room."

"Look, SPI knows nothing about your abilities. Best to keep it that way. You don't want this kind of trouble, believe me."

"But I want to help."

"Why?"

"Because at some point I'll have to fight them anyway. Better with somebody than alone, right?" He stood in front of her and blocked the door. "Come on. Every hero needs a sidekick."

"I'm not a hero, and this isn't a comic book movie. Now move out of the way."

"Lady—"

"The name is Eve. Not 'Lady'," she retorted.

"Eve, you're taking on an entire secret agency, and you're

not a hero? You're basically Bond with superpowers. You don't have to be humble with me."

She groaned. "I know this all sounds like fun to you, but it's not. There are real people after me, and they'll find me if I don't find them first. Right now, these people don't know about you or else you wouldn't be standing here. You know what that means?"

He shook his head.

"It means you can return to your regular life like none of this ever happened, like you have no special ability."

"What if I don't want—"

"Look, you have no idea what I'd give to go back to the anonymity of my old life. Stop trying to be a superhero, Niles, and live your boring ass life. Forget all this ever happened."

"And what about when they do come for me? Just because I hide my abilities and try not to draw any attention to myself doesn't mean they won't find me eventually. So, the way I see it, helping you means helping myself down the line."

"You have no idea what you're dealing with."

"I read the article about what happened to you and the others. I saw what happened tonight. I think I have an idea."

Images of Agent Grobeck pointing the Taser at her flashed before her eyes. "Listen to what I'm telling you. You don't want this life."

"I don't want this one either."

"Fine," she relented, shaking her head. "But don't say I didn't warn you."

As Eve plopped onto the new hotel bed in downtown Philadelphia, Niles stared at the small, black safe box she was holding.

"How many times have you tried it?"

"Fifteen? Twenty?" she said, sighing. She brought the box close to her eyes and searched for any inscriptions she'd missed. Nothing. "I don't know. I've lost count. I've tried every number combination I can think of. I don't get it...there can't be that many different number possibilities, can there?"

"SPI didn't give you the passcode?" He pulled up a chair in front of her. "Guess they didn't want you to see what was in it."

"Guess not."

"My cousin might have an idea how to unlock it." He scrolled through the contacts list on his phone.

She typed in another number combination using the keypad on the safe and waited for an indication that the number had worked. But nothing happened. Disappointed, she slipped the box inside the backpack and retrieved the flash drive AJ had stolen from her target, Andrew Wilder, the CEO of Generate, Inc. Perhaps it was connected to Salazar, Eve mused.

She inserted it in the computer and tensed.

To her surprise, several folders appeared. "Whoa," she exclaimed, and Niles looked at her. She clicked on one of the folders, only to be met with a box indicating that the folder was password-protected. Each folder she clicked on presented her with the same box. "Shit. We need to see what's in there."

"I can take a crack at it," said Niles. "I can crack relatively easy passwords."

"Hold on," she said, raising her hand. She typed furiously into the password box and waited. A box appeared on the screen with the words "Access Denied." She groaned and typed in another password. After two more tries, she was ready to scream.

"Eve," said Niles, "I'm sure it'll shut you out if you get the password wrong too many times."

"But we have to see what's in these folders."

Niles flashed her a sympathetic look and placed his hand

on her shoulder. "I know. But we'll find another way. I'll take a stab at it later."

With a sigh, Eve removed the flash drive, returned it to the bag, and shut down the computer.

She lay against a pillow. Her thoughts swam with more safe combinations and possible passwords as she stared at the ceiling. "You ever wonder what it'd be like to be the most powerful person in the world?"

"Like the president?" replied Niles, glancing sideways at her.

"No, like if you had the power to do something no other person could do? An ability that 99% of people would give their left tit to have?"

"Don't we have that?"

She shook her head. "No. Invisibility, teleporting, shapeshifting is all interesting. But I'm talking about real power. Something that would make you unstoppable."

"I guess I've never thought about it. What would that power be?"

"I don't know. But I think about it all the time. Maybe time travel," she said, lying back and staring at the cottage cheese ceiling. "That way I could go back in time and slap the disturbed person who came up with the notion of cottage cheese ceilings."

Niles laughed. "Hey, guess what I just read?" He turned his phone's screen to her.

"Something about cottage cheese ceilings?"

"No," he scoffed. "An article in *The Guardian*."

"Oh. Okay. Cool, I guess."

He rolled his eyes at her. "I thought it was about you at first. But this is about another one, a fader in London."

She sat up. "In England?"

"Yeah. You're mentioned, though."

Eve stared at the screen and read the headline. "This

means—"

"It means there are faders all over the world making themselves known now, coming out of hiding. We're not alone anymore."

"And we're not safe anywhere," she mumbled, flashing him a wary look.

"Is the glass ever half full with you?"

"Who was the fader in that article? Did they give their name?" She gestured for him to hand over the phone, her eyes glued to the screen.

He scrolled to the middle of the article. "His name is Orson. Orson Remington III. Maybe we should try to reach out to him?"

She didn't hear Niles' suggestion because at that moment an idea struck her like a boulder, and she popped up. "The fader we were looking for here...Samuel Kim? I know how to find him. We need to visit Agent Yu."

Agent Yu paced in front of the sooty, half-dressed man on his knees. He was looking at the wet floor. Clots of crusty, dark blood ornamented his hair.

"The guards have worked you over bad," she remarked, low enough so that only he could hear her. She glanced at Agent Grobeck. He was lingering near the door with his arms folded across his chest and watching her silently. As she turned her attention to the man on the floor, he was groveling at her feet and reaching out to grasp her ankles. "We don't have to keep doing this, you know."

Sobbing, the man rubbed his fists against his sides with so much force that it looked as though he was trying to rub off his skin. "I don't know anything more than I already told you. Please."

"Mr. Ellis, if you cooperate, you can be out of here in no time." Agent Yu stepped back and squatted to meet his eyes.

She coated her voice with as much sweetness as she could dig up. She leaned closer to him and whispered, "Just talk to me. Tell me the truth so I can help you."

"I don't know any more than I told you. I don't know where Eve is." Gabriel shivered and wiped away tears.

Agent Yu looked over her shoulder at Agent Grobeck and, after half a second, shook her head. She watched him pull out his cell phone, dial a number, and say, "Do it."

There came a shrill scream of terror from a room next door. Gabriel looked at the brick wall, searching for the source of the screaming. His eyes grew wider while the tears overflowed and dripped to the floor. When he turned to Agent Yu, he peered at her through eyes bloodshot clouded with tears. "Please. I don't know anything. I don't know anything."

"I can't stop it unless you talk."

The screams continued, louder with every passing moment.

He stared at Agent Yu. At last, his shoulders dropped, he lowered his gaze, and he cried. "I don't know. I don't know. I don't know. I don't know." He slurred the words and repeated them like a broken vinyl record, his shoulders bobbing in sync with his sobbing.

"Mr. Ellis?"

Gabriel mumbled the same three words again and again, rubbing his fists against his sides of his head.

After a disappointed sigh, Agent Yu rose up and leered at him. "Fine."

She followed Agent Grobeck out the room and, before shutting the door, looked at Gabriel. He was on the floor, balled up in the fetal position, and covering his ears with his fists to block out the sound of the woman's piercing screams from the next room.

"Did he give you anything?" Agent Grobeck asked.

She shook her head.

"That's disappointing. I thought he'd be more useful, given your description of his connection to Miss Cooper." He typed into the electronic tablet.

"That description came from my snitch who was obviously wrong." Holding her tongue, she deliberately relaxed and folded her arms across her chest.

He fixed his cold gaze on her. "Let this be a lesson, Agent: do not negotiate with terrorists." With a smirk, he proceeded down the hallway to the elevator.

Agent Yu rolled her eyes as she watched him walk away. Once he was gone, she darted toward the cell two doors down and typed a code into a small black box.

When the door opened, AJ Taylor was sitting on a small metal chair in the middle of the windowless room.

After a glance over her shoulder, Agent Yu entered, shut the door, and locked it.

"What do you want now?" asked AJ, her face covered with grime and soot, her feet and hands shackled to the chair. Unlike Gabriel, she wasn't beaten up or bruised.

"I want to make you a free woman and take down Agent Grobeck in the process," Agent Yu whispered, careful not to be overheard.

AJ laughed. "And I'm supposed to trust a cunt like you?"

"Yes, if you want to be free. Here's the deal. My snitch, the only person who can lead me to Eve, is God knows where, while I'm wasting time interrogating a couple of her friends. Now, ordinarily, this realization would have been enough to make me start drafting my resignation letter."

"Your snitch? I don't under—"

"But then an idea hit me." Kneeling, she unlocked AJ's hand and feet restraints.

"What are you—?"

"I'm proving to you that you can trust me," said Agent Yu

and stood. She reached into the pocket of her pants and brought out a loaded department-issued GLOCK. "Here. Take it. Shoot me right now if you like. I'm sure I've done more than enough to earn it. Or you can hear what I have to say first and then make your decision."

Without hesitation, AJ took the gun and pointed it at the agent's right temple. "You swore nobody would get hurt."

Agent Yu didn't flinch. Rather, she came closer to ensure that AJ had a good shot. "And nobody has to get hurt anymore if you help me finish this. If you help me find Miss Cooper."

AJ kept the gun steady and pressed against the agent's temple.

"Think back to your first month of training. How simple it all was, how you knew you were part of something noble and for the greater good. It can be that way again." She stood and stepped away. "Contrary to what you might think, I don't like doing this shit—torturing innocent people and all. I don't like being an evil bitch for pay and, honestly, the pay isn't that good."

"But let me guess. You're just doing your job."

With an exasperated nod, Agent Yu replied, "Yes. This is part of my job and, believe it or not, I take no pleasure in it. But I have bills and shit, okay? And, on top of that, a dick of a boss who makes each day hell. So cut me some slack."

AJ frowned. "You're going to complain about your own life while you're torturing me? Wow."

"I believed in this work, once upon a time. I did. This work saved me from a life of..." she trailed off, lowering her voice. "It gave me purpose. I saw that it gave you purpose, too. What I'm trying my best to do is get us back to that, to our mission of protecting this country. Believe me, this bullshit that Agent Grobeck has us doing is not the mission."

"Right, this is all his fault. You're not at all part of the problem."

Agent Yu approached her again, closing the space between them. "You can shoot me right now, Miss Taylor. Or you can be smart, do as I say, and get out of this cell. It's your choice."

"What will you do to her when you find her?" AJ asked, her voice trembling, her eyes wide.

"Lower the gun, and I'll tell you."

AJ's chest heaved as her finger tightened against the trigger. She glared at the agent but, after a second, lowered the gun.

When Agent Yu arrived at home that evening, she retreated in surprise at the sight of the two people sitting on her sofa. Not missing a beat, though, she stepped inside, hung her bag on the coat hook, locked the door, and headed straight for the kitchen.

"Well, aren't you the stealthy little fugitive, Miss Cooper," she said, reaching into the cabinet for a glass. "Do you have any idea how much I've been looking for you?"

Eve sneered at her.

"Would you like anything to drink? Water? Juice?" she asked.

Eve didn't say a word.

"Suit yourself," she said, smiling and turning her gaze on the man with the large light brown eyes set against a smooth almond complexion. "What about you?"

Niles merely stared at her.

Agent Yu shrugged and poured herself a glass of water. She refilled it before joining her uninvited guests in the living room. "I'm disappointed you stopped calling me, Miss Cooper. But I suppose this is a nice, unexpected change of pace."

Eve signaled to Niles, and he pulled a gun from his hoodie

jacket and pointed it at Agent Yu's head.

She smiled at Niles. "You're not the first person to point a gun at my head today." But when she noticed the silencer on the gun, her smile faded, and she turned to Eve. "Interesting. That's a SPI-issued silencer. We never supplied you with a GLOCK or a silencer. And we confiscated AJ's when we extracted her. Where did you get this?"

Eve glanced at the silencer that had belonged to Mauricio. She smiled and leaned forward. "I told you if you ever interfered with my plans, I'd make sure you regretted it. What part of that did you not understand?"

Agent Yu's thin lips formed into a smile once more as she sat the glass of water on the coffee table and relaxed in the comfy chair. "If you were going to shoot me, you would've done it as soon as I walked in."

Eve glowered at her and gestured to Niles. He lowered the gun.

"Good girl," said Agent Yu. "While this James Bond cosplay is cute, I can see that you're not about this lifestyle. You have to be—"

He fired two shots in quick succession, striking Agent Yu in each knee. She stared at him, her mouth hanging open. A second later, she whimpered in pain and clutched at her legs.

Eve gawked at him. "Hey, you didn't tell me you were a good shot."

"My grandpa took me hunting in Virginia when I was a kid," he said, staring in dismay at Agent Yu. He looked mortified about what he'd done. "I...I never shot anybody before now, though."

Eve turned to the woman. "As you were saying, Agent?"

She moaned, still clutching her legs. "You think just because you got this lapdog willing to pull the trigger for you, you're really something now, huh?"

Eve gestured to Niles, and he shakily handed her the gun.

She held it steady, pointed at Agent Yu's face. "Go ahead, keep talking shit."

"You think you know what's going on, but you have no idea."

"Well, I do know you should protect your computer better." Eve gestured toward the laptop that was sitting on the coffee table. "It didn't take me more than ten minutes to get past your password, and I'm not even tech-savvy."

"But I am," said Niles.

"So, who's Forest Sherman?"

Holding her leg and rocking in pain, Agent Yu cast Eve an inscrutable look.

"From what I saw in your files, you seem awfully worried about him messing things up for you. Who is he?" She paused, watching sweat roll down the agent's forehead as her face flushed bright red. "Whatever. That's not why I'm here anyway."

"Why are you here then?"

"To get a lead on Samuel Kim. Your computer was helpful on that front as well."

"Is that it?" asked Agent Yu.

"No. Are they still alive? Zoey, Gabe, AJ, Mauricio?"

"Yes."

"If you're lying to me, I'll put two more bullets in you."

Agent Yu rolled her eyes and clenched her teeth, wincing from the sharp pain shooting through her legs. "They're alive."

"Where's Zoey and Gabe?"

She looked away. "I don't know."

"She's lying," Niles observed.

A frantic gleam came over Agent Yu's face as her eyes swept from Niles to Eve. "They were moved today. I don't know where they are now. Agent Grobeck doesn't fill me in on these things."

Eve moved closer. "Why were they moved?"

"To get more information out of them about you. They weren't responding to my...tactics."

"More information about me? Like what?"

"About your whereabouts primarily."

Eve exchanged a glance with Niles. "Okay. Where's Mauricio? What did you do to him?"

Agent Yu grinned now and tried to laugh, but the pain in her knees transformed the laugh into a moan followed by a cough. "I freed him. It was the least I could do to reward him for leading us to you."

"Bullshit."

Niles put a hand on Eve's shoulder while keeping his eyes on the agent. "Eve. I don't think she's lying now."

Still smiling, Agent Yu tilted her head toward him. "Listen to your lapdog. After AJ got cold feet—"

"AJ? What are you talking about?"

"I got a surprise call from her when you were in Philly. She didn't trust Mauricio and wanted to protect you. Then, she developed a guilt complex and refused to help anymore. Lucky for me, Mauricio decided to give me a call shortly afterward. You know what they say...when one door closes, another opens."

Eve stood and kept the gun pointed at Agent Yu.

"Eve?" Niles whispered, cautiously placing his hand on her shoulder. "That's enough. Give me the gun."

"Tell me the truth. What have you done to him?" she asked, focused on Agent Yu.

"I'm telling you the truth. I haven't done anything to him. When AJ backed out of helping me, I thought it was all over. I figured I'd never find you, even after scaring your friends—Zoey and Gabriel—into contacting you again. I thought all hope was lost. Until Mauricio called my office the night you were heading to the house in Ardmore. I thought he might be setting us up." She shut her eyes for a second and squeezed her thighs near the wounds. "I don't know why he sold you out. But he did. And that's the truth."

"He did it to get his family back," said Eve, lowering the gun. "That's the only reason he'd do it. There was nothing he wouldn't do to get back to them."

"I did some digging, you know. He and Agent Grobeck have a special agreement. I don't know or understand the details, but that's what I found out. There's more to Mauricio than he told you."

"Clearly. Where's your cell phone?"

"In my bag, there." Agent Yu pointed to the coat hook near the door.

Eve handed Niles the gun, and he flicked on the safety. She went to Agent Yu's bag, dug inside it, retrieved the cell phone, and dialed 911. "A woman's been shot. She needs an ambulance," she said and hung up before the operator could respond. She dropped the phone on the floor and turned to Niles. "Let's go."

Agent Yu stared at the two of them as they hurried out the door.

At the elevator, Eve pressed the button for the ground floor. She didn't bother changing from her regular appearance.

When they reached the outside, they clasped hands and faded.

Bursting into a sprint, they didn't stop until they were a block away from the building. Niles teleported them back to the hotel in Philadelphia. "We have to remember to stay faded when we hop from place to place," Eve said, gazing around and hoping no one had witnessed their sudden appearance in the middle of the park.

"My bad. I can't seem to keep us from becoming visible during the move. I'll do some test hops later and see if I can work out the glitch." He hurried behind her as they crossed the street. "I think it worked."

"What? Oh, scaring the shit out of Agent Yu again? Yeah, it worked. Even better, she and her team will be looking for us in Chicago now, not Philly. We're in the clear for a while."

"Was that your plan? To trick her into taking her eyes off us here?"

"Part of it."

They rushed across the busy intersection, turned left toward the hotel, and walked along a vacant cobblestone street.

Just as they arrived outside the hotel, she stopped and looked around. A chill went through her, and she felt an intense urge to run. "Niles, I think there's somebody—"

Gripped by some invisible bind, she couldn't move. *Arms. Someone's holding me.* She tried to scream, but only muffled sounds came out. Someone's hand was covering her mouth.

"What's wrong?" He reached out to grab her, but when he did, her whole body lurched backward, as if pulled by something.

Eve fixed her watery gaze on Niles. "Get the hotel key out of my pocket," she gasped as a hand tightened around her neck.

He hesitated for a moment but agreed. As soon as he reached inside her pocket, he gripped her arm with his free hand and teleported them to the hotel room.

When he blinked, he saw a long-haired man standing behind Eve and holding a knife to her throat. "Try anything else, and I'll kill her."

Niles threw his hands up in surrender.

"Why've you been following me?" the man asked.

Eve recognized that voice, but she couldn't move or speak for fear that he'd slit her throat.

"Easy. I'm Niles Woodard. We're like you. Faders."

"I know what you are. Did they send you after me?"

Sam? Is that you?

There was no answer, just silence. It sent chills through Eve. Why couldn't she hear him? Why couldn't he hear her?

Niles took a step forward, looking as though he was trying to calm a wild dog. "Just listen—"

"I took out the chip days ago. How could they know where I am?" A large bandage was on his right forearm that was wrapped around Eve's midsection.

Niles held out his hands, taking another cautious step forward. "We're not SPI. We're trying to stay off the radar, too, just like you. Now, put the knife down. Let her go. We're on your side."

Sam? Can you hear me? We weren't sent by SPI. We're—"

"I'm not going back," he shouted at Niles. "Not after what they did...after what they made me do."

"Bro, we're not trying to make you go back. We're on your side."

"Nobody's on my side but me," he spat, squeezing Eve's midsection so tightly that she felt the air leaving her.

Sam, please?

In the next second and with one swift motion, he slid the knife against her throat.

As he released her, she stumbled from the blinding shock of it all. She watched the bloody knife fall to the floor at her feet. For a moment, everything stopped. Eve stood inert like a mannequin. A thick red line appeared along her throat, and an expression of surprise sailed across her face only to be replaced with a pained contortion.

She collapsed onto the floor.

On her stomach, she clenched her throat with one hand while clawing at the carpet with her other hand. She wasn't aware of the physical struggle that had commenced between the two men or the faint sound of the gun firing. Every breath she drew became more painful and more of an effort. Finally, she stopped scratching at the carpet, lay still, and watched it all—the carpet, the room, the men. It all melted away and receded into a vast array of brilliant colors until there was nothing and no one.

12

As Eve lurched to her feet, she looked around the strange room. Cement floor, four blank walls, steel door. A familiar feeling of terror crept up, and she ran to the door. Her hand closed around the knob, but it wouldn't turn.

"Help," she screamed, but all that came out was a choking sound. *Niles, anybody, please!*

Her feet felt ice-cold, and she looked down to find that she was standing in a puddle. Water gushed in from a vent on the back wall. Desperately, she tried to turn the doorknob.

"Help me," she called out, banging on the door as the cold water rose past her calves. "Please!"

For no reason that she could discern, the door swung open, and she fell forward. Her face slammed against the floor. Stars dancing before her eyes, she squinted at the shadowy figure approaching.

"Come on," said Agent Yu, helping Eve to her feet.

Coughing and struggling to catch her breath, she managed to dust herself off. *Why...how am I not wet?* She turned to reassure herself that she'd escaped the flooding room. But there was no water. No door. Only a blank, cement wall.

"Let's go." Agent Yu grabbed her arm and hoisted her. Together, they lumbered down a winding hallway.

Eve knew this hallway. It led to a room with rows of beds—like hospital gurneys—and wires. Wires they would attach to her body while her wrists and ankles were locked to a bed. Or maybe that was another hallway. Why did it feel like she was trapped within a maze of hallways lately?

Walking at a brisker pace than usual, Agent Yu glanced back now and then, as if worried that someone might be following them. Her dark hair hung past her shoulders, and the stern face Eve was so accustomed to seeing was nowhere to be found. In fact, Agent Yu looked younger.

As Eve began to speak, a piercing pain shot through her throat, and she massaged the tender skin of her neck. Her mind flashed to the long-haired man with the knife in the hotel room. "The fader—Sam—he cut me. Where is he? Where's Niles?"

Agent Yu didn't respond.

Eve stopped. Still rubbing her neck, she stared at Agent Yu. "Am I dead? Did I die?"

Agent Yu turned to her and shouted something that sounded like nothing more than gibberish.

"Agent—" Eve tried to speak again, but no sound came out this time. "Why can't I hear myself?" she screamed silently, staring at the woman, and mouthing the words with as much emphasis as possible.

The hysteria continued to swirl around her until a door appeared before them.

"Okay, that definitely wasn't there a second ago," Eve remarked, eyes wide.

The agent typed a code into a small box. The door made a creaky sound as it opened. The room looked almost like a hospital emergency room, except the beds had leg and foot restraints. The only people present, besides Eve and Agent Yu, were a middle-aged white woman in a lab coat standing over a black man strapped to one of the beds. The woman wore a disappointed expression as she stared at the man.

Eve drew closer and noticed the man was unconscious. It appeared he'd been dunked in a pool of water. Water was dripping from his clothes, spilling from the bed, and forming a small reservoir on the floor. She took another step toward the man, wanting a closer view, but Agent Yu pulled her away.

"Don't move," Agent Yu said. "Stay here."

Doctor Thomas frowned as Agent Yu approached her. "I didn't call for you, Agent."

Eve tried to get closer to hear what the women were saying, but something she couldn't see prevented her from moving forward. Holding her breath, she pushed against the invisible barrier but relented when Agent Yu turned around. "Agent Yu?"

With no warning, the agent took off running toward the door.

Eve thrust herself against the invisible barrier and hurried after Agent Yu. They stopped at a door, and the agent typed a code into another box.

"That fucker. That evil fucker," Agent Yu muttered once inside the office. She slammed the door and paced for a moment. When she stopped pacing, she groaned and sat in the leather chair behind a large desk.

"Agent?"

"They're not going to get away with this," she said, pecking at the keyboard. She gasped, covering her mouth and staring at the computer screen.

Eve watched all this with curiosity and increasing worry. "Agent?" She scurried around to get a look at the screen.

There was a video of a man, the man who had been unconscious on the bed. He was lying naked in a puddle of water in the middle of a cement room. His tattered clothes lay near him, and his body showed red and brown lines from lashings. The lines striped his whole body, neck to legs. He was shivering, and Eve couldn't be sure if her eyes were fooling her, but he seemed to be fading in and out. What's more, his hair was changing from dark brown to white to red with every passing second.

"What the...?" Eve began.

Agent Yu closed the video and moved it and several files, one of which was titled "Special Project Report, Part One," to a delete folder. Frantically, she moved several more files.

When she dragged the last file to the delete folder, Eve caught a glimpse of a familiar name: Forest Sherman. "Hey...why does that name sound—"

"They're not going to pin this on me. I had nothing to do with it. Nothing." The agent wiped away tears and paused. She looked upward, then rose to her feet and sniffled. "You have to go. Now."

"Who is he?"

"He's like you." She rushed to the door and turned to Eve. "He could do more than disappear. He could do...everything. I didn't tell anybody about it."

"Agent—"

"They only know about the disappearing bit. Not the rest. I made sure of that."

"Slow down..."

"He could've gotten free. The fool could've gotten out of here and never been found. Why did he stay?" She was speaking in a jagged, broken sort of way, partly to Eve and partly to herself. She looked at the ceiling again, as if she were seeing something Eve couldn't see. "You have to go."

The lights went out, and there was a sound of feet against the floor and the door opening.

"What's going on?" Eve whispered, her heart racing.

When the lights came on, she was standing next to Agent Yu, and they were both looking at a man lying on a hospital bed. His hands and feet were strapped to the bed, and he was dry now. Eve looked into his wide, lifeless brown eyes.

"Is he..." she said, turning to Agent Yu, but the woman was no longer there. Instead, Eve was staring at another set of familiar brown eyes.

Squatting over her, Niles sniffled and his tears dropped onto her face. But he stopped when he saw her eyes blink. Leaning in closer, he brought his face within inches of hers and turned his ear to her mouth. His hair hung over his forehead and draped his face and hers.

"Eve, how...?" he said, drawing back in shock. "How are you still...?"

She coughed a few times and focused her blurry gaze on him. Instinctively, her hand went to her neck, and she stared at her palms. *No blood?* From the corner of her eye, she noticed another man lying on the floor near the bathroom. He was squirming in pain and clenching his left arm.

Quivering, she sat up and tried to stand. Her knees shook as though she hadn't used them for years, but she managed to balance herself. She went to Samuel Kim and glared at him, his mouth hanging open and his eyes wide in astonishment. He flinched as she grabbed him by his shirt and pulled him up. For a moment, she regarded him with a mixture of confusion and fury.

She slapped him hard enough to split his lip.

He whimpered and averted his gaze.

"You tried to kill me. What the hell is wrong with you?" A wave of guilt flooded her as she watched him shrink and cower away from her, tears spilling. This wasn't the Samuel Kim she remembered. "Bring me a wet towel, Niles."

Staring at her like she was a ghost, Niles didn't move.

"Niles? Did you hear me?"

After a moment, he shuffled to the bathroom and

returned with a small towel.

"Let me see it," she said to Samuel, gesturing to his injured arm. With the warm, wet towel she dabbed at the wound, cleaned off the dried blood, and wrapped a dry towel around his arm. He slouched to the floor, and she realized she'd never seen so much sadness in anyone other than her mother. He looked like a dog that had been beaten one too many times. What had happened to him?

"Bring me a glass of water and my backpack," she ordered Niles.

Still not saying a word, he ran to the bathroom once more, filled a paper coffee cup with water, and brought it to her with the bag.

She handed Samuel four pills along with the cup of water. "Take it," she insisted when he hesitated.

"You were dead, Eve," Niles whispered, shaking his head. "There was so much blood and...you had no pulse. For at least five minutes, you were dead."

Her fingers swept over her neck. The skin was as smooth as it had always been, but the spot where the blade had cut through was still tender to touch.

"My grandpa died on our living room sofa when I was ten. Stroke. I was sitting right next to him when it happened, watching *Happy Days*. I'll never forget how he sounded when he took his last breaths, and how his eyes looked. You made the same exact sound, Eve. And your eyes...your eyes looked the same way." He touched her neck. "There's no trace of where he cut you. It's like it never happened."

She retreated from him.

Observing her like she was a circus animal, he cupped his hands around the back of his head. "It's impossible."

As she retreated from him, she glimpsed a spot on the floor. There was a large pool of blood on the area of the carpet where she'd fallen. "You know that feeling when you walk into a room and notice a picture on the wall is a little crooked, not quite level? That's how the world, all of this, feels right now. But no matter how hard I try, I can't level the picture."

"Eve?"

Walking past Niles and Samuel, she went to the window. Rain was falling in a slow trickle onto the alleyway below, and she wondered if it would turn to snow later in the evening. Was it snowing in Chicago right now? She missed the peaceful quiet of snowfall. She missed the simplicity of it.

"How is any of this possible?" asked Niles.

Leaning against the desk and watching the rain, she thought about the strange dream she'd had. She recalled Forest Sherman's still, wet body. Was any of it real, or was it a dream? If it was real, why had Agent Yu protected the man's secret? Did the flash drives contain information about him? She turned to Niles. "We need to take a look at the flash drives."

"Eve, we need to talk about how you—"

"Later."

"But—"

"Not now, Niles," she said, her tone shorter than usual.

"Fine," he replied, sighing. "But shouldn't we figure out what to do with him first?" He looked at Samuel who was staring at them in horror.

"What to do with him? He's with us now."

"He tried to kill you."

"Yes, but he failed. I doubt he'll try it again, especially not in the sorry state he's in." She turned an icy stare on Samuel. "You got any plans to try to kill me again?"

He shook his head.

"See? There you have it," she said, smiling at Niles.

"The man cut your throat."

"He's a victim, like the rest of us. He didn't know we

weren't sent by SPI."

"Whatever you say," Niles scoffed. "Look, I need to get some air."

Before she had a chance to respond, he teleported.

With a long sigh, she knelt and took another look at Samuel's injured arm. It appeared to be swelling. *You know I'm taking a big, fucking risk by trusting you, Sam. Don't prove him right.*

He grimaced in pain.

As Samuel rested half asleep against the sofa, Eve grabbed the backpack and sat on the floor. "Let's see," she mumbled, removing the computer, the small safe box, and AJ's flash drive from the bag. She turned the box over in her hand and pulled the tiny latch on the front. It didn't budge. She typed a few number combinations into the keypad. Nothing happened. No clicking noises. No beep.

"Did you ever get in touch with your hacker cousin?" she asked Niles, who'd returned after a half-hour away.

"Not yet."

She studied the safe box, her brow furrowed in deep concentration. *How the hell do I open this thing?* She tried the tiny latch. It didn't move.

Niles shook his head. "I think it's time you give up on that thing."

"Well, it was worth—"

A cracking sound stopped her mid-sentence. She examined the box and noticed a long fracture line along the center.

Niles tore his gaze away from the computer screen and looked at the safe box on Eve's lap.

So stupid. Why didn't I think of this ages ago?

Gently squeezing the box again, she smashed it just enough to make the fracture widen. Worried about accidentally smashing the flash drive within the box, Eve rolled her shoulders and applied a small amount of pressure. A second later, the tiny latch clicked and popped up.

Smiling, Eve lifted the hood of the safe box.

"No fucking way," Niles said, loud enough to wake up Samuel. "That was solid metal." He came from the desk and sat next to her to get a closer look at the contents of the box.

Inside the box was a flash drive nearly identical to the one AJ had retrieved. It was affixed to the floor of the box by a blue twist tie, the sort used to tie plastic bags. She untwisted the tie and removed the flash drive.

Rushing to the desk, she stuck it into the computer's USB port. One folder, labeled "Salazar," appeared on the otherwise blank computer screen.

Niles placed his hand on her shoulder and pointed at the screen. "What's that?"

The word "Salazar" had appeared at the center of a gray screen. Before she could make sense of what had happened, the word disappeared and was replaced by another screen displaying only a small gray button with the word "Welcome" on it. The button flashed.

"I have no idea." She clicked on the flashing button, and a page came up that resembled the previous screen of folders. There were two documents, marked "1" and "2." She clicked on document "1," and it brought up a twenty-page report, authored by Salazar. "Special Project Report, Part Two: Purpose, Market, and Findings," she said aloud, reading the title of the document.

They scanned the pages of the document, their eyebrows retreating farther and farther into their hairlines as they read page after page. Her heart thudded against her chest when she saw the name "Forest Sherman." After finishing the final page, she closed the file and opened document "2," a spreadsheet containing fifty items—company and organization names, contact information, and dollar figures that ranged from millions to billions of dollars.

She skimmed and re-skimmed the page several times before it all came together in her mind. "Oh, my God."

Samuel sat up, watching the two of them from the other side of the room.

Eve closed the document and the folder. She ejected the flash drive and inserted AJ's flash drive. Once more, she clicked on the folders and was met with the password box. "Fuck. How do we get in?"

Niles sighed. "I tried every password I could think of. I don't know."

"I can open it," said Samuel. He was sitting next to the sofa and holding a laptop computer now. "I have an application on my computer that should be able to access the files."

Eve rolled her eyes. "I'm sure your SPI-issued computer has a lot of applications like that, but—"

"It's not SPI-issued. Do you think I'd be carrying that around so they can track me? It's my personal computer."

"Oh," she replied. "In that case." She removed the flash drive from her computer and handed it to Samuel.

They sat next to him and stared at his computer screen as he inserted the flash drive.

"Give me a second. Sorry, my computer's not as fast as it used to be." With one hand, he typed something into a box that appeared, and more screens popped up and vanished. Then, the screen she'd seen before appeared followed by the password box. The password box disappeared and, suddenly, the screen displayed the name of the company, Generate, Inc., in large block letters. "We're in," said Samuel, standing up and taking his laptop to the desk. He offered the seat to Eve.

She sat and squinted at the small circular logo at the bottom left corner of the screen. It looked familiar. "That's

Salazar's logo."

"Are the two companies related?" asked Niles. The next screen displayed two documents, labeled "1" and "2." "They're duplicates of the documents on the other flash drive. Maybe they're the same company."

"Or Generate, Inc. is a subsidiary of Salazar's company," said Eve, opening the files.

"So, does all this mean what I think it means?" he asked.

She shot him a wary look. "Maybe I'm paranoid, but I have a feeling they're trying to figure out how to create or reproduce our ability. To sell it. Spies who can literally be invisible. Can you imagine a hotter commodity?"

He sat up straight. "Wait a minute. That spreadsheet is a list of buyers, isn't it?"

Eve nodded. "Potential buyers maybe."

"You don't think the product is available yet, do you? They haven't figured out how to reproduce our ability?"

"I don't know. But I bet SPI sent operatives to retrieve these flash drives because it wants the information for itself. If one of these companies has figured out how to create or reproduce the ability, we can intervene before it goes on the market. That's why SPI sent us on field missions to get these drives. It all makes sense now. If we can stop SPI from getting its hands on the information—"

"And expose them in the process," Samuel said, cutting in abruptly. "We win."

They turned to him.

"Exactly," said Eve, smiling. "Pack up. We're taking another little trip to Chicago tomorrow."

Eve and Niles sat in the corner of his favorite dive bar, a noisy hole in the wall in the heart of Germantown. They took turns taking shots of tequila while he regaled her with stories about all the places where he'd tended bar in the city. The normalcy of the evening was a welcome change to Eve, although her mind lingered on SPI. What were they doing to Zoey and Gabe right now? Were they still alive? These questions haunted her, and she tried to push them aside.

"You know I was a schoolteacher before all this," she said, her words slurred as she leaned across the table and dropped her hand on top of Niles'. "I was just a normal, underpaid high school English teacher. Nobody special."

He laughed. "I highly doubt you were ever normal."

"No, really. I was struggling to pay rent, dealing with past-due student loans, all that typical bullshit. Really. It was all so cliché, to be honest," she said, grinning stupidly. "I guess except the part where I was involved with a married couple."

Niles burst out laughing, and she joined in. They slapped the table, laughing loud enough to turn heads.

"Sounds complicated," said Niles, still laughing.

As the laughter faded, Eve fell silent and stared at her hand gripping the empty shot glass. For a moment, she felt Zoey's lips against her neck and Gabriel's arms around her. She smiled. "It wasn't. Actually," she said, mostly to herself. "It was so easy. I never loved anyone the way I loved them. You know they asked me to move in with them when I was struggling with bills? I was too stupid to say yes. Could've avoided all of this by just saying yes."

"Why didn't you?"

"Pride. Jealousy."

"Jealousy?"

She motioned her agreement. "I think at first I was jealous of Gabe, jealous that Zoey chose him. That she married him. But then, the more I was with them, the more they showered me with love, the more I realized I was wrong. It was possible to love two people at once, and she loved us both. She chose both of us."

Niles regarded her with an inquisitive expression. "That

couple you visited on the night of the..." he trailed off. "They're who you're talking about?"

She continued staring at her hand, hoping he wouldn't see the tears forming in her eyes. "I pulled them into my shit. They're suffering because of me. I don't even know if they're still alive."

"I'm sorry, Eve," he said, grasping her hands across the table.

"Probably if I'd done like Agent Grobeck said and kicked my useless father out of the family home, I could've set myself up financially and never needed to take the job at SPI. What can I say? I don't make the best decisions."

He regarded her with a sympathetic look.

"I probably *will* kick him out whenever I get out of this mess," she mumbled. She looked at Niles and tried to smile. *I came out for drinks, not therapy. Get it together, Eve.* "Hey, you want to do another round of shots and then get out of here?" she asked, hoping her voice sounded light-hearted.

For moment, he stared at her with the kindest eyes she'd ever seen. At last, he smiled and held up his hand to flag the server.

Just before dawn, she woke to Niles' incessant snoring. Sitting up, she groaned and looked across the room at Samuel on the pallet. His wounded arm lay awkwardly at his side. She got up and, hoping not to wake him, lightly placed her hand on his arm. It was warm and moist.

As she closed her eyes, she thought about how the wound on her neck had healed instantly. How had she done it? If she cut herself again, would the wound heal? "He could do everything," she murmured, repeating Agent Yu's words from her dream. *What does that mean?*

Samuel's eyes blinked open and shut twice before he opened them wide and stared at her. "What are you doing?"

He looked at his arm when she released him.

"Sorry," she said, shaken out of her daydream. She stood. "I was looking at your—"

"My arm..." Samuel pulled the bandages from his wound. He sat upright and rubbed the spot where the skin had been torn from the bullet. The skin showed no signs that a bullet had ever pierced it.

They locked gazes.

Holy shit. I didn't do that. I couldn't have—

"What are you?" He scooted to the headboard and away from her. "Look, it was weird enough during training when you could hear my thoughts. Then I find out you're...unkillable, and somehow strong enough to crush metal. And now this?"

Eve stared at his arm, not believing her eyes.

"You're not like the rest of us, are you?" asked Samuel, a mix of fascination and fear in his eyes.

"What's going on?" Niles yawned. He squinted at them.

Samuel held up his arm, his eyes fixed on Eve. "She healed my arm."

At that moment, Eve spotted something sparkling on the blanket and picked it up. Her hands shook as she examined the tiny bullet that had a minute earlier been lodged in Samuel's arm. There were flecks of blood on it.

Niles' eyes flitted from Samuel's arm to Eve. "Is it true, Eve?"

She turned to him, still in a daze, and holding the bullet up before her.

When he noticed the bullet in her hand, his mouth dropped open. "This is some X-Men shit."

Eve was speechless.

13

Her arms propped up on crutches, Olivia Yu hobbled down the hallway, hoping not to run into Grobeck. She wasn't in any mood to deal with his condescension, which had reached a fever pitch ever since he'd had to send emergency medics to her home after Cooper's unannounced visit. He'd made no attempt to disguise his intentions of treating this incident as an outstanding debt she owed him.

Agent Yu's patience was waning nowadays, and over and over she had to remind herself of her plan. In a week or less, she told herself, she'd have everything she needed to ruin him.

"Don't rush, Olivia. You're almost there," she told herself as she entered AJ's cell. "You can do this."

Dried blood lined the corners of AJ's mouth, and her right eye looked darker and puffy.

"Are you all right?"

Sitting upright in the chair, AJ scowled at her. "What do you think?"

Agent Yu rested the crutches against the door and ran her fingers through her hair. She removed a large hairpin, put it between her lips, gathered the crutches again, and shuffled to AJ. "It's a recording device," she said, handing the hairpin to her. "See? If you look closely at the open tip, there's a tiny switch. When you push the switch to the right, the hairpin starts recording. You can see a faint blinking red light."

AJ brought the hairpin close to her face and flipped the switch.

"Do you see it? The red light? Put the pin in your hair, close to the front where it can record everything in front of you. Agent Grobeck will be visiting you again for more questioning. See if you can get him to talk. Massaging his ego usually does the trick. I'm interested in what he has to say about Mauricio Candela."

"I have to endure more of this?" her voice cracked. "All he did was slap me around and ask about Eve."

"I'm sorry. I didn't have the device until now. It would've been useful to have him recorded doing that to you."

"You mean beating me?"

Agent Yu lowered her eyes. "When we get this recording, we'll have him."

"What does that mean? For me."

"It means I'll have the authority to get you out of here," said Agent Yu. "Like I said before, you'll be free."

"And if there's nothing useful on it? If I can't get him to talk about Mauricio?"

"Then, I'll have to find another way to get him, without your help," replied Agent Yu, sighing.

AJ frowned. "Which means what?"

"You'll be free, Miss Taylor. Regardless of what information you get on the recording. I give you my word."

AJ stuck the pin in her greasy hair and rolled her eyes. "I don't know why I'm trusting you."

"Because you're smart," said Agent Yu, looking at AJ one more time before shutting the door.

Crutches clinking against the floor, she hobbled to the elevator and pushed the up arrow. As it opened, she rushed past some colleagues. When she arrived back at her office that looked more like a large utility closet than an office, she picked up the phone and called Agent Grobeck.

"I'm off to a meeting. What do you want?" he answered.

"This'll just take a moment. I'm trying to finish up my report on Zoey and Gabriel Ellis, but I realized I need to talk with Doctor Thomas. I believe she did their psych eval...?"

"Yes, that's correct."

"Well, I can't find her contact information..."

"Check with my assistant. She can give you Doctor Thomas' information," he said, and then there was a click.

After obtaining the doctor's office number, she called her own assistant. "Creekmur, can you turn the cameras off outside Doctor Thomas' office?"

"Sure thing."

"Oh, and get me the code to her office, will you?"

"You're not going to tell me what this is about, are you?" he asked.

"No. It's best that you don't know."

"Of course," he said, with a bored sigh.

To Agent Yu's relief, the hallway was quiet outside Doctor Thomas' office. To avoid being seen lingering outside Doctor Thomas' office, she decided to stop at the end of the hallway. Gingerly, she rested the right crutch against the wall, reached in her pocket, and pulled out a small strip of paper. It contained the six-digit number Creekmur had given her. Scribbled on the back was a username and password.

She glanced around to make sure she was alone and looked at the two cameras. "Hurry up, Creekmur," she mumbled, tapping her feet against the concrete floor. When her phone buzzed, a message that read "Done" appeared on the screen. She slid the phone in her pocket. Thrusting her arm over the crutch, she rushed to the doctor's office and dialed the code into the box.

After a click, the door opened. The spacious, airy office was bare, except for a desk in front of a large window overlooking the dingy street below. "I get a damn closet, while Doctor Evil gets a view of the city. Figures," Agent Yu muttered.

She shut the door and made her way to the desk. On the desk, there was a small laptop, a couple of manila folders, and two framed photographs of Doctor Thomas presumably with her husband and daughter.

As Agent Yu sat, the crutches fell to the floor, causing quite a bang. She cast a frantic gaze at the door and realized she'd forgotten to lock it. Hit with an even greater sense of urgency, she turned to the computer and clicked the power button.

When the welcome screen appeared, she entered the username and password that Creekmur had provided. "Thank you, Creekmur," she said as a screen of file folders appeared.

She conducted a simple search for Zoey's and Gabriel's names, bringing up at least a dozen documents sorted by date. The most recent document contained Doctor Thomas' observations of the couple since Agent Grobeck had moved them from the Chicago facility. Skimming the document and looking for any mention of the facility, she scrolled down page after page. "Where are you?"

A moment later, she stopped at a section where Doctor Thomas was discussing Gabriel Ellis' responsiveness to Agent Grobeck's new enhanced interrogation methods. Prolonged solitary confinement.

"Bingo."

After saving the document onto a flash drive, she closed the folder and shut down the computer. Crutches under both arms, she bolted out the office to a nearby empty restroom and locked the door.

Leaning against the door of a stall, she puzzled over what she'd learned. "We only take high-risk terrorist suspects to the Galena facility. Grobeck can't think these people are that important. What the hell isn't he telling me?"

When she emerged from the restroom, she saw Doctor Thomas entering a code into the box outside the office.

Agent Yu inhaled and approached the doctor, careful not to look suspicious.

"Agent, can I help you?" The doctor's smile revealed coffee-stained teeth.

"I'm glad I ran into you. I'm trying to finish up my progress report on Zoey and Gabriel Ellis, but I have some quick questions about them. Is now a good time?"

"Sure. I have about fifteen minutes."

Agent Yu followed her into the office and took a seat in front of the desk. Meanwhile, she pulled another small hairpin from her pocket and flipped the power switch on it.

"Fire away," said the doctor, sitting behind the desk. She turned on the computer and glanced at the screen before giving Agent Yu her full attention.

"I'm trying to get a sense of how pliable the couple appears to be at the moment. Given the mild interrogation methods we've employed so far, do you think they'll be more forthcoming as we move forward with our information gathering? What methods would you say have demonstrated the most success or the greatest potential for success so far?"

Doctor Thomas' face lit up with a satisfied smile, and she leaned forward. At once, she launched into a lengthy summary of her observations.

Agent Yu noted how the doctor looked positively excited to discuss the barbaric treatment of the couple. In fact, she wasn't sure if it was a trick of the light, but the doctor's pupils seemed to expand and drown out the blue of her irises. Her impassioned voice and mannerisms sent chills through Agent

Yu. Something about the woman was downright terrifying.

"As you can see, we're exploring all avenues to retrieve the intel from them," said Doctor Thomas.

"Thank you. This is helpful." Suppressing her desire to ask an additional question, Agent Yu stood and made her way to the door. "I don't mean to keep you from your meeting."

She rose and walked with Agent Yu to the door. "Not a problem, Agent. If you need anything else, feel free to stop by or call."

Agent Yu wondered if she'd ever seen the woman look so cheerful and eager to help. "Actually. I'd love to know who did your hair. Do you mind?" She reached out to touch the doctor's hair that was pinned up in some sort of pompadour.

Clearly flattered, she patted her hair and smiled. "Oh, there's a little salon in the South Loop at the corner of Wabash and Balbo, called Hair Karma. Ask for Vanessa. She's a miracle worker."

"I'll take your word for it," said Agent Yu and nodded, relieved to be leaving the office.

"Do you think she has any more information yet?" whispered Niles, sitting on the sofa and looking around the apartment.

Samuel and Eve sat next to him. They all faded and waited in silence.

"I mean," said Niles, interrupting the brief quiet. "I'd be kind of surprised if she has much yet."

The door creaked. "Shush. I think that's her now. Remember the plan, okay?"

"Got it," said Niles and Samuel in unison.

The door swung open and in walked Agent Yu supported by crutches. A man with eyes nearly identical to hers followed behind her and closed the door.

As planned, Niles crept to the opposite side of the room, while Samuel went to the front door and Eve remained close to the sofa. Agent Yu hobbled to the lounge chair and plopped down. Her companion sat on the sofa directly across from her. He reached for the crutches and laid them against the coffee table.

"How long are you going to need those?" he asked.

"A couple of weeks they say," said Agent Yu, rubbing her feet.

"I wish you'd tell me what happened."

"Don't start—"

"Or at least let me move in here for a week or two and help you out. You shouldn't have to do this alone."

"Isn't he sweet?" said Eve, appearing in front of the television.

Agent Yu registered no shock but held Eve's gaze, not blinking. "It's okay, Ian," she said, not turning to look at him. His eyes were wide, and beads of sweat formed on his forehead.

"Who's your new friend, Olivia?" asked Eve.

"My brother."

"Ah, that's right. Ian Yu. Yes, I know all about your family situation. Did a little bit a research during all the spare time I've had lately."

"Speaking of new friends, I see you've brought along Mr. Kim," Agent Yu remarked, her stony gaze flashing on Samuel. "How are you?"

"Your boss tied me to a chair, stripped me, and poured freezing water on me. After he Tasered me and starved me while you did nothing but watch," said Samuel, his voice deeper than usual. "How do you think I've been?"

Eve and Niles stared at Samuel, who was pointing his gun straight at Agent Yu's chest.

"You had a choice, Mr. Kim, and you chose unwisely. You chose to renege on your duty to complete the assignment and retrieve the drive. There was nothing I could do to help you," said Agent Yu.

He advanced toward her.

"Sam, stay where you are," said Eve. She raised her hand and shot him a dangerous glare. *If you fuck up our plan, I swear to God I'll shoot you.*

He looked from Agent Yu to Eve and, after a moment, stepped back.

Eve turned to Agent Yu. "Do you have a conscience in there? At all?"

"I've done a lot of things I'm not exactly fond of remembering, Miss Cooper."

"How much do you remember about Forest Sherman?"

At the mention of the name, Agent Yu averted her eyes and looked at her hands.

"Those little flash drives you all have us recovering, they have some wild stories on them," said Eve. "Special Operative Forest Sherman: a fader SPI captured. From what I've pieced together, SPI tortured him, but he wouldn't break. Tell me, why do you all think torturing us works?"

"That's a better question for Agent Grobeck," she replied.

"Well anyway," Eve said, shrugging. "The problem is that's about as far as I've gotten with the information on the flash drives. But I also had a weird dream recently about you and this Forest guy, and I'm wondering how close my dream is to reality. See, in this dream, he was unconscious in his cell, emaciated and, for all intents and purposes, dead. What did you and Grobeck do to him?"

Agent Yu kept her eyes lowered. "His sensitivity training didn't take, so we shut down the project."

The unusual quiet tone of her voice made the hairs stand up on Eve's neck. "Sensitivity training?"

"Yes, an earlier version of the training you went through. We called it the Special Project, Part One."

Eve's stomach turned. "By 'training' you mean 'torture'.

You tortured him to death?"

"The training was intended to desensitize the subjects and ensure they were ready for the field."

"Why didn't you offer him a cushy spy job like you did me and the others?"

"We were experimenting with different recruitment models," said Agent Yu.

"So you figured you'd brainwash him to work for SPI?"

"That was Agent Grobeck's brilliant idea."

"But you went along with it. And when he wouldn't comply, you all tortured him until he died."

Agent Yu sighed. "Physical conditioning was not intended to be the primary method. I developed the pilot with Doctor—"

"You developed it? It was your idea to torture people?"

She looked at Eve and was silent for a moment. "I developed a program focused on desensitizing through enhanced psychological conditioning. No physical conditioning, except as a last resort. The elements of the pilot all but eliminated the possibility that the physical conditioning exception would ever be necessary to employ.

"But David—Agent Grobeck—had different ideas. I didn't expect him to exploit the exception in the program. The exception spelled out that physical conditioning was only allowed for subjects presenting an immediate threat to national security. I developed the pilot right after the 2015 terror attack in DC, so we had to be particularly vigilant, do some things we didn't want to do.

"When we launched the pilot, however, there was no immediate security threat. We were playing offense. We were experimenting with options in case an immediate threat arose. But mid-way through—when we were actually making progress with Sherman—Grobeck got impatient. He found an excuse to justify using the exception."

"And what excuse was that?" Samuel interjected.

"The very existence of your kind. Specifically, the threat of your kind falling into the hands of enemies and terrorist cells that could exploit your ability and use it against our country. As Grobeck saw it, that sort of threat made us immediately vulnerable. It triggered the exception." Agent Yu stopped and exhaled. "I was naive not to see what he would do. And by the time I did see it...it was too late. I tried to protect Sherman. But I couldn't. And when Grobeck started the physical conditioning phase—"

"Conditioning," Eve scoffed, rolling her eyes. "For fuck's sake, just call it what it is. Torture."

"When Grobeck started it, Sherman didn't last a week. I was bringing him his meal one afternoon when I found him dead," said Agent Yu.

"So, he really is dead?"

"Yes."

"You people are sick," said Eve, barely above a whisper.

"Sherman was the only operative who died as a result of or during the intensive training. As for the program, it's now—"

"A run of the mill, good old-fashioned torture program. I mean, who doesn't have one these days?" Eve smacked her lips, hot with rage as she thought about what Sherman endured. The Tasers. The electric shocks. The beatings.

"Essentially, yes, that's what it is now. Agent Grobeck and Doctor Thomas corrupted it. They like the torture. They get off on it. Thankfully, they've restructured and rewritten it, so my name's no longer on it. It's their program now."

"Because that's all that matters. Your name and keeping your hands clean. Of course," Samuel replied, fuming.

Agent Yu looked from him to Eve and fixed her eyes on Niles, the one semi-neutral face in the room. "Try to imagine creating something, spending months creating something that's supposed to help do some good, only to have your boss take it and turn it into something perverse and totally unrecognizable. Imagine how that feels."

Niles looked at her with revulsion. "It was already perverse. Mental torture is as bad as physical torture. Maybe worse."

"Don't try to put yourself on a higher moral ground. You're just as disgusting as Grobeck and Doctor Thomas," said Eve.

Agent Yu cracked a smile. "You have no idea the levels of depravity human beings can sink to. At least there's a limit to my depravity. I'd never have done to Sherman or anybody the sick things they did to him."

"Just answer one question for me. Was Forest Sherman capable of other things?"

Agent Yu sat up straight and regarded her with increased interest. "Yes."

"But you hid this information from everyone else, didn't you?"

"Yes. How do you know this?"

"Like I said, I had a weird dream." A familiar image flashed in Eve's mind—an image of Sherman naked and writhing on the wet floor, fading in and out and his hair changing colors. She shut and opened her eyes, trying to erase the image. "I'm wondering why you kept the information about him to yourself. Why you went out of your way to conceal it?"

"Isn't it obvious?" said Agent Yu, incredulously. "Agent Grobeck and Doctor Thomas are monsters. Genocidal. They were already terrified of your kind. Imagine what they would've done with that information."

Eve shuddered.

"I couldn't live with that. I couldn't," Agent Yu added.

Eve stared at the agent. She hadn't expected to feel sympathy for the woman.

Zoey and Gabe. You're here for them, and for AJ. Focus.

"Look, as much as I'd love to sit here and listen to the rest of your shameless attempt to avoid accountability, that's not why we're here. You're going to tell us where Zoey, Gabe, and AJ are, and you're going to help us extract them."

Agent Yu mouthed the word "extract" and snickered.

"Then—"

"You want the contact list of all the trainees," Agent Yu muttered, bored. "I already have the list ready for you on a flash drive." She pulled a flash drive from her pocket and handed it to Eve.

"What is it with you people and flash drives?" asked Samuel. "Ever heard of secure cloud storage?"

Agent Yu smiled, smugly. "Keyword: secure. Which cloud storage is not."

"I don't just want the list of faders," said Eve. "I want the whole file on the Special Project."

Agent Yu's smile vanished. "What if I'm tired of complying with your demands?"

Eve approached Ian Yu and lowered her gun so that it was level with his chest. She looked at him, realizing he couldn't be more than nineteen years old or so. "Ian, I imagine this is all very upsetting to you right now. All these horrible things you've heard and your sister's role in it all. I imagine you're thinking you don't know who she is. How could your own sister do these horrible things? Believe me, I know the feeling. Families are so complicated. And I'm sorry you've had to hear all of these things. But this is your sister's chance to rectify the damage she's caused to many people. Wouldn't you say it's wise for her to accept this opportunity?"

He stared at her before nodding.

"Your brother's got the right idea," Eve remarked, turning to Agent Yu. "You should listen to him."

Agent Yu straightened her posture.

"Now, first off," said Eve. "Where are my friends?"

"Zoey and Gabriel Ellis are at the Galena facility. Grobeck transferred them for enhanced interrogation. I don't know how long they'll be there."

"What's the address?"

"I don't know."

She raised the gun and pointed it at Ian. He shrank away. "What's the address?" she asked again, not taking her eyes off the agent.

"Advanced locations are not generally disclosed to lower level agents. But I can find out tomorrow. I can check the database." Her voice wavered as she looked at her brother's panic-stricken face.

"Good. Where's AJ?"

"She's at the facility here in the city. On North Elston. The big gray warehouse building where you were held. She's helping me set up Grobeck."

Eve lowered the gun. "You're setting up Grobeck? Why?"

"He literally enjoys torturing people. He's a psycho who needs to be put down."

"You're calling somebody else a psycho?" Samuel sneered. "Irony truly is dead."

Niles chuckled.

"Say I believe you. I mean, I don't, but say I do. Why would AJ help you?" Eve asked.

"I promised her freedom."

"And she believed you?"

Agent Yu shrugged. "She's cooperating, which is all that matters to me."

"So," said Eve, regarding her with suspicion, "what's this plan and how far along are you?"

Niles stepped forward. "Eve, you don't believe her, do you?"

"Why would I lie?" asked Agent Yu, smiling.

Eyebrows raised, they all stared at her, their incredulity undisguised.

"Fine," said Eve, at last. "Ian, hand me my laptop from that bag there."

With shaky hands, he did as told, watching Eve's hand on the gun.

Agent Yu removed a black hairpin from her hair, attached it to a flash drive she retrieved from the breast pocket of her blouse, and inserted it into the computer. "This should bring up the live feed from the recording device Miss Taylor is wearing. I also placed one on Doctor Thomas—she should be meeting with your friends and Grobeck this evening for more interrogations. Obviously, I planned to use the most damaging clips from the recordings, assuming I manage to get any damaging footage. There's seventy-two hours of memory available on each device." She extended a black cord to Eve. "I need you to turn on the TV and hook this cord into it."

Eve handed the cord to Samuel and kept her attention on Agent Yu. Once the cord was plugged into the television, the laptop's desktop screen appeared on the television.

Agent Yu clicked on a video icon. It brought up a screen showing a blank gray wall and a steel door. "Looks like we have nothing so far. But we're live right now in Miss Taylor's cell. From the looks of it, she must be sitting in the chair and facing the door. As for Doctor Thomas..." she went on, minimizing the video screen and maximizing another screen that showed Agent Grobeck talking inaudibly. "What's going on here?"

When Samuel increased the volume, they could hear Agent Grobeck saying, "If we can't get anything out of them, we're going to have to suspend this investigation and move them."

"Good," said Doctor Thomas. "I would like to continue my work with them. It may require experimenting with more traditional EITs."

"Let's try other methods before we do that."

"It's been three days, and they've given us nothing on Miss Cooper's whereabouts. What other method do you suggest?"

"One that we tend to save for high-value targets," he said, turning to someone else who wasn't visible in the camera frame. Although his voice grew faint when he walked out of the frame, he could be heard saying, "Bring in subject two."

A man moaned and muttered indistinctly. The moans became louder but stopped the moment Agent Grobeck returned. Zoey Ellis, wearing tattered, dirty clothes, stood with her head lowered in front of Agent Grobeck. Her face was smudged, and she was shivering. Not saying a word, Agent Grobeck ripped the clothes off her body.

There was a commotion off camera and someone—Eve assumed it was Gabriel—yelled, "No, please. We don't know anything."

Zoey appeared too weak to do anything other than try to cover herself as tears escaped her eyes. There were bruises on her chest and stomach where she'd been beaten. Her abusers had spared her face.

"This can go easy if you tell us what we want to know, Mr. Ellis. What do you know about the whereabouts of Eve Cooper?"

The camera turned to reveal Gabriel slumped in a chair, crying and struggling to free himself. His limbs were tied to the chair. His shoulders rose and fell as he sobbed and shook his head. "Please. I don't know anything. We don't know anything."

When Agent Grobeck and Zoey came into focus again, Gabriel still could be heard crying out and begging. "This doesn't have to be so hard, Mr. Ellis. I want to help you."

Agent Grobeck looked at Doctor Thomas, bringing his empty gaze into focus with the camera.

"Stop, please," Gabriel appealed. "We don't know anything."

Zoey kept her eyes lowered while Agent Grobeck studied her. Without warning, he smacked her face once then twice. She didn't move or make a sound until he grabbed the back of her head and brought out a large plastic rod. He rubbed it against her cheek.

Gabriel went from moaning and pleading to hurling every threat conceivable at Agent Grobeck.

"Mr. Ellis, what do you know about the whereabouts of Eve Cooper?" asked Doctor Thomas.

This time, Gabriel stared at her with a venomous gleam in his eyes. His face was wet, but he was no longer crying. His nostrils flared as he pulled himself forward against the restraints.

"Answer the question, Mr. Ellis," Doctor Thomas demanded.

When Gabriel spit on the ground at her feet, she took a step away and turned to Agent Grobeck. "I think we're done here."

Gabriel turned to his wife, fresh tears glistening on his cheeks. "Zo, I love you. I love you so much."

Unable to watch another second, Eve ran out the room and down the hallway to the bathroom. She dropped onto her knees at the toilet, gripped both sides of the bowl, and vomited.

She wondered if she'd ever be okay again. Would she ever be able to unsee that terrified, defeated look on Zoey's face again? Would she ever be able to forget the agonizing cries of Gabriel trying to protect his wife? She vomited again, her body convulsing and her chest burning as all her lunch seemed to come up at once.

"Eve?" Niles said. He knelt and touched her gently. "Eve, are you all right?"

"I did this to them. I got them involved. I called them. I never—I never should've gotten them involved." She pulled at her hair and rocked back and forth.

Niles wiped her mouth with a tissue and flushed the toilet. "Listen, this isn't your fault. SPI did this. Not you."

"If I'd never called them—"

"Eve, you have to pull yourself together. We're going to find them. Remember the plan," he said, his palms cradling her face. "You can't afford to fall apart right now. They need you. We need you."

"What they've done to her, Niles. To Gabe," said Eve, shaking her head and sobbing. "What they've done. I can't...I can't undo it. Oh, God. I can't fix it."

He sighed and stood, pulling her up with him. He blotted her wet cheeks. "No, you can't undo it. But you can stop it. You can save them."

"Turn it off," said Eve, emerging from the bathroom with Niles beside her. "Turn it off, now."

Agent Yu closed the video and shut down the computer. A triumphant smile settled on her face. "I got him."

"Liv, what the hell was that?" Ian Yu asked, gaping at his sister. "What is going on?"

When she looked at him, her expression went from satisfied to apologetic in an instant. "I need to explain something—"

He stood. "No, what was—"

"Look, you two can finish this tender family moment later," said Eve. "Sit down, Ian."

He continued staring at his sister and didn't move.

"I said sit."

With a wary glance at Eve, he sat.

"All right," she said, looking at Agent Yu. "You're going to take us to AJ tonight, and you're going to get me that Galena address tonight. We're not waiting until tomorrow."

Not wasting another minute, she laid out a plan.

"Everyone has their assignment and deadline. Are there any questions?" She turned to Samuel and Niles. "Sam, you stay and don't let little Ian out of your sight. Meanwhile, keep your cell phone on you in case I need you. Niles, I'm coming with you and Agent Yu to the Chicago facility to get the Galena address. Once I have it, I'll leave you with her. Get AJ and make Agent Yu provide you the file. Do whatever it takes, and don't let her out of your sight. If she tries anything, shoot her. Kill her if you need to. I don't care. But not before you have the file and AJ. Got it?"

"Yeah." For the first time that evening, he looked worried. "I got it."

"Good. Ian, hand me that pack and the flash drive from Olivia's computer," said Eve.

She pulled her laptop from the backpack, inserted the flash drive, and saved the clip of the torture. As a backup, she saved a copy on the hard drive of the computer. Then, she opened up her email, found the email addresses of the journalist contacts Zoey had provided, the journalists who had covered her story. She pulled out the business card from Landrien Moriset.

Eve typed up a brief email that concluded with, "Can you run this tonight?" Giving a deep sigh, she cc'd Landrien, Zoey's journalist contacts, and some local news reporters. She hit send and closed the laptop.

"Sam, check social media and the news outlets, and keep the TV on. If we're lucky, TV news networks might run that video this evening. Text me to let me know if the networks are showing it. It's a shot in the dark, but let's keep our fingers crossed."

"I hope you're right," he said.

Eve glimpsed the clock on the wall—5:50pm—and turned to Agent Yu and Niles. "All right, let's go." She handed him the flash drive. "Hang on to that."

Agent Yu reached for her crutches and rose. As she approached Niles and Eve, Ian stirred.

"Liv? You can't leave me here," he said in a small voice, his eyes darting from Samuel to his sister.

She stopped but didn't turn to her brother. "Just do as he says. This'll all be over in a few hours."

"But—"

She caught Samuel's gaze. "Please don't hurt him."

He glared at her. "I'm not like you."

Niles scoffed at Samuel. "Well, you did try to kill Eve."

"What?" asked Agent Yu, looking from Niles to Eve.

Eve frowned. "None of your business. Let's go."

With a look of increased concern, Agent Yu cast a glance at her brother. As she exited the apartment, Niles and Eve faded and followed behind her.

14

The setting sun cast a warm glow over the warehouse and the vacant parking lot. Squatting behind a bush, Eve peeked over the shrubbery to check that no one was near the entrance. After releasing some tension, she held up the cell phone to check for her reflection, happy to see nothing there other than the trees across the street and the cars behind her. *All right. You got this.*

She pocketed the phone and set off toward the entrance of the warehouse building.

There was a small box next to the door handle. She stared at the touchscreen on the box. As she placed her palm flat against the box, it lit up and two words appeared—"Not Recognized."

At first, she groaned and stomped her feet in frustration. But as soon as the anger swept over her, it was replaced by an overpowering calm and confidence she'd never felt before. *Just hop, silly. Why are you even tripping over this box?*

"Okay," she mumbled, closing her eyes for a moment and concentrating as she'd done before when practicing with Niles. *I need to get in.* She repeated this a few times, and just as she was about to give up, there was a familiar tug at her belly button.

When she opened her eyes, she peered down the long hallway illuminated by a dim strip of light. As far as she could see, she was the only soul nearby. The place stunk of bleach, and she wasn't sure if it was the dingy navy-blue carpet or the beige walls, but something about the place felt outdated and old. It reminded her of the place where she'd been trapped so many months before. Indeed, the hallway was indistinguishable from the long hallways she'd been led through during her captivity. The stale odor, the coldness, the damp floor of her room, the four walls that seemed to be constantly closing in, suffocating her. It was all too familiar.

Several moments passed before she realized she was leaning against the wall and covering her mouth, struggling to keep from vomiting. She bent over and dry heaved, sinking to the floor. As she brought her hand up to cover her mouth, she noticed her hand was visible and appeared to be floating in the air all by itself.

The fade is wearing off. Shit.

Panicking, she tried to steady herself and stand upright. She rested against the wall, her heart racing. The dry heaving lessened second by second, but her head was spinning. *Keep it together. You have to keep it together.* She stood there for a moment until the heaving ceased, and her hand faded. "You can do this," she whispered.

Taking deep breaths and counting one to ten, Eve headed out.

She stopped in front of a steel door at the end of the hall and looked at the small box. Once more, she closed her eyes and went into her mind until she felt the tingle in her stomach.

When she opened her eyes, she was standing in the middle of yet another long hallway. *All these fucking hallways.*

"Go to the northern-most wing on the first floor," she whispered, recalling Agent Yu's directions. *Room C120.* She began walking, noting the room numbers. C101, C103, C115. She stopped for a moment.

There were two guards standing in front of a door with a tiny window at the end of the hallway.

Drawing closer, she noticed the men wore belts around their waists, a GLOCK and a Taser in each belt. Her eyes focused on the batons they were holding. She walked as lightly as possible, holding her breath as she got closer to them. The larger guard was playing a game on his cell phone, while the shorter guard seemed to be lost in his thoughts as his feet tapped against the floor.

Barely breathing, she leaned between them and peeked through the window. In the empty room, sat a man strapped to a metal chair with his head hanging past his shoulders. He appeared to be asleep. The setting looked the same as what she'd seen on the recording. She tried not to recall the sound of Gabriel begging Agent Grobeck not to hurt Zoey. But she couldn't block it out. Something akin to fury rose within her as she stood there, staring at Gabriel.

A movement from one of the guards startled her, and she covered her mouth. To her relief, they hadn't detected her presence. *Get it together, Eve.* Reminded of her objective, she backed away, pulled the gun from her pocket, and examined it. The silencer was on properly, but she knew it would still make enough noise to draw attention. She had to be quick. She turned off the safety, looked at the two guards, and inhaled. *Here we go.*

In an instant, she let off two bullets into the feet of the taller guard, one bullet for each foot. He tumbled forward; his mouth opened in a silent scream before he hit the ground. The carpeted floor muted the sound of his fall. As he gripped his wounded feet, she snatched his gun and tossed it out of reach. The smaller guard's head swiveled around, searching for the assailant, and his hand went to his waistband. When she fired two shots into his feet, he collapsed next to his partner.

She seized their weapons as the men thrashed and convulsed. "Shut up!" she whispered, afraid the noise would draw unwanted attention.

To control them, she used the Taser on the men. The smaller guard fell unconscious after a few seconds, while the other guard twisted in pain, trying to pull out the Taser clamps. The moment he began to scream, she delivered a forceful kick to his head, and he moved no more.

Heart racing and palms sweaty, she switched on the safety locks on the guns and stuffed them inside her backpack. She picked up the now heavy bag and slung it over her shoulder. "At least the fade is holding up," she muttered when she didn't see her reflection in the window. She glanced at the camera over the door.

When she looked down, she was surprised to find no box next to the door. She turned the knob, and the door creaked open. The room smelled of sweat and something metallic. Blood.

As she walked in, she saw her own fragile body naked and curled up on the floor, jerking about as Agent Grobeck Tasered her. She inhaled and exhaled. *Keep it together.* There was no time to waste.

She ran to Gabriel, who was asleep, his snoring low and ragged. He reeked.

"Gabe?" she whispered, making herself visible.

He didn't stir.

She slapped his face and cast an anxious glance over her shoulder. "Wake up," she said, slapping him again.

He looked at her, and she froze, taken aback by his weary eyes. He looked nothing like the Gabriel she'd seen mere days ago. Where was the sparkle she'd always seen in his eyes? She remembered what her mother looked like during the last months of chemotherapy, how her mother had withered away, how her eyes sunk in and lost their light. In the end, Marie Cooper had transformed into a skeletal shadow of her former self. Gabriel's eyes similarly had lost their light.

"We have to hurry, Gabe." She bent and untied the four ropes.

"You're not here." His words were slurred and his voice barely audible.

"Yes, I am," she said, untying the last rope and extending her hand so that he could lift himself up. "We need to find Zoey and get out of this place. Come on." She grabbed his thin arm and pulled him up. It was easier than it should have been.

His knees shook, and he swayed like a drunk. "This isn't a dream?" he whispered, gazing at her.

The rotten smell of his breath almost knocked her off balance. Cringing, she covered her nose. He stumbled, but she caught him before he fell.

"You're really here?"

"Yes. I'm here. Now stand up."

With some fumbles and his arms extended, he stood upright at last.

She handed him a Taser and a weapon. "Don't hesitate to use them. Let's get Zoey."

The hallway was still empty and quiet. They stepped over the two unconscious guards, and Gabriel stared at them. Eve noticed that rage seemed to bring back some of the light in his eyes.

"They're the ones. The ones who hurt her." His voice was cold enough to freeze boiling water.

"You don't know that. There are lots of guards here, I'm sure—"

"Yes, I do. The agent...he..."

"Agent Grobeck made you watch them beat her?"

No sooner than the words were out of Eve's mouth, Gabriel let off two bullets, one in the chest of each guard.

Covering her mouth, she looked away. "Let's go," she said, wishing she could unsee what had just happened.

He lowered the gun and spat on them.

"Gabe," she said, tugging his arm. "We need to go."

Nodding absently, he tore his attention away from the dead guards and followed her.

They headed into the hallway, but the sound of a woman's screams cut through the quiet and halted them before they'd gone more than a few feet.

"Zoey?" he called, going to the steel door and fumbling with the knob. The door didn't budge. "Zo?"

Eve pushed him aside and turned the knob. Taking a deep breath, she applied as much force as she could. It swung open and clanged against the wall.

"How did you—"

"Not now, Gabe," she replied, darting inside the room.

Zoey was sitting tied to a metal chair in the middle of an empty room, asleep and thrashing about.

"Zoey, wake up. You hear me?" said Eve, trying frantically to untie the ropes around her wrists and ankles. "Wake up."

Gabriel, all the while, stood at the door and looked on in silence.

"Don't just stand there, Gabe! Help me," she hollered, trying to work out the knots in the rope as Zoey stirred and mumbled something incoherent.

Gabriel appeared to be frozen in shock.

"It's me, Zoey. Just hold still, so I can undo these ropes," she said, pulling at the final knot.

"What's going on?" Zoey mumbled, opening her eyes. She looked at Eve as the rope dropped to the floor.

Eve helped her stand, and she looked like she might fall

for a moment. Then, she rushed into the arms of Gabriel, and the two sobbed uncontrollably.

They threw their arms around Eve, who was staring at the door. At any moment, guards would come rushing into the room. "Not now. We need to go," she yelled, pulling them apart and pushing the extra Taser into Zoey's hand.

Footsteps and voices came from the hallway. Knowing they were mere seconds from being discovered and killed, Eve brought her arms around them and shut her eyes. She concentrated on an image of Agent Yu's living room, focusing so hard that it made her head ache. *Please. Please. Work. This has to work.*

The voices from the hallway grew closer and louder.

She felt a tug somewhere deep in her stomach, and the voices became fainter until she could no longer hear them.

In the next moment, she found herself staring into Samuel's eyes. She almost collapsed in relief. Trembling, she released Zoey and Gabriel.

"We're safe now," she said, stumbling and falling against the comfy chair. She waited for the walls to stop spinning. "Every time I do that it feels like being held under water."

"Are you all right?" asked Samuel.

"I'm fine," she breathed. "What time is it?"

"About twenty-five minutes after eight. Have you heard from Niles?"

She shook her head. "No. That means he's doing fine, too. We have less than half an hour until we meet him at the facility." She looked at Gabriel and Zoey.

"Where are we?" asked Gabriel.

"At Agent Yu's house."

"Agent Yu?" said Gabriel. "This is her apartment?"

"Yes. I had Sam—he's a former colleague of mine at SPI—stationed here to watch over Agent Yu's brother. I'll explain later."

They looked at the man on the sofa.

"He looks just like her," said Gabriel, scowling and advancing toward Ian who retreated in fear.

Eve stepped in front of him. "Gabe. Ian is innocent in all of this."

"His sister did this to me. She was there. She helped them...do things to me."

His eyes were fixed on Ian as he spoke. Eve saw in his eyes the same rage she'd seen in the hallway with the guards. She put her hand against his chest. "I know, Gabe." She looked over his shoulder at Zoey who seemed to be in a state of stunned silence. "I'm so sorry this happened to you. I should've never involved you and Zoey."

"They wanted you. Just you," said Zoey, her voice hoarse.

"I know."

"The Agent—she said your friend Mauricio did this. That he tipped her off."

Eve frowned and nodded. "He gave us to them. In exchange for his freedom, so he could get back to his family."

"The *Post* has published the video," shouted Samuel, jumping up and startling everyone. He was on his feet at the bar and running his finger over the touchscreen of the laptop. "They linked it to the previous article about the faders and the black sites."

Eve looked at the clock on the wall. "Any news stations running it on TV?" She spun around, reached for the television remote control on the coffee table, and flipped through the news channel apps. She clicked on the *CNN* icon and turned up the volume. "They're not running it yet. Let me check something," she said, hurrying to the computer. "Nothing on their website either. I didn't expect them to run it so fast, to be honest. But I had to try. They may run it days from now, who knows."

Meanwhile, Samuel took the remote and tried the other

news apps. "Nothing so far on any other news channels."

"It's all right." Eve hit play on the video from the *Post's* website. As soon as it started playing, Eve saw Zoey and Gabriel clasp hands and turn away. She lowered the volume and turned the computer screen away from them.

An apologetic look clouded his face when Zoey and Gabriel looked from him to Eve.

"This was part of your plan?" Gabriel asked Eve. "To show the world what they did to us?"

Just as she rose to go to them, her phone buzzed and vibrated inside her jacket pocket. "It's a message from Niles," she said. "It's done. He has the file and AJ."

"Are we really doing this? Is it going to work?" Samuel looked worried. "Is it going to work?"

She smiled and stuffed the phone inside her pocket. "It is, Sam."

"Eve," said Zoey. "Is this part of your plan? The video?" She pointed at the television.

Eve turned to her and Gabriel. "Agent Yu showed us what they did to you. She recorded this. I didn't want them to get away with it, so I sent it to your media contacts. I'm sorry you have to see it, and I wish I could've stopped all of this before it happened. But people need to see what they've done."

Zoey leaned against Eve and cried, sniffling and coughing. As she held Zoey, she stared at Gabriel. She could see he was trying to be strong for them.

"I don't mean to interrupt," said Samuel. "But we don't have a lot of time, Eve. We have to get to Niles."

Although she didn't want to let go, she released Zoey. She cleared her throat and wiped her own wet cheeks. "There's a shower past the kitchen. Get cleaned up and, afterward, I'll tell you everything. I promise. This is almost over."

"Eve," said Samuel, and they all turned to him. "Can I also suggest a slight change to the plan?"

She regarded him with curiosity. "I'm listening."

He held up a tiny black hairpin and smiled. "I hope you're okay with becoming a YouTube celebrity."

Eve studied the outside of the building where she'd been held and tortured not long ago. From behind an azalea bush alongside a boarded-up and abandoned house, she watched several men in military fatigues make their way to the side entrance of the facility. The men's weapons weren't drawn, and they weren't running. If they were responding to the presence of Niles and the escape of AJ, they seemed rather calm.

She adjusted the hairpin to make sure it could capture everything in front of her.

"What's your game plan for getting in?" asked Samuel, his voice loud and piercing through the earplug.

She wiggled the wireless earplug in her left ear and pulled the cell phone from her pocket to turn the volume down. "You don't have to yell. This thing is loud enough in my ear. Can you see everything clearly?"

"I can see. You know we're way outgunned, right?"

"Yeah, but I don't think Niles and the others have been detected. So that's good. Also, thanks for the idea about using the hairpin Agent Yu left behind."

"You're welcome."

She smiled. "Don't be smug. Are you live-streaming this right now?"

"Yeah, from your YouTube account." He paused. "Eve, are you sure about this? There are at least a dozen men over there, and who knows how many more inside already. It's suicidal."

She held up her hand to quiet him. "I know. Just give me a minute." She whipped out the cell phone and opened her email.

"What are you doing?" asked Samuel.

She clicked "reply all" to the email she'd sent to the press contacts, typed in the address of the facility, and hit send. She figured she had a half-hour at best before press began to show up at the location. "All right. I'm going in."

After fading, she sprinted across the street to the building, repeating the room number Niles had texted to her. Room A3330. Room A3330. *I got this. I got this.*

Before she realized it, she was standing inside an office and tripping to avoid running into a solid wall. Lightheaded, she held her arms out to balance herself. *Okay...accidentally teleporting wasn't part of the plan.*

"Eve, what happened? Are you already in the room?" Samuel's voice came through the earplug.

She focused her eyes and waved her hand in front of her face. *Good. At least the fade's still working.*

As she turned around to take in the room, a lump settled in her throat. Doctor Thomas and Agent Grobeck were standing behind a desk, and a middle-aged man with gray-streaked dark hair lingered next to them.

"Did you hear something?" asked the man.

Doctor Thomas and Agent Grobeck looked around and shook their heads.

Taking a step back, Eve hit a wall. Someone gasped.

When she turned around, her face was inches away from AJ's bruised face. Eve moved aside, watching AJ blink and peer around in confusion. Standing next to AJ, Niles had a gun pointed at Agent Yu and another pointed at the trio around the desk. Eve's eyebrows went up as her gaze swept over the guns and his determined face. *Damn, Niles. Impressive.*

Turning to Agent Grobeck and Doctor Thomas, Eve fixed her attention on the strange man. He casually stroked his well-groomed beard. Something about that mannerism made a light bulb flicker on in her mind. Indeed, the déjà vu of the scene knocked the wind out of her, and she covered her mouth to silence her panicked breathing.

"Eve? What the hell...?" AJ exclaimed, ogling at her.

Agent Grobeck and Doctor Thomas gasped.

"Fuck. The fade wore off. I'll explain later," Eve replied. She reached for the gun in her pocket, all the while keeping her attention on Agent Grobeck and his colleagues. To her surprise, neither he nor his two colleagues were armed. Rather, they were standing close together at the desk. *Like cornered dogs.* Niles and AJ had caught them off guard, she surmised. A smile pursed her lips as she pointed the gun at Agent Grobeck. "So, who's your friend?"

"This is Charlie Ford," said Doctor Thomas.

"I wasn't talking to you, Doctor." Eve moved the gun to the left a few inches to point it at the woman. "But thank you for the lovely video. It helped speed things along. Now we have the list of trained faders, the Special Project files, and your little torture video has gone viral. It'll be playing on every single news station."

"You have no idea what you've done, Miss Cooper," said Charlie Ford.

Ignoring him, she kept her eyes locked on Agent Grobeck and Doctor Thomas. "It's over, at least for you two," she added, before shifting her gaze to the other man. "As for you, I don't know who you are, and I don't care."

Agent Grobeck shook his head. "You foolish girl."

"The whole country knows who you are, you and Doctor Thomas. Everyone with an internet connection and a Twitter account has seen what you did to Zoey and Gabriel Ellis. People *saw* it. You know, there's just something about seeing a person tortured. Folks don't forget that kind of shit. Not to mention the optics of a couple of sadistic white people torturing two defenseless black people." She smirked, bringing the gun closer to his head. "You're pariahs now. You won't be able to go anywhere without people seeing you for the monsters you are. How does it feel?"

He looked at her with a hint of admiration in his eyes. "While what you've managed to do is impressive, don't start thinking you're smarter than you actually are. You may have been clever enough to elude us since Philadelphia, but you're not that clever. Do you think we didn't have a contingency plan in the event of your escape? Do you think we were unprepared for that? I have to give Olivia credit. She read you well."

Eve looked over her shoulder at Agent Yu.

"SPI's decision not to pursue you right away was her idea. The hope, as Olivia put it, was that you would gather the other faders and help them hone their skills. Sure, you might attack SPI in your desperation to stay free. But it was a risk we accepted. We knew we were ill-equipped to train your kind, and with the program being so new, we had no elder pool of faders to enlist as trainers. If we could put you in a position to train other faders, even outside the agency, and then bring you in—"

Eve snickered. "That's the dumbest idea."

"I know. It wasn't the smartest. I didn't say it was my idea," he retorted.

Agent Yu glowered at him.

"But we were desperate, you see. The potential that your kind offered to our efforts....We had to exhaust every option."

"What about the flash drives? Why did you send us searching for them?" Eve asked.

He sighed. "Stopping the dissemination of the data on those drives, that data from our experimental attempts to replicate the ability, is crucial."

"So you lost a bunch of your own research, and we were expected to do damage control?"

"You could say that. We set out to reacquire those drives before they could fall into the hands of terrorists."

"I'm afraid that ship likely has already sailed," said Doctor Thomas.

Agent Grobeck went on. "When we failed to recover Salazar's drive, I knew matters had already gone beyond our control. I realized then that we needed to evolve. We'd been playing offense for so long that we'd forgotten the importance of defense. We needed you and your kind as soldiers, as our first line of defense against those who seek to destroy this country."

"And to that end, you thought torturing us would encourage what...loyalty?" Eve replied. "How stupid are you people?"

"It was a short-sighted strategy, I admit," he said, shrugging. "As you know, we tried softer methods. But apparently a generous salary, excellent health coverage, a 401k, and paid vacation wasn't enough for you and your peers."

Eve rolled her eyes.

"You really are an entitled generation," Doctor Thomas replied.

"Right, we totally turned all that down because we're entitled. Not because we have, say...a conscience, a moral compass."

Doctor Thomas chuckled and stared at Eve with the look of a disappointed mother.

"Anyway," said Eve, ignoring the woman and looking at Agent Grobeck. "You mentioned the drives contain information about how to replicate the ability. So by 'evolve' you mean make more of us, create your own enhanced military of people like us so we can continue doing your dirty work."

Agent Grobeck's head tilted to the right, and he smiled.

"We were initially hoping to prevent exactly that by stopping the trade of the information on those drives. But you've unfortunately left us with no other choice, Miss Cooper," said Charlie, placing his hand on Agent Grobeck's shoulder to silence him. "Let me give you some background here that David has neglected. SPI discovered those like you—the ones you call 'faders'—several years ago when there was an incident in a small town in Alberta."

"Canada?"

"Yes, Miss Cooper. In that small town, an ordinary family man walked into his neighborhood grocery store, just as he did every Sunday afternoon, to shop for the next week. But everything changed this Sunday afternoon in October. From the moment he entered the store, he became invisible, unseen. He didn't realize this, of course. And when another shopper bumped into him and fell, naturally he bent to help her up. Not surprisingly, the woman screamed and caused quite a racket when this invisible man grabbed her hand. The man apologized profusely and tried to help the woman up, but she kept screaming and flailing about until she'd drawn a sizable crowd in the store. Unbeknownst to the man, he began 'flickering'—coming in and out of sight second by second—and this rather terrified the crowd as you can imagine. They screamed and threw things at him, forced him to flee from the store and speed off in his minivan.

"Of course, this story made the local news, and SPI took notice. As an agent at SPI at the time, I went to that town, spoke with Canadian intelligence, and viewed the security camera footage that had been shown on the local news corroborating the townsfolks' story.

"When Canadian intelligence and our agency located the man, which didn't take long, he was brought in and quarantined. Since he was American, originally from Florida, he was turned over to us. He was the first...that we discovered anyway. Through my leadership, SPI studied the man and began to watch for other extraordinary incidents in other towns and cities. The agency began searching for other people like this man."

"Dude, have you ever considered doing audiobooks? Because that was riveting," AJ quipped.

Eve glared at him. "So a normal man trying to live a normal life had some weird shit happen to him one day. And now he's dead. Because of you people."

"Dead?" said Doctor Thomas.

Eve regarded her with increasing venom. "Forest Sherman deserves justice, and I'm going to make sure he gets it."

"Ah," Charlie replied. "Please let me clarify, Miss Cooper. This was before Mr. Sherman. You know this man as Mauricio Candela. He came to work for SPI shortly after the incident."

"Why is there no record of him in our personnel files?" Agent Yu interrupted, and everyone turned to her. "Or in any of our files, actually. The records show Forest Sherman as the first one of them we found."

"Because Mr. Candela's employment with us was not what you'd call 'official'," said Charlie. "For our purposes, he was a ghost and of no concern to you."

Agent Yu stepped forward, but AJ held her back. "Are you serious? I was second in command over the development of the project—"

"Keyword: second. I was in charge of matters relating to these people. And David was hired to replace me as lead. As such, Mr. Candela was none of your concern, Agent."

Eve looked between an incensed Agent Yu and an extremely smug Charlie Ford. For a brief moment, she sympathized with the agent.

"Mauricio was just the beginning. When Charlie found Forest Sherman in Louisiana a year later, I thought we might be able to use him to find out more about the ability, where it comes from. That if we ran enough tests on both of the men, we could get to some answers. But Mr. Sherman was less resilient than Mr. Candela. We went too hard on Mr. Sherman. His death was a major setback," Doctor Thomas chimed in, throwing a cautious glance at her colleagues.

Charlie cleared his throat. "Afterward, SPI continued locating subjects with this extraordinary ability and spent months observing them from a distance, to no avail. Meanwhile, I transitioned out of SPI and Agent Grobeck took the reins. Eventually and thanks to Agent Yu's guidance, he decided to deploy the recruiting and training program that you became part of last year, Miss Cooper. This would enable SPI to bring more of those with abilities under our control so that we could learn about you."

"Hold up. If you don't work at SPI anymore, what the hell are you doing here now?" asked Eve.

"I'm the CEO and founder of FordTech International, a security consulting firm. Agent Grobeck enlisted my company's help in studying the trainees. Unfortunately, just before your training began, FordTech was breached. One of our own employees decided it would be worthwhile to sell to Salazar and our other competitors the information we had compiled for SPI regarding those with your ability. Somehow, this employee breached all of our safeguards.

"As Agent Grobeck indicated, we never found the perpetrator. The employee was gone before we even noticed the breach. I alerted Agent Grobeck, and he smartly created a set of assignments for the operative trainees. You would be responsible for retrieving the information from our competitors and other illegal purchasers. We believed others would use the information to create—or, at the very least, gather—individuals like you and use these enhanced individuals for God knows what purposes. We at least needed to try to stop that from happening.

"With someone like you on board, we were hopeful. We needed a person with abilities who could lead the others, teach them. We had high hopes, until your resignation. And then Samuel Kim resigned not long after. I assumed all was lost at that point. But Agent Grobeck refused to give up. He reverted to old methods, methods we had abandoned after Mr. Sherman, for obvious reasons. I was intrigued to learn that during interrogation you responded a lot like Mr. Sherman. Your blood pressure was not as elevated after a round of shocks. Your brain wave patterns showed little change during questioning and conditioning. And you were tough. All reports indicated you were special.

"At any rate, we don't know how many flash drives are out there. But we knew people like you were the only hope for getting them and shutting down the black market. Unlike me, Agent Grobeck still had a slight bit of hope that we could retrieve the drives and stop the spread of the information.

"And we were making progress until you leaked to the media. Anyone who didn't know we were actively searching for and retrieving the stolen information now knows, including the illegal purchasers. You've shown them our hand, Miss Cooper. You've effectively undone this whole operation and put everything and every person in this country, on this planet, in great peril. You've put us all at the mercy of people who will stop at nothing for money, power, or revenge."

Eve snorted, looking at Charlie, Agent Grobeck, and Doctor Thomas. "You mean people like you."

"If you think we're the ones you should be worried about, you really are naive," said Charlie. He looked disappointed with her.

Agent Grobeck shot her an annoyed look. "We're stuck playing defense against terrorists now, thanks to you."

Her mind looped and turned, digesting all that she'd heard from them. Then, it grabbed onto the one thing that puzzled her most. "But Mauricio...if he was working for you, why did he help me escape?"

"Mauricio's only job was to remain a ghost and keep an eye on your kind. See, I may be in the minority here, but I never trusted you or any other faders," said Agent Grobeck, sneering. "If it weren't for the drives, I'd be ready to put your kind down. You're a threat to all of us."

"Where is Mauricio now?" she asked through clenched teeth.

Agent Grobeck shrugged.

Confusion mixed with indignation rushed through Eve, filling her veins, as she stared at him. Without trying, she vanished, teleported several feet forward, appeared again, and clasped her hands around Agent Grobeck's beefy neck. His eyes widened, and a look of terror clouded his face for the first time.

But the fearful look was gone in an instant and replaced with a smile. When Eve squeezed, he coughed, and the fearful look returned. He stared at her with petrified eyes as his hands grasped her wrists, trying but unable to detach her grip.

"How...?" he mouthed.

"Where is he?"

"I don't know," Agent Grobeck wheezed, struggling to free himself from her.

She squeezed harder.

"I swear I don't know. He's been AWOL since you escaped," he managed.

"We assumed he was helping you," said Charlie. "But we've had no luck locating him."

Eve shot a glance at Agent Yu who suddenly wore a pleased expression. "Agent Yu made a deal with him."

He looked at his subordinate, and his expression went from surprised to hostile.

Eve grinned, looking at Agent Yu with deep admiration. She released him.

"How are you able to...your strength...how...?" he said, rubbing his neck.

"I'm pretty sure she's the smartest person in this room." Eve gestured toward Agent Yu but kept her eyes on Agent Grobeck. "Now I can see why she set you up." From the corner of her eye, she saw the perturbed looks on the faces of Charlie Ford and Doctor Thomas.

A raucous, guttural sound came out of nowhere, and her chest was heaving in and out, causing pain in her upper abdomen. Laughter.

Eve was laughing harder than she'd ever laughed. She laughed so much that she bent over and held her thighs to catch her breath. "You people are the worst." She laughed so hard she didn't hear the noise outside the room. The noise of boots against the floor.

AJ grasped Eve's arm and pulled her away. "We need to fade before the cops get here, Eve."

Eve glanced at Agent Yu. She'd stepped aside once AJ released her and was watching her boss with a look of profound delight.

Charlie sat behind the desk, while Agent Grobeck and Doctor Thomas remained standing. Warily, they stared at the door.

Observing their anxiousness, Eve smiled with satisfaction and folded her arms across her chest.

"Eve," AJ said, tugging at her again. "We need to go."

She turned to Niles and AJ, grasping their hands as relief swept over her. "It's finally over."

"I wish it was, Miss Cooper," said Charlie, buttoning his blazer. "For your sake and all of ours, I wish it were. Because of your actions, the world is going to look quite different soon, and I'm afraid there's nothing men like me can do about it now."

As she stared at him, she saw something new in his eyes. Fear. "There was never anything men like you could do about it. That's why you beat us, imprisoned us...killed us. Because you couldn't control us," she said, smiling. "The world doesn't belong to you. Not anymore."

Holding hands, she and her friends faded.

As they hurried away from the building, Eve felt as though she was walking in a daze, as if she'd been hit over the head. Charlie's last words rang in her ears.

"Eve?" said Niles. "Where're Sam and the others?"

They stopped next to the boarded-up greystone across the street from the SPI facility. Absently, she removed the hairpin from her hair. Before she turned it off, she said, "Sam, get Gabe and Zoey and bring them here."

Niles slid the gun into his pocket and stared at her with a quizzical look.

Samuel appeared in front of them, with Gabriel and Zoey standing next to him. She rushed into the arms of Zoey and Gabriel, kissing their faces and hugging them as though she hadn't seen them in ages.

"I wasn't sure if I could do that, Eve. I felt like I was standing in place forever trying to get us here," said Samuel, his breathing labored as though he'd run a marathon. "You and Niles make hopping seem so easy. It's not."

"What's going on? How did he know to—" Niles began.

"Eve used Agent Yu's hairpin recording thing, and I live-streamed the whole showdown," replied Samuel, looking around. "Speaking of...where's Agent Yu?"

Niles pointed at the building. "Back there."

Samuel gaped at Eve and Niles in disbelief. "You let her

go?"

"This wasn't about her," AJ replied.

Samuel groaned but kept quiet.

"Is it over now?" Zoey asked, propped against Eve and observing the chaos across the street.

Like a distant and detached spectator at a movie, Eve watched the activity across the street. The scene in front of the building seemed so far away. "I don't know."

"What about Mauricio? Do they know where he is?" asked Gabriel.

She shook her head. "There's a silver lining, though. They don't seem to know about our abilities beyond the fading."

"Except for Agent Yu. She said at her apartment that she knew Forest Sherman could do other things," said Niles.

Eve nodded. "But that she kept it to herself because she feared what Grobeck and Doctor Thomas would do. They still have no idea we're capable of more than just fading. I hate to admit it, but she may have saved us. I suppose she has some sort of moral code. Warped as it may be."

"Well, they know that you're Wonder Woman strong now," AJ remarked, grinning. "I have to admit watching you almost choke out that psycho was the most satisfying moment of this whole night."

Eve flushed bright red.

"So, where to now?" asked Niles.

Eve looked at the building. The crowd had begun to disperse, and the cop cars were departing. A dozen individuals in agent uniforms hung back and lingered outside the building. The last media crews were leaving. Within minutes, the parking lot was vacant.

"I mean, we can go pretty much anywhere," said Samuel.

She thought about the money in her backpack and dug her hands inside her jeans pocket. When she felt a hard piece of paper in her pocket, she pulled it out. A business card from

Moriset & Granger, LLP. She glanced at Gabriel and Zoey and stuffed the card in her pocket. "Mr. Pebbles? Where is he?"

"We left him with our neighbor again. They love him. He's fine," Zoey answered.

Eve exhaled.

"Okay, so what's the plan?" asked AJ, growing impatient. "I'm ready to get far away from here."

"Well, I say we go pick up Mr. Pebbles and head somewhere that's warm in late January. An island in the Caribbean," Eve suggested. She thought about the house in Indiana. It was time for her to do what she should've done years ago. "But first, I need to make a stop in Indiana. There's something there that belongs to me."

"So it looks like the itinerary is Chicago, then Indiana, then the Caribbean?" Niles grinned.

AJ smiled. "Sounds fucking fantastic to me. I hear good things about Aruba."

"Then that settles it," said Eve. "Come on."

They all linked hands, and when Eve closed her eyes, she felt that familiar tug in her stomach.

EPILOGUE

Mauricio turned over and rubbed sleep from his eyes. Stretching and yawning, he gazed around the large room and looked at the vaulted ceiling. He rolled out of bed, still wearing his jeans and sweater from the previous night, empty bottles of cheap wine strewn about the floor.

As he squatted to collect the bottles, he cried out in pain and pressed his palm against his forehead. It throbbed as though he'd been repeatedly punched in the face. *"¡Coño!"*

Dropping to the floor, he held his palm firmly against his forehead and massaged it in a futile effort to soothe the pain. He panted, and tears threatened to pour down his face.

With scrunched up lips and a look of determination, he brought himself to his feet and stood. He wouldn't give in again. He promised himself he wouldn't have another drink to block out the images of Zoey Ellis' bruised body. He wouldn't sleep away another day trying to silence the shrill screams of these innocent people he'd led into the web of SPI, all for the sake of securing his own freedom.

But what was this? Was this freedom, being cooped up in a hotel room away from home and unable to be with his family? What had his betrayal purchased but a flimsy, temporary freedom that all ended when Eve's video aired and

Charlie Ford uttered his name? He promised himself he wouldn't sleep away another day trying to replay all the ways things had gone wrong. Dwelling on the "what ifs," "shouldas," and "couldas" was nothing more than an exercise in masochism.

Even as he promised he'd stop wallowing in self-pity and bygone possibilities, he knew he'd break this promise in a matter of hours. Just as he'd done yesterday and the day before that and the day before that.

He squatted and scooped up bottle after bottle, depositing each in the trash. By the time he'd cleared all the bottles off the floor, each of the three trash bins in the room was full.

Next, he dragged himself to the tiny bathroom and went straight to the shower. He turned on the cold water. His body shivered violently as the frigid water hit him, but he was glad for the distraction from his miserable thoughts.

He wasn't sure how long he stood under the water, but he stepped out when he heard the phone ring. Throwing a towel around his waist and still dripping wet, he ran to grab the phone from the nightstand. It stopped ringing just as he reached it. It was probably the hotel's receptionists, he figured. It couldn't be anybody else he knew because he'd dropped completely off the map.

He was safe. Finally.

Sitting on the bed, he looked at his briefcase that contained around five thousand dollars or, as Olivia Yu had referred to it, "get lost money." It wouldn't last him long in London. He needed a plan.

A knock came at the door, and he hopped up like a man on fire.

He waited to hear "Housekeeping," but the word never came. Silence followed and then another knock.

"No. It's not possible. I covered all my tracks."

When another knock came, he cautiously approached the

door and looked through the peephole. No one was there. Another knock. He pressed his eye against the peephole. Still, no one was there.

"Am I going crazy? Or..." He opened the door but left the chain up. "Who's there?"

"Mr. Candela, may I have a word?" said a man he couldn't see.

Mauricio stayed quiet, frozen still. How had they found him? He'd done everything to stay hidden.

"My name is Orson Remington III. I'm like you," the man whispered in a thick English accent.

Mauricio could smell mint on his breath. He was leaning in close. "Wait, that name rings a bell. You're not with SPI?"

"If I may have a word, I can explain."

Hesitantly, he undid the chain and opened the door wider. Although he couldn't see him, he felt the man pass by and enter the room. Casting a final glance at the hallway to ensure nobody else was there, Mauricio shut the door and locked it.

When he turned around, he was facing a towering and exceedingly well-dressed man with chestnut hair. The man extended his hand, and his eyes lit up with excitement as he smiled. Mauricio looked at the man's hand but didn't shake it.

"Your fear is understandable."

"You say your name is Orson? Where do I know that name from?"

"The papers, I suspect."

Mauricio folded his arms across his chest and regarded him with distrust.

Orson's smile faltered, and he cleared his throat. "I'm an MP."

"Parliament?" Mauricio's eyes widened.

He nodded.

Mauricio's posture stiffened, and he seemed to grow an inch taller as he straightened up and dropped his hands to his sides. "And you're a fader, too? But your country doesn't know. They don't know what you are, do they?"

"I take it you don't read the papers?"

He narrowed his eyes on the man. "What do you want from me?"

"I have a job offer for you?"

"Yeah, been there done that. My answer is no."

"I know all about you, Mauricio Candela. I know about your exploits in the United States with the other fader, Eve Cooper. You two have been doing a lot of PR over the past weeks. And my contact in Chicago told me quite a bit about you."

"Your contact?"

"Yes. Mr. Ford found it necessary after the events of recent to divulge information about you, in hopes that I could assist with locating you. He was under the impression that you'd managed to move your family to England. He's extremely unhappy with you. It's all rather complex and convoluted, but he believes you are an imminent danger to the national security of the States. The Americans, always so worried about bloody terrorism. Nevertheless, it didn't take much to find you once I sniffed around enough. I caught a whiff of you while I was on a business trip in Philadelphia. I ran into a lovely redhead in the restaurant of the hotel you happened to be staying at. I will admit I tried but failed to chat her up—something about fit ginger women is simply irresistible. However, imagine my surprise when I followed her—I was invisible, of course—and saw that she was sharing a hotel room with you and another fit young woman. You, my fellow, are a lucky man."

Mauricio sighed. "Look, I said I'm not inter—"

"I confess I lost your trail a little while after that—had to attend an all-day meeting. Duty calls, you know. But the next thing I know, you turn up on my side of the pond.

McDonald's isn't the best place for healthy eating, and even fugitives should take heed of what they put into their bodies."

"You stalked me?"

"Well, in fact, I was simply passing by the McDonald's next door when I saw you walk out two mornings ago. I followed you up to your room but thought I'd be polite enough to wait for you to arrive at the McDonald's the next morning. But you didn't. And you didn't this morning either. Hence, my untimely visit to your room. From the odor, it's safe to assume that you haven't left this room during the past two days. Or showered, for that matter. Is that so?"

Mauricio didn't nod or offer any response other than a confused stare.

"I understand that those poor chaps on the torture video were acquaintances? Bloody savage Americans. How awful."

Mauricio studied the man's face for any signs of sincere sympathy. "Look, I'm not interested in anything you have to offer me. You can leave now."

"Oh, I think you might be interested in this opportunity. After all, I'm sure you'd like to return to your family," said Orson.

"Forgive me if I'm not in the trusting spirit, but the last time someone offered me a job I didn't apply for, I ended up losing my family. Then, the minute I get back to them, I'm forced to leave again."

"If you don't mind me asking," Orson interjected, "why did you leave them again? Surely you could've stayed with them and kept yourself off the radar, so to speak."

Mauricio glared at him. "How could I remain with them after the whole world learned my name? Where could I hide from SPI, from Ford, with the whole world knowing who I am? Look at how easily you found me."

Orson nodded. "Yes, but lucky for you I'm not here on behalf of SPI or Ford. I'm here because you shouldn't have to hide. My science, research, and development firm hopes to create a world where you never have to fear being a post-human, where you never have to worry about your friends or family being made to suffer because you are different. I'd like for you to work for my firm."

"Post-human?"

Orson came a step closer, and Mauricio could make out the freckles on his nose. "I believe we're the next stage in human evolution. We're what comes after human."

Mauricio shook his head. "We're freaks."

Now Orson looked genuinely sad for a moment. "One day, I hope you realize that's internalized prejudice."

"Whatever. I don't want the job. You can go now," said Mauricio, frowning.

"Are you sure?"

"Yes."

Orson buttoned his blazer jacket. "As you wish." He headed to the door but turned once more. "My brother Cornelius may have another opportunity more suitable for your talents and interests. Here's my card." He reached out to hand him a small business card, but Mauricio didn't take it. Orson, instead, laid the card on the desk. "Whenever you're ready, call that number and leave a message. Meanwhile, I've paid up your room for a month. Cheerio."

Without another word, Orson Remington III disappeared, and the door opened and closed. He was gone.

For two more days, Mauricio didn't leave the room. Instead, he ordered up more food and bottles of wine and drank himself into a stupor. He flipped through the channels on the television, stopping on the *BBC*, where an anchor discussed the details of the Ellis' torture video. The anchor was interviewing a human rights expert about what it meant for the world that faders existed and that the government was willing to torture innocent citizens to find them.

Night had fallen outside, and Mauricio muted the television while he gazed at the London skyline, at the BT tower in the distance. How far he was from home. He thought about his wife and kids. He wondered what it would be like if he could go home to them; if he'd never been pursued by SPI in the first place. If he'd never been born a fader. He didn't dare close his eyes to try to envision this alternate reality. Doing so produced greater despair.

In fact, closing his eyes nowadays only yielded images of Zoey Ellis' tearful face, or images of Gabriel Ellis beaten bloody and strapped to a chair. With those images came the terrible recognition that they may never have endured such torment had he not made a call to Agent Yu. No, he didn't dare close his eyes. He imagined he'd mastered the art of sleeping with his eyes open during the past couple of weeks.

When he looked at the television, he saw Eve's face alongside some of the quotes and headlines from papers that had leaked her story. He wondered if he'd ever be able to look at her in the face again and explain what he'd done or why he'd done it. Would he be able to explain that those blissful days he got to spend with his family again had been worth the cost?

Mauricio fell against the bed and stared at the ceiling. Tears dampened the pillow. Turning over onto his side, he saw the card on the desk. He thought about the man who had visited him, about the offer.

He got up, went to the desk, and looked at the business card for the third time in as many days. Wiping his face, he abruptly picked up the card and headed to the bathroom. He dropped the card in the toilet and stared at it floating in the urine and water.

As he sat on the bed again, he opened another bottle of wine and turned it up. It heated his chest and stirred up a flavor of vomit in his mouth, but he held it in. He increased the volume on the television, thankful that the *BBC* news anchor had moved on to a story about the success of wind energy in northern Europe. He drained the bottle of wine and fell onto his back.

It wasn't long before the vomit flavor returned and rose up his throat. There was no holding it in this time. Mauricio bolted to the bathroom, knelt in front of the toilet, and vomited.

He wasn't sure which was worse—the stench of the urine or the putrid smell of the vomit. The turkey sandwich and potatoes he'd eaten earlier came up and floated in the toilet around the business card. Through the chunks of meat, he could see the name on the card.

Mauricio reached in and retrieved the card. He pulled himself up and went to the sink, where he rinsed off the card and his hands. After splashing water on his face, he lumbered back to the room, found the remote, and turned off the television. His head spinning, he rested one hand against the wall to steady himself.

After composing himself, he picked up the phone and dialed the number on the card. It went straight to voice mail and, at the beep, he said the only words he could manage to say without slurring his speech. "This is Mauricio Candela. I'm ready."

He put the phone on its hook and collapsed onto the bed.

That night Mauricio slept with his eyes closed. That night, he dreamed of everything. He dreamed of his wife and children. He dreamed of Eve.

ACKNOWLEDGMENTS

Special thanks all our friends and fellow book lovers, including Doris Haynes and Maria Bryson, who served as great readers and guides for the development of this story. Thanks to Mary-Theresa Hussey, for her fantastic edits and passion for the characters. We wrote this story because we sought to create a space for unconventional heroes, particularly queer women and people of color, in the fantasy and speculative fiction space. We are grateful for every invisible hero who inspired us to craft this story.

ABOUT THE AUTHORS

Berneta L. Haynes was born and raised in Little Rock, Arkansas but has lived everywhere from Missouri, England, Iowa, Chicago, and Philadelphia. Her first novel, *Landrien Moriset,* debuted in 2015. An environmental attorney and founding editor of Waking Writer, Berneta lives in Atlanta with her partner and co-author, **Lornett B. Vestal**. A Chicago native, Lornett served in the U.S. Navy and traveled the world before attending the University of Chicago. An environmentalist, social worker, and politics junkie, he runs the Evolving Man Project, a website centered on promoting social change through insightful discussion, activism, and idea sharing. *Eve and the Faders* is Lornett's debut novel. They are working on upcoming speculative fiction and blogging joyously.

Official Site: www.bernetahaynes.com | Twitter: @BernetaWrites | Twitter: @EvolvingManLBV

Made in USA - Kendallville, IN
1209909_9781735985008